PRAISE FOR RISE OF THE PHOENIX

Nominated for four Indieverse Awards including Book of the Year and Best Fantasy.

Winner of three Bookstagram Awards including Debut Author of the Year, Cover of the Year and Young Adult Book of the Year.

"Rise of the Phoenix is the kind of queer fantasy that reminds you why stories about self-discovery and belonging matter. Brendan created an engaging adventure filled with magic, danger, and heart. With themes of found family, friendship, and slow burn romance. It's an exciting start to this series and a MUST read for people looking for an LGBTQ+ fantasy filled with adventure and representation. Extremely proud of you, Brendan. Love you dearly!" – Jacob

"Brendan creates bold and vastly imaginative fantasy worlds that you will become obsessed with!" – Bestselling and award-winning author, B.J Twigg

"Brendan beautifully crafts the magical world of Arulean with a horde of lovable and love to hate characters. What leapt out the most during the read was the emotional stakes and growth of all characters throughout the novel. Not just our heroes but our main villain as well." – Chloe Jayne, author of Squid Ward

"Brendan Arnold masterfully weaves this breathtaking fantasy, creating unforgettable characters you'll gladly lose your heart to, set against a world overflowing with magic, wonder, love, and emotion." – Rachel Jones, author of Dead Horizon and Under a Fractured Sky

"Rise of the Phoenix hooked me from the beginning and didn't let me go! It was fast-paced, but slowed down when needed to. Brendan builds a new world with a rich history and amazing characters too! The whole book was a ride! A pure gem hidden within the fantasy genre that the world is sleeping on." – Anthony Parody

"Rise of the Phoenix left me wanting more of the story and needing to know what happens next.... It left me with tons of theories, questions and the promise of, we have only seen the start of Brendan Arnold's beautifully crafted storytelling." – Paige

"I love the world Brendan has created; there's so much detail I felt like I was there and experiencing the journey our trio was on. I'm really big on connecting with the characters, and I found them all relatable. I genuinely cared for them and had so many emotions ranging from joy to heartache. The pacing and writing style are phenomenal, and this was such a page turner for me. I stayed up well past my bedtime to read (and finish) this book." – Marco Lopez

"Brendan crafts a rich, breathing world filled with heart and soul, incredible adventure, and complex characters. With vivid and immersive writing, this is fantasy storytelling at its most fabulous." – Dave Lee, Dave Lee Down Under

RISE OF THE PHOENIX

RISE OF THE PHOENIX

Brendan Arnold

Second Edition

10 9 8 7 6 5 4 3 2

ISBN: 978-1-7640475-0-0 (PB)
ISBN: 978-1-7640475-1-7 (HB)
ISBN: 978-1-7640475-2-4 (eBook)

First Published in 2025

To Damien, who has walked every step of this journey with me.

From the brightest of highs and the darkest of lows,

thank you for always believing in me.

My cover art is dedicated to my loving grandparents Doreen and Stan,

who nurtured my love of the arts from a young age. My loving Pop,

this cover would not exist without you. Rest easy with Nan,

knowing you live on in my heart and my art.

ARULEAN
BASILIUM
HAVEN'S REST
FAWKESTON
TERCET
CROFTWOOD
WESTVALE BEACH
AMARANTHINE FOREST
OLDWELL
STARKHOLD
KORGUN
RAVENROCK
DRAGON'S JAW
VANDFALL
ORORO'S PEAK
FORTRESS OF THE FLAMES
GREGARON
SUNSCYTHE
LARASGATE
BAY OF SLAYERS
EMERALD GROVE
CYANDRA
JEAN ISLANDS
N
E
S
W

~ PROLOGUE ~
Eighteen years ago

A ray of sunlight brushed across the pages of the book Daemoon Torvinya was reading. He glanced up from the old tome about magical stones and gems, and gazed out the window. As the sun was setting behind the Coronet Mountains, snowflakes danced around the highest peaks on the cloudless late-winter's day. Like all fae, he had keen eyesight: he could see far off into the distance, and minute details hidden to the human eye were visible with perfect clarity. He pulled his attention back to the book, eager to finish the last passage before he took himself home for the evening.

Realm gems are the most powerful and rarest of magical stones. The gems are the keys that unlock the gateways from our realm into the three known realms beyond. When used correctly, the gems will open the gateways, allowing safe passage between each realm.

In the under-realm, the land where the darkest of beings were born and the barrier between the realm of the living and the under-realm is the weakest. Temporary openings have appeared, created by magic from either realm over the centuries. These openings are the reason horrid creatures and beasts of the under-realm can be found around Arulean.

The eternal realm is the place that the spirits of the worthy ascend to after death. The barrier to the eternal realm is the most sacred and treasured. A realm gem powered in a crysorium by a skilled mage is required to open the gateway and commune with the spirits.

The magic realm is the most powerful and ancient of the known realms. It is the home of the mystical creatures and the source of magic. It is believed the first fae came from the magical realm, entering the realm of the living with dragons and phoenixes over ten thousand years ago. Only those who hone their abilities to the masterful magical levels can open the gateways and tap into the source of magic.

Daemoon placed a marker in the book and began packing up his belongings. He returned the book to his book tray at the front of the library. The librarian had already placed the books he had requested earlier in the day into his book tray. The two large volumes were about Arulean history, and they would help him with his preparations for the new initiates class he was due to teach about the phoenix wars of the fourth age in a few days' time. As a guardian at the Tower of Wisdom, Daemoon was responsible for safeguarding the lore and history of Arulean. Magical lore, historical texts and artifacts, knowledge, and most importantly, records of all prophecies were stored in the tower. All guardians were required to teach the initiates, and this semester, he was tasked with teaching history. To be accepted as a guardian was considered an honour of the highest degree in Vandfall, many fae applied and few were accepted.

He wrapped his cloak around his shoulders and began his long descent down the tower. At each landing, hallways annexed out in six directions. When flying above Vandfall on a dashia – the majestic, winged horses that were often riding companions to the fae – the tower resembled a six-pointed star.

Daemoon had walked down two flights of stairs before a familiar sensation flickered through his mind. He stopped walking as his whole body came alive with magical awareness. The air around him shifted, changing direction wildly. It wasn't an ordinary wind blowing through the tower: traces of magic weaved through the air. Daemoon was an elemental fae – he could wield the elements to his command – and nature had a way of informing elementals when danger was about.

He stepped off the stairs onto the landing, following the sound of the wind whistling along the corridor. Torches flickered in the brackets along the wall as he walked. The whistling transformed into an eerie howl, leading Daemoon into a section of the corridor that was bathed in darkness. His eyes instantly adjusted to shadows creeping around him as he stepped forward.

The door to the prophecy chamber ahead of him was ajar. The tingling along his body intensified with each step. The hairs on the back of his arm stood at attention, goosebumps appearing across his skin. Where were the guards that should be stationed at the entrance? Traces of magic lingering on both sides of the door as he stepped into the room, drawing it closed behind him.

The chamber was dead silent. Daemoon gazed into the room: nothing seemed out of the ordinary. Large shelves were stacked high with vessels containing prophecies, crystal orbs, obsidian capsules and phoenix eggs. Each vessel was sealed with fae magic and phoenix flames. Phoenix eggs were reserved for the most important and sacred prophecies. The pungent smell of sealing magic lingered in the air... Which was rather peculiar for this late hour.

Daemoon paced between the stacks. Prophecies were neatly lined up, glowing in the soft light radiating from each timber shelf. His cloak fluttered by his feet and his hair swept across his face as a wind blew through the room. He followed the source, quickening his pace along the stacks. Turning between two shelves, he stopped by a mass on the floor. Daemoon reached down to the guardian lying motionless. Traces of magic lingered around the guardian: he had been knocked out with magic.

A glimmer caught his attention, and he spun towards the shelf lined with vessels. Fire swirled in the empty space where a phoenix egg should have been.

He tensed as an icy chill passed through him. A prophecy had been removed from its place and a guardian had been enchanted to sleep! His pointed fae ears prickled with attention. The wind brushed across Daemoon's face again, urging him to follow a new trail. He ran and rushed between two stacks, charging towards the opposite side of the room. Adrenaline coursed through him as he found himself face to face with two guardians, the door guards! They stood in front of a wide-open door leading into another corridor, eyes glowing a soft yellow-green before they collapsed into each other, passing out on the floor.

Daemoon leapt over the guardians and ran into the corridor. He looked from left to right along the empty space. A flash of golden hair caught his eye.

"Alert! Intruder in the prophecy chamber!" he called out loudly, hoping to stir his fellow guardians into action.

He surged after the figure. Each gulping breath filled his lungs with strength and clarity, even as the adrenaline rushed through his body. Flashes of light caught Daemoon's attention, traces of the magic that sealed the phoenix egg left a trail to follow. Two floors down, he exited onto a landing and pursued the golden-haired intruder. He followed the trail onto a terrace outside the building. The intruder stood on the edge, glancing back towards him. Her face was mostly covered by a large hood. Even with his keen fae eyesight, he couldn't see her face clearly.

"Hand it over and you walk away," he commanded, holding his hand out towards her.

She smirked at Daemoon and ran along the terrace. He followed her as she ran to the end of the terrace and leapt from the edge. Daemoon didn't flinch as he ran forward, following her. As he sped towards the ground, preparing to land effortlessly one hundred feet below, the intruder was gliding towards the other side of the river, two hundred feet away.

Fae magic? Daemoon wondered: he hadn't expected that. He would have glided after her otherwise. He ran towards the river, desperate to shorten the distance between them. She seemed to know the land well: weaving away from the tower she darted left and right, slipping through areas where she would easily be seen. The only traces of her were the magical tendrils left behind by the prophecy.

"Alert! Intruder fleeing the tower!" Daemoon boomed, hoping to draw the guards' attention.

The intruder ran towards the dense forest. The tall mountains surrounding Vandfall were excellent cover for anyone looking to escape, particularly as darkness set in. Daemoon quickened his pace and sighed with relief as guards began to move in their direction. He had stirred help; he might just capture her yet. Daemoon summoned a wind to push him faster along the road. The air swirled around him, cooling his sweat-covered body. He leapt into the air, the strong current whirling behind him and thrusting him forward. As he sailed through the air, the intruder glanced back and leapt away from him.

He sailed closer to the intruder, but as he stretched forward to secure her, she turned quickly on the spot, golden energy enclosing her. Daemoon's outstretched hand was clutching her hood when she disappeared. He dropped to the ground, grunting as he hit the hard earth right where she had just been standing.

"Daemoon, what's happened here?" a guard called out, charging towards him on a horse.

"An intruder stole a prophecy, she..." He paused, panting and trying to catch his breath.

"Blinked before our very eyes." The guard finished Daemoon's sentence.

Daemoon looked down at the cloak in his hand. His blood ran cold and every inch of him tensed as he stared down at the clasp on the front of the cloak.

"Call the grand masters now. We need to see Queen Keeva immediately."

"What's wrong?" the guard replied.

"Just do it," he directed impatiently, turning back towards the city.

He ran out of the forest back towards the tower, clutching the cloak tightly. His first stop was to investigate the prophecy room. It was crucial to learn which prophecy had been stolen before he and the grand masters met with the queen.

By the time he was finished in the prophecy room, he had more questions than answers. None of the guards could recall what had happened to them, nor could they identify the intruder. As Daemoon made his way out of the tower with the panicked grand masters, he sensed their troubles were far from over.

~ CHAPTER ONE ~

Will Tavner's heart pounded in his chest. He panted, as the muscles in his legs burned. He was wading waist-deep in the ocean, pushing against the pull of the water rushing back out to sea.

"Faster, Will," Seb called out from the shoreline.

Will fought against the pull of the current. He usually found the smell of the salt water and the feel of the ocean breeze across his skin quite calming. Anytime he found himself by the ocean, he would close his eyes and inhale the salty sea air: it always felt like home. Today, even the ocean couldn't calm him as he emerged from the sea and ran towards his friend. Seb picked up their shirts and boots and threw them into their horse's saddle bags.

A patrol of city guards galloped along the beach in their direction. Basilium – the capital city of Arulean – towered over the beach in the distance. Will counted six guards riding towards them.

"Curse the gods," Will shouted, running towards Seb. "This wasn't my best idea."

City guards didn't usually stray this far from Basilium, nor did citizens like to stray too close to them. Smuggler's Cove was miles away from Basilium. People frequently visited it in the warmer months for a leisurely swim.

Will ran straight to his horse and pulled himself up onto her. Will and Seb spurred their horses into a gallop, racing away from the beach towards the royal road. Will glanced back towards the city guards: they had not bothered to turn from the sand to chase the boys. Instead, they continued along the beach, ignoring Will and Seb completely.

"Oh," Seb sighed deeply as he slowed his horse, "that's a relief."

"Back to the water then?" Will asked hopefully.

"Can't we just go back home?" Seb sighed. "This isn't the post-graduation excitement I was looking for."

To be fair, excitement *never* seemed to be something Seb was looking for: he was shy and reserved. And yet, somehow, Seb often followed Will around when Will had some wild idea for a new adventure.

"Throw my shirt back, will you? Will asked, dropping his horse's reins as Seb threw his shirt over to him. He caught it easily. "Thanks!" Will winked and pulled the shirt over his head.

"Show off!" Seb called out, rolling his eyes at Will.

For an eighteen-year-old, Will was quite strong, although you wouldn't know from looking at him, he had a slim and agile body, not the typical strong and bulky type you would see from other boys around the city. Will's clothing covered his defined muscles on his six-foot frame, his golden brown hair was short, and he often pushed it to the side to keep his hair out of vivid green eyes. Will was known as a bit of a charmer in his hometown of Fawkeston, south of Basilium.

Seb was slightly shorter than Will and had a slimmer, less athletic build. His dark brown mop of hair always swept into his brown eyes. Will often joked that he used his hair to hide and blend into the crowds, which Seb never seemed to find funny. Seb's family were originally from Sunscythe, the exotic city on the eastern side of Arulean. Sunscythians were known for their darker features and olive-coloured skin, and Seb was no exception. Every summer, Seb's complexion darkened so deeply, you would think he had just spent six months relaxing in a villa on the Jean Islands.

"Can we please just go find Aylise and go into the forest? Seb pleaded. "We've been out of school for one day."

Will, Seb and their friend Lady Aylise Rotherwell – the daughter of Lord Nathaniel Rotherwell of Fawkeston, and his wife Lady Ana – had just finished their last year of schooling. Now that they were eighteen, it was time to discover the joys and wonders of Arulean. That was all that Will yearned for: to go on a grand adventure around Arulean and beyond.

Will, Aylise and Seb had grown up together in Fawkeston. Will and Seb's parents had worked for Lord Nathaniel and Lady Ana for years. When the three women fell pregnant around the same time, their bond grew deeper. Although it was unconventional for lords and ladies to spend leisure time with ordinary citizens, no one in Fawkeston seemed fazed by their friendship.

"Aylise is in Basilium with her father today. Do you want to go and find her there?" Will smiled at him, grinning mischievously.

Seb looked horrified momentarily before composing himself. "By all means, you go." Seb looked at him deadpan. "Just don't blame me when your parents keep you housebound for a month."

"Where's your sense of adventure?" Will quipped in reply.

"I left it at home in Fawkeston," Seb replied, laughing. "Maybe it's time we started to explore some of the eastern beaches."

"Okay, Sensible Seb," Will teased.

"If I had a sword on me, I'd throw it at you," Seb laughed back. "I'm as adventurous as any old grandmother. Besides, if you didn't have me to stop you acting on your every impulse, you'd be dead by now." He paused for a moment. "Reckless Will."

"Reckless Will?" he replied, laughing. "That's a new one."

A rattling noise drew Will and Seb's attention along the road. Two carriages travelled along the road with a patrol of guards. The sounds of horses trotting and rickety carriage wheels grew louder. Will noticed the family crest too late and his heart sank.

"Oh shit," he called out, pointing towards the crest.

Seb's eyes widened with fear as the carriages slowed to a stop.

"Will Tavner and Sebastian Estermont!" a large man called out from the carriage door. "Dismount from those horses and get in this carriage immediately." His voice was commanding, with just the subtlest undertones of alarm.

Lord Nathaniel Rotherwell's eyes were wide as he gazed down at them. He was of average height and had a large muscular build. Although he was an excellent swordsman, he preferred to fight his battles behind closed doors. "Diplomacy will achieve much better outcomes than a sword," Lord Nathaniel would say. He had short greying hair, which he often blamed Aylise, Will and Seb for causing.

Lord Nathaniel was a firm but fair lord. On top of his duties to Fawkeston, he was also the High Lord of the crown lands. It was the High Lord's responsibility to oversee matters relating to citizens of the region, while the Crown oversaw matters for all of Arulean. Although it was much more of a ceremonial position in recent years, King Rickard and Queen Haveena had no interest in working with the five High Lords and Ladies, who governed the five regions of Arulean. Each region was separated by large rivers that flowed from the Coronet Mountains surrounding Vandfall.

"We're sorry, Lord Rotherwell. We were just..." Seb spoke softly, not daring to look Lord Nathaniel in the eye. "We were..." He paused.

"Far too close to Basilium," Lord Nathaniel interjected firmly. "You both know better." His voice was deep and commanding. Lord Nathaniel's close friendship with Will's mother and father, Selina and Darian, certainly meant that he would inform them where he found Will.

"We know." Will bowed his head respectfully. "We're sorry, Lord Rotherwell."

"In. Now!" he commanded, stepping out of the carriage.

Will climbed into the carriage and sighed, unsure whether he was nervous or ready for the argument he was sure to face when he got home. Will's parents were protective, or so they would say. Will would describe them as overbearing, with a tendency for odd rules without any reasonable explanation. Will had hoped that turning eighteen and completing his school education would have eased some of their rules, though perhaps Seb had been right. Maybe they should have waited a few more days before "pushing the boundaries" as his parents would say.

It wasn't all bad for Will growing up. In fact, he had quite a pleasant upbringing. Will's mother was loving and attentive, and together they spent countless hours in the garden, nurturing Will's passion for gardening. While he loved growing his own crops on the property, he had a fondness for a rose bush that his mother grew. He loved the sweet and fragrant smell of the white, yellow and pink petals that bloomed every spring. He would often cut flowers from the bush and bring them into the house to decorate the table where they ate their meals. Selina would beam at him whenever he brought them in.

Seb stepped into the carriage after Will, looking rather relieved. The Rotherwell name certainly demanded respect, and they were far less likely to come across trouble in their company. Sitting next to Seb was Will and Seb's best friend, Aylise Rotherwell. Her sapphire blue eyes sparkled with a glint of mischief. Her long copper coloured hair was tied in an elaborate bun on her head, and she wore a beautiful cerulean-blue gown with a dark blue travelling cloak. Will locked eyes with her and fumbled the rest of the way into the carriage, practically falling into his seat.

"What were you two up to?" she asked, laughing and twisting a tendril of hair between her fingers.

"We were swimming," Will replied, mumbling the words out.

"So, you both travelled to Basilium," Aylise began.

'Smuggler's Cove," Seb interjected.

"Smuggler's Cove," Aylise corrected herself, "on a day when you both knew I was going to Basilium with my father. You're both idiots. Of course you were going to be caught." She paused for a moment. "Now, what's the story we're going to tell your parents?" She looked at Will.

"Great question!" He perked up. "How in the gods names, am I going to spin this one?" He thought on that while the carriage travelled close to home.

"Smuggler's Cove? Thank the shield you weren't hurt!" Will's mother Selina shouted across the kitchen.

It was never a good sign when his mother started referencing the gods. Will sighed and prepared himself for the inevitable. Will realised on the way home that he wasn't going to be able to spin the situation. Therefore, he decided it was best to be honest with his parents – before Lord Nathaniel was. His mother fidgeted with her hands, holding them tightly together. She sighed deeply between ragged breaths, her eyes kept gazing towards the front door like she was expecting someone to burst in at any moment. *Oh great*, Will thought, each little gesture and action a sign that his mother had worked herself into an emotional state.

"How many guards were there?" his father Darian asked firmly. He stood over Will, his brown skin glistening with sweat after a day's work in the blacksmith's shop.

"There were six," he replied, "but they weren't even interested in us. They just rode straight by." He tried to keep his voice neutral.

His father glanced at his mother. They both kept gazing towards the door, to each other and back at Will, like they were boring into his soul.

"Did they see you with Lord Rotherwell? Did they get close to you?" His father was erratic as he spoke, his tone switching from rage to an urgent panic. "Did they see your face?"

"No," he replied, exasperated. "They barely paid us any attention."

His parents sighed. Their anxious breaths in perfect rhythm. They gazed towards the door again.

"Why do you both keep doing that?" Will shouted. "Can you both calm down? No one is going to barge in!"

"Don't you tell us to calm down!" Darian shouted. "We've had enough of your childish and frankly irresponsible behaviour." His tone more heated with each word. "We'd expected this from you when you were a child, not an eighteen-year-old."

"It was just the beach," Will replied, exasperated. "We weren't doing anything wrong, we were just..." Will paused.

"Just what?" His father boomed.

"Just too close to the capital," he replied.

"Why can't you stay within Fawkeston?" Selina pleaded. "Isn't there enough around here to explore?"

"Oh Mama," Will rolled his eyes, "there's more to life than this boring town." He sighed, deciding to speak frankly with his parents. "I want adventure. I want to explore Arulean. I want some excitement in my life."

He also wanted desperately to end this conversation, but his overprotective parents were unlikely to change their ways now. His father was a blacksmith – and quite a good one, too. His shop produced all the weapons for Lord Rotherwell's army. His father was also a fair swordsman himself, often found training with the guards behind the closed walls of Fawkeston Castle. Darian also spent a fair amount of time training Will in the forest behind their home since he was old enough to hold a sword. His mother was a seamstress, creating some of the most elaborate and beautiful designs for the residents of Fawkeston. People often told her she should expand her business, but she was content to live her life creating for the locals in Fawkeston. Will often felt weighed down by their rules and their contentedness to stay in Fawkeston. They were not fond of him straying too far from home, but now that he had graduated from school and come of age, he was ready to leave Fawkeston behind. He yearned for a life away from this town: away from their rules.

"Will, are you even listening to us?" his mother asked.

"I'm sorry," he replied belligerently, snapped out of his daydream.

"Don't take that tone with us," Darian barked at him. "We're trying our best to protect you."

"Protect me! Protect me from what?" Will snapped back.

"You're only eighteen." Selina's lip quivered as she gazed at her son.

"You didn't answer my question!" Will responded, becoming more irritated at his parents' lack of answers. "What are you trying to protect me from?"

"That's enough now, Will." His father glanced at his mother as he spoke. "Go and get cleaned up for dinner." His father walked out of the room.

"That's all you have to say?" Will tried to argue, sensing his parents shutting him down.

"That's enough, Will!" growled his father from the other room. "Go and do as I ask."

Furious, Will stood up and marched off towards the base of the stairs.

"I'm not a child anymore," he protested as he began to march up the stairs to his room. "You can't protect me forever."

Selina watched Will walk up the stairs, her lip quivered as the wooden stairs creaked under the weight of Will's stomping feet. Tears streamed down her face as he slammed his bedroom door shut. Darian walked back into the room and wrapped his arms around his wife. He stroked her hair as he comforted her.

"That's what we're afraid of, my darling boy," she whispered, looking up towards her husband. She kissed him softly and held him tighter.

They had made a promise a long time ago. It had seemed like the logical thing to do then, but now it felt so wrong. Surely just a little more time was okay? Did everything have to change now?

Selina picked up her goblet and the decanter of red wine, filling her glass. She drank deeply, barely tasting the sweet and rich wine that Darian's father had shipped up from the Jean Islands.

Surely just a little more time before everything changes. She said the prayer silently.

Will was soaring through the sky, flying higher and higher into the endless blue expanse. Winds streamed past his face and his shirt flapped behind him. He laughed as he dipped down through the clouds to reveal snow-capped mountains below. He dived down towards the earth, pulling up sharply to soar above the clouds as the sun beamed on him, filling him with warmth. He rolled over, facing the blue sky above and dove through the clouds, racing towards the mountains.

"Ah-ha!" he shouted, pulling out of the dive.

How was he flying? People couldn't fly. Was this real, or was he dreaming? It didn't feel like a dream. Will normally felt aware of his dreams: that strange feeling you have where you know you're asleep, even if the dream feels real. Well, this felt different: this felt magical. A sudden movement close-by caught his attention. A girl was flying close to him. Her hair was a light sandy blonde colour, and it was flowing through the air, just like her long silky white gown. As she smiled at him, her gaze filled with warmth and familiarity. She plunged towards the mountains, and Will followed her.

"Will," she called to him, drawing closer to the mountains.

"How do you know my name?" He asked, as a warmth spread through his body. He tried to follow her.

"Come to me, Will," she called, diving faster to the ground. "Will!"

Will woke from the dream, startled and confused. It took a moment for him to realise he was still lying in bed. He gazed around his dark room, a faint light from the night sky crept in through the window. His body was dripping with sweat, even though it was a cool night. His wrists were itchy, almost like they were burning. He scratched at them, rubbing his fingers back and forth until the sensation disappeared. A faint smell of smoke hung in the dark room. Perhaps a candle had burnt out somewhere in the house?

He threw his shirt onto the floor, gulped down some water, and rolled over, slipping smoothly back into sleep.

~ CHAPTER TWO ~

Will had forgotten about his dream when he woke up the next morning. He pondered why he had removed his shirt during the night. Perhaps he was hot in the middle of the night and took it off while he was half asleep? He was relieved to find his father had left for work when he came down the stairs. His mother was making breakfast in the kitchen, and she was the softer of both his parents.

"What are you doing today?" Selina asked gently, handing him a bowl of porridge.

"Studying with Aylise and Seb in the castle library." He tried to remove the iciness from his tone.

"You're still angry with us then," she responded, tutting and shaking her head. "Studying for what? You've graduated."

Will wondered if there was any point arguing back. Anytime he tried to have a reasonable conversation with his parents, they backed away and shut the conversation down. It began to feel too hard to argue with them some time ago, so now he barely bothered. Sure, he fired up yesterday, but that wasn't completely unreasonable, was it? He gazed down at his breakfast, choosing to focus on the oats, although he could feel his mother's gaze upon him.

"Studying for life!" he snapped back.

"Will, I wish you…" Selina began.

"I should get going," he cut her off, shovelling another spoonful of oats into his mouth. "I'll be late otherwise," he mumbled as he ate. He left the table and marched out of the house.

Fawkeston was nestled into the northern edge of the Amaranthine Forest, which covered over one-third of the Coronet Mountains. Fawkeston was a short distance from the royal road, which connected the regions of Arulean. Farmers with large properties surrounded Fawkeston, and the area had declined year on year. Growing crops had become significantly more challenging. As rain became less common, the rivers dried up and the rich, fertile fields dried out. Despite the dryness, grey clouds often blanketed the skies around Fawkeston, yellowing the crops away to nothing. Lord Rotherwell ensured the farmers never went hungry: each citizen was always clothed and kept warm. Fawkestonians took care of each other.

Will's back door led directly into the Amaranthine Forest, on the southern side of town. His parents said they liked the tranquillity of the forest on their doorstep. This was one occasion where Will couldn't argue with them: he loved living on the forest's edge. It was a short walk to Fawkeston Square – the vibrant trading hub – but Will loved that his home was away from the hustle and bustle of the town. Will would normally stop into his father's shop on his way into town, however after the argument, he didn't feel like seeing him today.

Aylise was waiting for him at the edge of the square, standing by the road that led to her castle. She wore her hair in a braid, and her green dress had accents of gold woven intricately across the bodice. Will wouldn't dare dream of saying it aloud, but his stomach felt like it was full of butterflies as she walked towards him. Aylise often took his breath away. She was a striking beauty – there was no doubt about that – but it was the kindness and soft-hearted nature beneath her bravery that sent Will weak at the knees.

"How much trouble are you in?" Aylise smiled at him mischievously.

"Let's not ruin the morning already," he replied.

"That bad, huh?" Her eyes softened and she frowned at him. "Seb's not here yet," she said, looking around the busy square.

Aylise always looked at him fondly after a fight with his parents. She understood his frustrations, although she always did her best to look at arguments from both sides. Aylise would often try to see things from other people's perspectives, offering alternative ways to think about things. Will believed she would make a terrific diplomat.

"He won't be too long," he replied, looking into the square.

As always, the town square was bustling with people. Merchants and farmers were setting up their stalls, ready to start selling their goods for the day. Customers wandered through the stalls, seeking out their regular sellers. Horses were hitched at the stables outside the tavern, which was already full. Travellers rode out of the square, talking happily to each other with their wagon full of supplies. Will looked at them leaving town and envied them. His desire to leave Fawkeston on an adventure of his own was fuelled even more so after the confrontation.

"You'll get out of here one day." Aylise looked at him. "Though it would be nice if you remembered to come back and visit me occasionally," she added bashfully.

"Or you could come with me?" he replied, his cheeks reddening at his boldness. He quickly averted his eyes.

Will had known Aylise longer than he had known Seb. Aylise was born three months before Will and because their parents had such a close bond, Will and Aylise had been inseparable since they could walk. They had always been friendly with each other, preferring to spend hours together. Where Will moved, Aylise moved and vice versa. It had been a subtle change – a few years back – when Will started to see her differently. He found himself getting butterflies, becoming tongue-tied and losing his train of thought when she was close. He often thought about telling her how he felt, because sometimes he thought he saw her looking at him the same way too. He wondered, though, if that was him just seeing what he wanted to see.

"The heir of Fawkeston isn't simply allowed to adventure into the wild with Will Tavner," she smiled at him, "even if she wants to." She spoke softly under her breath with a bashful smile.

Will could barely contain the wild thoughts running through his head. Did she just say that? Gods, *say something, you idiot.*

"Here he comes," he called out, pointing towards Seb, who was walking between two stalls with another friend of theirs, Rupert Sadlyn. *Well done, idiot.* He thought to himself.

Seb and Rupert stopped at the edge of a stall. They were talking animatedly to each other, laughing and glancing at passersby. Rupert patted Seb on the arm and walked around the edge of a stall, disappearing into the sea of people. Will waved at Seb, whose eyes grew wide when he locked eyes with Will and Aylise.

"How bad was it?" he asked Will.

When Will finished telling Seb about the confrontation, Aylise linked her arm around Will's.

"I miss the simple days when our biggest concern was where to play," Will replied. Wrapping his arm around Seb's shoulder. "The good times, my friend. The good times."

"I'm sorry," Seb replied softly, smiling gently at Will, "I miss those times too." He chuckled to himself. "Except when you two would get us into trouble."

"How dare you," Aylise chuckled. She playfully smacked Seb's arm. "Anyway, whatever you had in mind for today, we're skipping it," Aylise said mischievously, her eyes gleeful.

"Why?" Seb and Will replied in unison.

"Because I got my hands on several banned books from my father's private study." She spoke softly, her voice barely above a whisper. Her eyes were wide with delight. "All thanks to you, Will. While he was talking to your parents, I slipped into his office."

When Rickard and Haveena usurped the throne, one of their first acts was to burn books and records of history, fables and magic. Thousands of years of records were destroyed in an instant. Stories of magical creatures, legends of the fae, ancient spell books, and texts of magical temples and buildings were burnt in a blaze of fire and ash.

"You don't mean to say..." Will paused as various thoughts swam through his mind. "How does he still have them?" He asked. Oh, how he would love to get his hands on some of those volumes.

"Oh, he's in the queen's good graces. She stopped snooping around our house a long time ago," Aylise replied, linking her arm around Will's again. "To the forest then?"

Will beamed at her, his smile from ear to ear. He started to walk out of the square heading straight for the forest.

Will, Aylise and Seb had built a little camp in the Amaranthine Forest when they were eight years old. Their fathers had built them a tree house up on the branches of a thick old tree. Not long after, they built another structure on the ground below it, allowing the three kids to climb easily between each level. Over the years, Will, Seb and Aylise made additions to their camp. They added targets for archery practice and dummies for sword play. They built swings on ropes for the times they simply wanted to relax, adding areas to sit and escape from other kids in town. Their parents had always allowed the kids their privacy in the camp, as long as they were home by nightfall. The camp was only sixty yards away from Will's home, which meant his parents were far less anxious about Will being too far away.

"They're just so overprotective," Will complained, recounting the fight with his parents as he placed a log into the fire pit.

Flames hissed around the log, sending sparks and fire into the air. Will sat down on one of the large logs that surrounded the fire. The smell of burning maple branches mixed with the scent of the tall kamar trees around them.

"But they've always been like that." Seb sat down on a log by the fire. Aylise nodded in agreement.

Will, Aylise and Seb had added the large fire pit to their camp when they were young teenagers. They had become far less inclined to want to play in the tree house, and found it much more enjoyable to sit around the fire and gossip.

"But I'm not a kid anymore," Will huffed in reply, "and what exactly do I need protecting *from*?" He stoked the fire with a large stick. Aylise disappeared behind a wall of flames at least five feet high. "I just want some freedom." He looked at Seb. "I want the freedom to be me."

"Don't we all?" Aylise looked at him knowingly as she moved around the billowing flames. "Also, your parents would not be happy with you doing that," she pointed at the stick in his hand.

Will smirked as he stoked the fire again, sending sparks flying into the air. One of his parents' strangest rules was that Will had to stay away from fire. They didn't like him lighting the fire at home or even lighting his own candles in his room. No matter how many times he asked why, he never got a response.

"Anyway," Will raised his eyebrows and grinned, "What books do you have?"

Aylise pulled three large books out of her bag. The leather bindings were old and tattered on two of the books. The last book looked new. She passed one of the older books to Will: the pages were a deep golden yellow, and their leather smelled of smoke and ash. It felt warm in his hands.

He ran his hands over the title stamped into the cover. "*The Phoenix Wars of the Fourth Age*," he whispered in awe. "A book from the fourth age? This book is at least a thousand years old... But what are the phoenix wars?" He opened the book, carefully lifting the pages. The sharp scent of burnt paper curled through the air. A mixture of charred ink and smouldering parchment permeated from the pages. It sparked a curiosity inside him.

"This one is called. *The Fables and Legends of the Fae*," Seb called out in awe. "Wow, you did get the goods, Aylise!" Seb looked longingly at the book. "I wish magic didn't die out with the fae."

"It didn't completely die out, Seb," Aylise replied. "Queen Haveena and King Rickard have magic, everyone knows that. And the fae in Vandfall still have magic, even though..."

Aylise's sudden silence pulled Will away from the pages of the book in his hands. "What is it?" Her mouth was hanging open as she stared at the book.

"This book," Aylise spoke softly, like she was in some trance like state. "It hasn't been finished," she said, turning the pages. "I understand why my father wouldn't want the king and queen seeing this." She passed the book to Will.

"*The Fall of House Kyllarian and the Siege of Basilium*," Will read the cover out quietly.

A shiver spread through Will as he ran his hand over the cover. Stamped below the title of the book was a bird with its wings outstretched and its head turned to the side. As he ran his fingers over the bird, his head felt foggy, like some unseen force was plucking the strands of every thought from his mind and placing it within the pages of the book.

"Do you know what this symbol is?" he asked Aylise, handing her the book. Was the fire burning too hot? Was he too close? Heat seared under his flesh, spreading through his body rapidly.

"I don't." Aylise looked curiously down at the cover. "A mark of the author perhaps?" She guessed. "The handwriting seems familiar." Aylise flipped through the pages again, her eyes darted back and forth across the pages. "Looks like someone is in the process of writing about the end of the Kyllarian dynasty." Aylise looked towards Will and Seb. "Do either of you know the story?"

"Not really," Will replied. "I've heard whispers of them around Fawkeston, but that's about it."

"Same for me," Seb responded.

"It was brutal. Let's see." Aylise continued flipping through the pages until she settled on a page and began to read the passage aloud.

The queen's lady-in-waiting recalled the morning of the siege. Basilium was bustling with regular trade. The winter and early spring harvests had produced an abundance of produce for sale. Citizens were going about their day, purchasing goods from the markets, visiting traders at the docklands – the port master navigating the many ships coming in and out of the docks with their trades.

As Aylise read from the passage, the fog in Will's mind continued to grow. Heat waves from their fire warmed Will's face and he closed his eyes. He was lost in Aylise's soothing voice.

Queen Dyana was heavily pregnant at the time. We were standing together on the balcony in her private chambers, watching over the golden city, the crowning jewel of Arulean.

Aylise's voice became faint, distant. When he opened his eyes, he was standing on the balcony next to the heavily pregnant queen. She had dark golden hair and green eyes. Her eyes twinkled in the sunlight as she smiled warmly at him. *I'm dreaming*, he told himself. How else could he explain his sudden appearance in Basilium?

"*A dark fog rolled in from the south,*" Aylise's soft voice continued, from somewhere close by. It felt peculiar to be able to hear her but not see her. Was she close? Or hidden somewhere in the distance? Will turned towards the southern walls of the city and watched the dark clouds roll in. The fog was dark, and streaks of what looked like lightning lit up sections of the cloud with bright lights. Instinct told Will it was unnatural. Red-orange hues illuminated the fog too. Was that fire?

There was no time to prepare for the assault or evacuate the city. The dark magic blanketed us the moment it reached our walls.

Was he there? Was he seeing Basilium during the siege? Aylise's voice faded in and out, where was she? Was she here too? He wanted to walk to the edge of the balcony, but his legs wouldn't move. He looked at Queen Dyana, hoping to ask for her help. She was watching him, smiling, but with a sadness in her eyes too. A tear fell down her cheek.

"We need to move now," he said to the queen as the fog rolled in over the castle.

The fog crept along the balcony, obscuring Will's vision. The fog reeked of death and decay. Will was starting to lose sight of the queen, but he could still see her face. She continued to smile at him, choosing to ignore the fog completely.

King Eramund died first. We watched Rickard strike him down as he tried to defend the queen.

The sounds of clashing swords and falling stone echoed from a hallway in the castle. Will watched as a man – he presumed Rickard – charged down the hall. King Eramund's men raised their swords, slicing across the gaps in his armour and attempting to thrust their swords into his neck. Their swords bounced off him, seemingly unable to penetrate his flesh. Magic? Will wondered. Rickard swung his large arm in front of him. Eramund's men soared through the air, hitting the stone walls hard, their blood splaying along the stone before they collapsed on the floor.

The fog began to creep through the castle. King Eramund and his soldiers were left disadvantaged. The fog blinding us as it crept along.

King Eramund lunged at Rickard and the two men parried back and forth. Rickard lunged for Eramund and wrapped his hands around his neck. Eramund's sword was useless against Rickard's armour. Rickard drove his sword through Eramund. His body became limp, and Rickard threw him to the floor like he was throwing a shirt over his shoulder.

The queen and I tried to flee the castle, but we were separated. She instructed me to leave the castle as someone had to inform our allies.

Will turned back towards the queen. A large fire began to materialise behind her. Will fought against the force rooting him in place, desperate and panicked to escape the fireball sailing towards them.

"Move, now!" he shouted. Shivers ran up his whole body as he tried to force his legs to move.

"Will!" the queen screamed at him as the flames engulfed her. "Run. Now. Run. Don't stay here," she screamed, her high-pitched voice echoing around him.

Will shouted as he opened his eyes. He leapt to his feet. The queen, the castle and flames had disappeared. He was in his camp with his friends.

"Will, are you okay?" Seb and Aylise asked together, leaping from their own seats as he floundered through the camp, gasping for breath. He heaved, choking on the hot air in his lungs as he tried to shake the vision from his mind.

"Look out!" Seb screamed.

Will tripped, hitting the edge of the firepit. He slammed into the flaming logs and collapsed into the centre of the fire. His body was engulfed in flames. Seb and Aylise screamed out, standing by the fire in utter shock, unable to pull Will out without placing themselves at risk of the fire, which had now risen to over seven feet.

Will opened his eyes, the hot air soared through his body as he tried to breathe. The sharp aroma of thick smoke and cinders stung his nose. He writhed around, stoking the logs and causing the flames to fly around him in a frenzy. He struggled to lift himself out of the fire, searing hot logs disintegrated underneath his body. He was anticipating the searing pain as his flesh burnt, but it didn't come, only an internal heat that started in his chest and rapidly spread through him. He stopped writhing: instead focusing on the flames licking his body, he felt the heat of the flames, but they did not hurt him. He placed his hands on a burning log and pushed himself to his feet. His shirt was burning on his body, though his leather pants had been saved from the flames. He leapt out of the fire and attempted to snuff out the flames, feeling the flames tickle his flesh as they seared every last inch of his shirt. He looked down at his naked torso, which was completely unmarked. *How am I not burnt to a crisp?* Was the only thought racing through his mind.

"Will!" Seb called out, his whole body trembling, "what are those?" pointing at Will's forearms.

Will was transfixed by the bright orange glowing marks on his wrists. They looked like a sigil or crest. They were raised from his skin, like a burn, except they didn't hurt him. The bird-like mark grew brighter as he gazed at them.

"Have you ever seen a burn like this before?" Will asked.

"That's not a burn," Seb replied. He was still staring at Will wide-eyed.

"Then what is it?" he replied.

"Will?" Aylise spoke softly, her eyes moving up and down his body. "There's not a burn on you. How?"

"I don't know," Will replied, running his hands along his body.

"Are you in pain?" Seb asked, running his hand down Will's back.

"Not at all," he replied, watching Seb and Aylise steal glances at each other.

"These feel warm," Will said, running his hands along the glowing marks.

"They don't for me," Seb replied, running his hands along both marks. "You try, Aylise."

"They don't feel warm for me either." Aylise continued to speak softly, her eyes darting from Will to Seb.

Will sat down on the ground, bewildered. His hands began to shake, so he wrapped them around his legs. A quick glance at Seb and Aylise didn't confirm if they noticed his nervous reaction or not. The marks began to dim slowly.

"What happened before you fell on the fire?" Aylise asked, rubbing her hands along his back. The rhythm of her soft skin on his back soothed him. "You screamed out."

Will told them about his strange experience, analysing every small detail he could remember. Will wasn't sure how long they sat in the camp discussing "the dream" – which seemed to be the most logical thing to call it. Although the longer they spoke, the more they were weighed down with unanswered questions.

"I think the more pressing question is, what is this crest?" Aylise said, running her soft hands over Will's wrist.

Her touch sent a different energy surging through Will, easing his mind from his panicked thoughts. "There must be a mention of them in a book somewhere, right?" Will asked, gazing into her eyes.

"Possibly," Aylise replied, returning his gaze. "We could search my library as a starting point?" Aylise looked confused. "Why are you only seeing these marks now? Do you think it was the flames?"

"The flames," Will exclaimed. Jumping to his feet. "Of course it's the flames, that's the rule, isn't it. *Stay away from fire.*" He gasped as he recalled his parents' words.

Will marched over to the fire pit, knelt and placed his arm out into the flames. The heat of the fire warmed his body and licked across his skin. He didn't flinch, he didn't burn, he felt no pain. He did feel the mark on his arm come alive. A spark started in the middle of his wrist and the first strands of the raised mark appeared. It began to glow and spread out across his skin like fire. He lifted his arm out of the blaze and turned to face Aylise and Seb. He held out his glowing wrist.

"Oh, Will, this is unbelievable," Aylise gasped, running her hands along his wrist again. "You're invulnerable to fire."

Will ran his fingers through his hair and pulled his arm away from Aylise. His heart was beating fast and his stomach felt uneasy. What was happening to him? Was he cursed? Was he born like this? He paced back and forth, too many questions running through his mind.

"Will!" Seb called out, standing tall. "I know you, Will Tavner. Whatever you're thinking, stop, now."

"It's just..." Will replied.

"It's just nothing," Seb replied, cutting him off. "We're here with you and whatever this is." He gestured towards Will's wrists. "We'll work it out together." Will smiled warmly at his friend.

"Your parents obviously know about the marks, right?" Aylise said matter-of-factly. "Why would they have that rule otherwise?"

"Oh, I have no doubt they know." Will pulled away from his friends.

"Are you going to ask them about it?" Aylise replied.

"Yes!" Will exclaimed, but then he thought about it for a moment. That could be a tough argument to have. Did he really want to put himself through that? "Actually, they've kept it from me for this long. We're on our own for this one."

"Okay." Aylise tried to keep her groan quiet. "Where do we start?"

"Exactly where you said," Will replied. "Your library. And we're going there right now. But first, I need a shirt," he chuckled, trying to keep his tone casual.

~ CHAPTER THREE ~

Fawkeston Square was still bustling in the afternoon as Will ate his pie by the baker's shop. He chanced a glance in Aylise's direction: she hadn't taken her eyes off him since they left the library.

"Are you feeling any better now?" she ventured.

"I'm fine," Will snapped in reply. He stood in silence for a moment, resisting the urge to stomp his feet like a sullen child. "You would think," he huffed, "that we would have found something in all the hours we spent scouring through your library. We looked through how many healers' records? Volumes about magic and frankly far too many books on runes and symbols than I ever needed to see in my life, and still we came up with nothing. What a waste of time."

"It was a start, Will," Aylise replied softly. "We'll go back tomorrow. There's still the rest of the library to search."

His skin prickled as she interlaced her fingers through his, every inch of him warming at her touch.

"Is Seb here yet?"

"Maybe." His response was less sullen than he was a moment ago.

Not long after they began searching through volumes in the library, Seb stood from their table, mumbling a muffled apology.

"Meet me in the square when you're done," he called back towards them as he ran out of the library and down the hallway.

Will looked around the square, searching for Seb among the crowds of people. The town seemed to be making the most of the sunshine, and it was quite delightful to see it breaking through the clouds as they left the library. It was a small comfort, after leaving empty-handed. Will admired the resilience of the people in Fawkeston: rivers continued to run dry, and their lands turned brown, but each day they found hope and joy that things might get better one day. Why, then, did he fear that things were about to get much darker than he had ever known them to be?

The crackling sound of a fire caught Will's attention. One of the cooks stirred a large pot of stew over a pit of coals. He was mesmerised by the fire. How many times had his parents kept him away from flames? Will had always found their fearful reactions to fire strange. Was the symbol the reason why? He wanted to ask them about it. Could they tell him everything he wanted to know? Or would it just end up in another fight?

"Why don't you ask them about it?" Aylise asked.

"Who?" Will retorted sharply.

"Your parents. Let's go right now and ask them," she pleaded.

"How did you know?" He snapped back, more harshly than he intended.

"I don't need magic to know what you're thinking." Aylise didn't mask the hurt in her voice. "I'm just trying to help you."

"Hmm," Will huffed.

Aylise turned away from him. *Shit, you idiot.* He slumped his shoulders, while his stomach twisted in knots. This whole afternoon made him feel awful. A familiar face caught Will's attention as Seb walked out of an alley. His eyes searched the square before turning back to talk to the boy walking next to him. Will didn't recognise the boy walking with Seb at first, but then he tossed his light blonde hair out of his eyes. What were Seb and Rupert doing together again? Rupert was softly-spoken and always adored spending time with Seb. The four of them had grown up together because Rupert's father was an archivist in the Rotherwell's Library, a career that Rupert would no doubt follow in the future. He was one of the smartest people Will knew, though Will had become jealous of the amount of time Seb had been spending with Rupert. Seb and Rupert paused several feet away from them, talking rapidly to each other. Seb walked towards Will, leaving Rupert lingering behind.

"Hi," Seb stuttered slightly as he spoke and fidgeted with his hands. "I had an idea, Rupert's really good with symbols and I…"

"You told him?" Will said angrily, cutting him off.

"I told him that we were looking into a symbol," Seb said pointedly.

"And what if he tells someone?" Will said sharply.

"Calm down, Will," Seb replied equally as sharply. "I never said it was on you."

"Stop it, both of you." Aylise stepped in between them. "Quiet." She looked pointedly at Will. Her piercing blue eyes boring into him. She turned towards Seb. "How good is he with symbols?"

"He's the best chance we have at answers." Seb smiled softly, looking towards Will.

"I need a moment." Will crossed his arms and walked away.

Why didn't Seb ask him first? This was about him, he had the right to decide who knew about the symbols, didn't he? He trusted Rupert, it wasn't that. But… but what? Why was he so angry?

"You should have asked me first, Seb," he snapped, walking back to Seb and Aylise.

"And how did you go at the library?" Seb's sharp tone cut through the air like a knife. "Because I'm guessing by your attitude that it didn't go well." He crossed his arms and puffed his chest. "So, what's it going to be Will, are you going to accept Rupert's help? Or are you going to finally grow up and talk to your parents?"

"Both of you calm down, please," Aylise pleaded.

Will didn't like the idea of someone else knowing yet, but he was out of options.

"I'm sorry." He bowed his head. "I shouldn't have snapped like that." He hugged Seb. "Just speak to me about it first next time, okay?"

"Sure," Seb replied. "I'm sorry too." Seb waved Rupert over, his smile growing wide. "Tell them what you told me."

"Hi!" Rupert greeted them eagerly, smiling softly and acting like he hadn't just witnessed that confrontation.

"What do you know?" Will said hurriedly. *Gods, you can be a dick sometimes.* Seb shot him an irritated look, which Will ignored.

"My father took me to Gregaron a few months ago." Rupert began, stepping closer. "He was down there to work in their library. They have some great volumes catalogued. It's the second-largest library in Arulean."

"And?" Will replied, hoping that it sounded less impatient than it felt.

"Well, there's a rather obscure section in part of the library. One day I was reading about Arulean history and there was an old archivist working on the same table. One of his books had a strange symbol on the cover." Rupert looked pointedly at Will. "When I asked him about the book, he said it was an ancient volume on the magical history of Arulean. The symbol is the same one you're looking for."

"How do you know what symbol we're looking for?" Will asked. Turning towards Seb without waiting for Rupert's answer.

"Seb drew it for me," Rupert replied, holding a piece of paper in his hand.

Will's chest tightened and his body shook with rage as he looked down at the drawing of the symbol in Rupert's hand.

"Don't flash that about," Will barked as the anger poured out of him.

Rupert jumped back, shoving the piece of paper back in his pocket.

"Will," Aylise called out, admonishing him. "Please. Calm down." She spoke each word slowly, her eyes silently pleading with him. Will looked into her eyes, he inhaled and exhaled deeply three times.

"How do you propose we get that volume from Gregaron, Rupert? We can't just go riding down there, it would take weeks," Will said, the irritated icy tone not completely gone from his voice.

"No, you can't, but I'm fairly sure you'll find what you're looking for in the Great Library of Basilium," Rupert said smugly.

"I thought Rickard and Haveena destroyed most of the library when they seized Basilium?" Will replied.

"But not everything," Aylise responded. "Not according to my father." They all turned towards her. "As Rupert said, the library in Basilium is the largest in Arulean. There are hundreds of thousands of volumes in the main reading room alone, and that's just one part of the library. There are two other floors on top of that one, and the lower levels where some of the most ancient texts are kept. She wouldn't have been able to destroy everything."

This is becoming more complex by the minute. Entering Basilium unnoticed by their parents would be hard enough. The city is a dangerous place, or so he'd been told.

"Have any of you ever been to Basilium before?" he asked. Aylise and Rupert both nodded in reply. "Good, because I haven't."

"So, what do you say, Will?" Seb asked.

"You don't actually want to go into the city, do you?" Will replied, rather shocked.

"Not particularly, but I'd go there for you," Seb replied. "You didn't have any luck in the library here, did you?" Seb replied.

"No," Will replied shortly.

"Well then now, you have a place to start," Rupert said matter-of-factly.

"Rupert, would you mind giving us a moment alone please?" Aylise said gently, but the command was evident in the way she spoke.

"Of course." He paused momentarily, "My Lady."

Seb pulled Rupert away. They spoke softly to each other, their heads so close they were almost touching.

"Come find me later," Rupert said, smiling at Seb.

"Of course," Seb replied.

Rupert walked back through the busy square and disappeared from view. Aylise was watching Seb curiously.

"What exactly did you tell him, Seb?" Aylise asked, her voice quite stern and direct.

It was moments like this that Will was reminded of Aylise's station. She was their friend, born and raised together. She had always been Aylise, but she was also the heir of Fawkeston and with that title came her commanding presence.

"I didn't tell him the symbol was on you, Will, I promise," Seb replied nervously. "I just told him we were looking into the symbol. That we were trying to research it."

"But why did you tell him?" Will asked.

"Because it was a good idea," Seb became defensive. "And as it stands, he gave you the best lead you have."

Seb wasn't normally this forthright. The usually timid, awkward and shy Seb was nowhere to be seen right now. Seb was radiating confidence, and Will liked this side of him.

"It's fine, Seb," Aylise said softly. "You're right, this is the best lead we have. But Will." Aylise turned towards him, "I think going into Basilium is a bad idea."

"You do?" Will and Seb said in unison.

"Yes," she replied firmly. "It's a dangerous city, and frankly, going in there unchaperoned would be even more dangerous for the four of us."

"I need to know, Aylise," Will pleaded. "I have to do something."

"You could just ask your parents about it. They clearly already know," she replied firmly. "So why don't you tell them you know too."

"No, I can't do that," he replied. He wasn't ready for that yet. "Do you want to stay behind?" he asked Aylise gently.

"I want us all to stay behind, but I'm coming with you," she paused again. "Someone has to get you to the library."

"We'll get in the city and head straight there, take what we can, and get out."

"When do we leave?" Seb asked.

"Tomorrow," Will replied. "Will you be able to get horses?"

"It shouldn't be an issue," Aylise replied. "Mother and Father are leaving early tomorrow. So, they won't be a problem."

"Good. Seb, go to Rupert, tell him the plan," said Will. "And thank him for his help."

"Okay, bye," Seb replied, turning on his heels and walking away.

Will watched him walk away. He glanced between Seb and Aylise. He felt queasy at the thought of what was to come. They were used to exploring together. As much as exploring the Amaranthine Forest or the lands around home seemed dangerous and exciting. It was vastly different to walking straight into Basilium. Was it reckless? Yes. But he felt like he didn't have any choice. Asking his friends to go to dangerous places for him felt odd, and as much as he didn't want to put them in danger, he needed their guidance and help.

Will woke the next morning wishing he could have slept for a few more hours, having tossed and turned through the night, unable to escape the debilitating thoughts running wildly through his mind. Was he really going to sneak into a dangerous city to steal a book? He rolled over in his bed and stared out his window. The sun was peeking through the clouds: perhaps that was a good sign for them. He pulled himself out of bed, took a deep breath and prepared himself to face his parents. He had rehearsed the lie over and over last night. Will walked down the stairs and into the kitchen. His mother and father were sitting at the dining table drinking tea, a plate of fresh-cut fruit sitting on the table in front of them.

"Good morning, I was beginning to wonder if you would ever rise?" his mother said to him, smiling.

"Growing boys need to sleep," he replied, smiling.

He rummaged through the fruit bowl and picked up a keoa, a sweet and juicy fruit that grew in the Jean Islands. He bit into its soft flesh, and its sweet aroma filled the room.

"When did these arrive?" he asked.

"We got a shipment in yesterday," his father replied.

"From Grandpa?"

"Of course," Darian replied. "He wrote that he would like us to come home to visit. He said it's been far too long."

"Maybe we should then," Will replied, smiling and biting into the fruit. Will's parents raised their eyebrows at each other and smiled softly.

"Will, what have you planned for today?" His mother asked.

Will took another bite of the keoa, exaggerating each chewing motion to give himself time to prepare himself.

"Aylise, Seb and I were planning to spend the day in Aylise's library."

"Oh?" His mother replied, pausing. "Wonderful, we were going to suggest you spend the day there."

"You were?" Will replied, confused and slightly suspicious.

"Yes, we have matters to attend to out of town today."

"You do? How long will you be gone?" Will tried to keep his voice neutral.

"All day, it would seem. We won't be back until later tonight."

Will stopped the smile he felt inside from creeping up onto his face. If his parents were out of the village all day, they would never know he was gone. He paused, remembering what Aylise said yesterday. Her mother and father were away all day, too. Were they going away together? It wasn't normal for a blacksmith and his dressmaker wife to be attending to business with a lord and lady.

"When do you leave?" he asked them, suddenly realising he would have to plan their exit from Fawkeston carefully.

"We're leaving in a few moments' time. Why don't you get ready, and we'll take you up to the castle?"

"Okay sure," he replied, running up the stairs to get what he needed.

Fawkeston Castle had stood for over two thousand years. Its walls and turrets towered over Fawkeston. The castle was built as the gateway to the Amaranthine Forest as a line of defence if the fae ever revolted against humans. Over the centuries, it had been used as a base for the fae when they had been called to aid.

Like most of Arulean, since the siege of Basilium, the castle had seen better days. If Will squinted, he could just make out the white stone that had once adorned the castle walls, now replaced with the dull and dirty grey build-up that had seemed to blanket most of the region. Seasonal rains used to sweep through Fawkeston, washing away the natural dirt that would be expected in a city or town. After each downpour, the town had glistened like new, but with each passing year, Arulean itself seemed to fade into despair.

Will and his parents walked through the castle gates into the bailey. Lord Nathaniel was inspecting his carriages by the stables. His footman pointed towards Will's family as they walked. Two carriages were being prepared for travel.

"Ah, Darian, it's wonderful to see you, my friend," Lord Nathaniel called out in greeting, happily.

"You too, my friend," his father replied, walking towards Nathaniel and embracing him.

Their families were often informal with each other in private. Will appreciated the relaxed nature of their friendship, but he never quite understood it. His parents always followed protocol in society, so what made it so different this time?

"Come ride with me today, I'm sure Selina and Ana would happily ride together in the other carriage."

They *were* going somewhere together! But where? His eyes darted from his father to Lord Nathaniel, then scanned the carriages. He wasn't sure what he was looking for, but anything that ascertained where they were going would be helpful.

"Young Will!" Lord Nathaniel turned towards him. "Try to keep out of trouble today." He chuckled to himself. "Go on in. Aylise is waiting for you."

"I will, thank you, Lord Nathaniel," Will replied, turning towards his parents. Gods, if only they knew exactly what trouble he was getting into.

"Stay in the keep today, Will!" his mother called out pleadingly.

"Goodbye, Mama," he replied, not letting her see him roll his eyes.

Aylise was waiting for him at the bottom of the stairs that led into the keep. She marched over to him as soon as she noticed him.

"Where are they going?" she asked him in hushed tones.

"Oh," he replied, crestfallen. 'I was hoping you'd know."

"And I was hoping you did."

"No," he huffed. "Damn it."

"Will, what if they're going to Basilium?"

The thought had crossed his mind. Their parents could upend their plans with a snap. They could be seen and dragged home, and with that, any chance of finding helpful information in the library would be gone.

"We'll be fine, we'll be careful," he told himself, as much as he told Aylise. "Come with me."

Will walked back towards the gates, Aylise followed closely behind. Lord Nathaniel's men were moving around the carriages, mounting their horses and preparing to move out. The bailey was bustling with servants, who all seemed to be preparing for the journey. Three familiar people came walking to the courtyard from the town, one of them was looking rather surprised to see Will standing there.

"It's Seb, look." Will pointed out to the gates as he spoke.

"Are his parents going with them too?" Aylise sounded and looked incredulous.

"They must be."

Seb's parents hugged him and ushered him towards Will and Aylise. Seb kept looking back at his parents as he walked over. He looked as confused as Will and Aylise. His parents walked over to Lord Nathaniel and Will's father.

"What are they up to?" Seb asked, not even bothering to hug Aylise and Will. Instead, he turned around and watched his parents.

"Your guess is as good as ours. What did your parents say to you?" Will asked.

"That they had business out of town today."

"Same as mine," Will replied.

"What about yours, Aylise?"

"If I knew where they were going, I would have told you already," she replied.

"Rupert is in Basilium already," Seb paused, looking over his shoulder. "He came to see me late yesterday afternoon. He told me his father had to go there urgently. So, he'll meet us at the library."

Will watched the procession leave the courtyard. He wrapped his hands around his stomach, which felt like it was tumbling. He couldn't shake the sense that something didn't feel right.

"Okay, we just have to get into the city and find a useful book and get out." Will tried to sound confident. He prayed to the gods that everything would go smoothly.

Will stared up at the dark grey walls of Basilium towering above him. His stomach still felt like it was tumbling and churning. The horrible sense of foreboding increased as they rode closer to Basilium. Will, Aylise and Seb had arrived at the eastern gates of the city without running into any problems. They tied their horses in the stables, Aylise paid the stable boy a hefty amount for watching the horses, and promised the same if the horses were still there when they returned. City guards were stationed on both sides of the gates. Their polished black armour was pristine, thick, and battle-ready. The guards stood in stark contrast to the rundown and dirty city walls. The city was far more dilapidated than Will had thought. Will followed Seb and Aylise under the sharp metal portcullis, passed the grey wooden gates and entered the city for the first time.

"Why does it look like everything is covered in ash and dirt?" Will asked, appalled at the lack of care or upkeep. The wooden buildings around them were falling apart, most of the windows were missing their glass panes and instead were covered in dirty rags that flapped in the wind. Dense grey smoke blanketed the city. The acrid smell of large fires burning across the city lingered in the air. "Gods, what are they burning?" He covered his nose. "I thought the wealthy lived in the eastern region of Basilium city."

"They do," Aylise said. "Appalling, isn't it?"

They moved deeper into the city, following the hard-packed earth around a corner. Will glanced back towards the gates, several guards moved across the open gates. Before he could give it any more thought, they disappeared out of sight.

The city of Basilium truly opened in front of them now. The city's royal quarter rose directly in front of Will. The quarter rose higher and higher along the hillside. Will paused for a moment. His skin felt hot, in fact, he felt hot all over. He looked up in disgust, the filthy street he walked along stood in stark contrast to the clean, polished and maintained buildings that adorned the hill. Aylise was right, the wealthy did live here, their large homes and manors the dazzling jewels of Arulean, leading up to the royal palace, looking down upon the less fortunate.

A large black wall had been erected around the royal quarter. He couldn't see the gates from where he was standing, but he had no doubt that they were guarded.

"Let me guess, only the select few are allowed in there," Will said, turning towards Aylise.

"It wasn't always the case." Aylise looked back towards them. "It was built three years ago. But you're right. Only the select few."

"Just another way for Rickard and Haveena to segregate the people," Will commented. "The Great Library isn't in there, is it?"

"No, thankfully. Stay close to me."

Run-down and dirty homes were replaced with modest buildings and shops. They were by no means the pristine manor homes of the royal quarter, but the difference was staggering. The air smelt cleaner, too: gone was the smell of sewage and unwashed bodies, not that it had been replaced with anything sweet or refreshing.

"Did they push all the homeless and less fortunate people to the city edge?" Will asked, looking around.

"It gets worse every day," Aylise responded.

"I hate being in here, it feels…" Seb paused, "It feels wrong. I can sense it."

"This way," Aylise said, turning towards the royal quarter.

Aylise led them to a wide street. The large wall segregating the city stood to their right. Will's assumption had been correct: guards blocked the entrance, watching every soul who walked through.

"I thought you said the library wasn't in there?" Will asked.

"It's not, it's just down here," Aylise said, pointing down the street. Aylise walked further along and stopped. "Oh no," Aylise gasped, "Look."

Ten guards were standing in front of the library, blocking anyone from entering.

"Move on or lose your head," a guard called out to an elderly man trying to enter the library.

"What do we do now?" Seb asked.

"Can you get us in there, Aylise?" Will asked. "You are a lady after all."

"If my father was here, maybe, but not alone," she slumped her shoulders.

"I think it's far too dangerous for us to be trying that anyway," Seb said, fidgeting with his hands.

Seb was starting to get nervous. Will could sense the change in Seb's mannerisms easily: his swift change of tone from casual to weary told Will that he didn't have much longer before Seb turned them back. Will dropped his gaze, the disappointment lingering. *What now, then?* he thought to himself. How was he going to find the truth?

"Is there anything else we can do?" He asked his friends.

"You could always ask your parents about it, Will," Seb replied.

"Would they even tell me the truth though?"

"Maybe you need to give them the chance," Seb was almost pleading.

Will thought over Seb's words. Was it so bad to go home and ask his parents about the symbols? Though his parents had always been secretive, maybe if he told them he knew, they would be forthright? They had to know about them, all the signs led that way. But if he told them, they would start to ask questions.

"What are we going to do?" Aylise asked.

"I need a moment to think," he replied, walking to the edge of the street.

Will gazed at the city around him. The citizens seemed to have a knack of dispersing every time a patrol of city guards rounded a corner. They darted left and right, disappearing down alleys or ducking into buildings. The guards seemed to relish the fear and power they wielded over the city.

"How do people live like this?" Will asked, tension rising in his chest. Will had always known the guards in Basilium were rough and dangerous, but he didn't imagine it would be like this. A yearning grew in him, pulling at every fibre of his consciousness. "This isn't right." He spoke with sadness and anger in his voice.

"They're too afraid, Will, they've seen their homes and their lives taken away. There wasn't anyone to stop it," Aylise said softly.

"It's not right," Will said firmly, raising his voice.

"Will, be quiet," Seb said in a reprimanding tone. "You can't walk around here saying things like that. Let's go home."

A guttural scream pierced the air. Will turned, looking for the cause. A guard held a young man by the throat, pushing him against a brick wall close by. The man screamed again, before going silent and turning a nasty shade of red. The tension building in Will turned to rage. He clenched his fists as the rage spread through his body, taking over all his senses. The guard threw the man into an alleyway. He landed hard into the dirt, sobbing and gasping for air while he scurried backwards. People around the area quickly dispersed, leaving the man alone with the guard.

Without thinking, Will moved towards them, the simmering rage propelling him forward. He wanted to hurt this guard, he wanted to hurt all the guards. His whole body felt like fire as he moved forward.

"Will," Seb hissed, grabbing his hand. Seb screamed, retracting his hand and clutching it.

Will stopped moving, the rage subsided as quickly as it came, his body cooling down quickly. He looked to Seb, who was still clutching his hand.

"Are you okay?" Will asked, not taking his eyes off Seb's hand.

"What the hell were you doing?" Seb replied, looking Will directly in the eye. "And why does your skin feel like it's on fire?" he hissed.

"I'm sorry, Seb." He paused. "I don't know what happened." Will looked down at his arms, bewildered. What was happening to him?

Will hated the way his friends were looking at him: quiet, motionless and a little fearful.

"I'm sorry, but can't you see what's happening here?" Will said.

"We are powerless to stop it, Will. This is not the time or the place," Aylise said firmly. "Remember where we are."

"Can we please go home now? I don't want to spend any more time in here," Seb said, his voice giving away to fear.

"Okay let's go," Will replied reluctantly.

Will wasn't ready to go just yet, but he didn't want to make Aylise and Seb feel any worse. Leaving meant the whole day was for nothing. He looked back towards the alley, where the young man lay unmoving on the dirt. The guard moved away from the alley, smirking and laughing as he joined his patrol. Will seethed as they walked past him, feeling a new appreciation for his life in Fawkeston, the sense of community, the safety, and his overbearingly protective parents. It was one thing to hear the stories about the dangers of Basilium, but it was another thing to witness the injustices being dished out to its people.

People started following the guards and crowds started to form as people pushed their way through the streets. As they were inched slowly forward, the crowds became louder, the shouting growing with every step.

"Something's happening," Will murmured.

He ran ahead, following the crowd as they marched down the street. The sea of people turned a corner to the left, down a wide road. He paused, soaking up the scene around him. Basilium Square loomed in front of him. Will had never seen such a large gathering of people. The square was full to the brim, stalls erected tightly in the market area, though nobody seemed to be shopping now. Large broken stone pillars rose from the ground in a circle around the square. Will had heard the stories about the Kyllarian family statues that had once adorned the top of the pillars: the kings and queens who had held the seat of the Basilium. Queen Haveena and King Rickard had crushed the statues into powders.

In the distance, the royal road wound towards the far side of the royal quarter. From his vantage point, the black stone castle shadowed over the whole city, perched high upon the seaside cliff. The differences between the royal quarter and the square weren't as stark as the other areas he had ventured to today. The town square was the most upkept place that Will had seen in Basilium.

Will couldn't control the urge and kept moving into the square, each step taking him deeper into the crowds.

"Will, wait a moment," Seb called out, shuffling up next to him.

"Something's happening, Seb. I can't see," Will replied, trying to move further into the crowd.

"We shouldn't be here," Aylise hissed.

A short man turned a corner on the royal road. Dressed in all black, he was round and bald with only a few sparse hairs perched on his head. His face was covered in boils and moles. He continued to walk down the royal road into the square. He stopped on a large wide step towards the end of the road, separated from the crowds. He looked down at the people. His smile was full of malice, there was no kindness in his eyes. His mouth was missing quite a few teeth, and those that were present were brown and chipped.

"We need to leave now." Aylise's voice shook as she spoke. "We don't want to see what comes next."

"Why, what comes next?" Will asked.

"That's Andeux, the royal executioner," Aylise replied, pausing. "He only makes appearances in public for one purpose," she continued.

"Will, we need to go," Seb pleaded.

Will agreed with them, but he couldn't move. Andeux had stirred something in him that he didn't quite understand. Who was this man that caused Will to feel so off? And why was he familiar?

Two royal guards marched down the royal road holding a shackled man, his face covered by a hood. Behind them, two large squads of royal guards led a party towards the square. King Rickard and Queen Haveena walked in the middle of the squads. King Rickard was tall and muscular, his large frame towered over those around him. His arms were so large that Will had no doubt he could crush a person with his bare hands. A black spiked crown rested on Rickard's dark hair, and he wore black leathers, his large sword sheathed in his scabbard by his side. He thought back to the dreamlike vision he had at the campfire, recognising the brutal warrior easily. The queen wore a black and silver gown; the elegant bodice was covered in black leathers. Even from this distance, Will could feel a coldness radiating from her. She wore a similar crown to her husband: it rested atop her bright blonde hair, which was curled up in a bun. She wore an elaborate jewelled necklace, and in its centre, a sapphire sparkled for all to see.

Will moved further into the square as the king and queen paused at the top of the steps. Their faces were cold and unreadable as they lingered close to Andeux and the gathering royal guards. Andeux removed the hood from the shackled person. It wasn't a man, as Will had thought. It was a boy. Will froze, every part of him felt alert and icy cold.

"Seb," he whispered, looking back towards his friend. His body erupted in goosebumps.

Seb's eyes grew wide as his body trembled uncontrollably. He moved towards Will, tripping over himself and stumbling into Will.

"Rupert, Rupert," Seb mumbled. Will held him in place as he tried to move closer to Rupert.

Will looked up at Rupert. He was dirty and tears streamed down his face as he looked out towards the crowd. His arms were covered in red sores, the flesh around them blackened. He was still wearing the same clothes he had been wearing yesterday. The guards gripped his arms tightly.

"Rupert... Will... We...' Seb gasped, choking on each word. "Please, Will... please.' He spoke in hushed tones, tears streaming down his face.

Will stared wide-eyed at Aylise. Her eyes darted from Will and Seb to Rupert and back, tears streaming down her face. Will didn't know what to do, he felt helpless.

"We did this." She spoke softly. Covering her mouth with her hands. "We did this to him, I know it. Look at his sleeves."

The words repeated in his head as he stared at Rupert's shirt, the arms were ripped and burnt. Oh gods, the symbols? He looked down at his wrists, smooth and bare, the symbol remained hidden away. They had burnt his arms, but how would they know about the symbols?

"The paper," Will said, Seb and Aylise stared at him confused. "He kept the drawing of the symbol. He came into the city last night with his father." He looked up towards Rupert. "The king and queen know what the symbol means, and they don't want anyone else to know. This is all my fault."

Will looked towards Seb and Aylise. Tears streamed down Seb's face and his lips quivered. Aylise looked shocked as all the puzzle pieces fell into place for her. Will's body began to heat up, the same fire he felt earlier burning inside him.

"Stay here. Stay together. Don't move," he called to Seb and Aylise.

"Will, what are you doing?" Aylise asked as he moved further into the crowd.

The fire burned in Will, spreading through him and taking over. He had to do something, he couldn't let him die. He pushed closer towards the steps.

Rickard and Haveena moved towards the edge of the step. The queen sneered down at the gathered crowd. The king placed his hand out, stopping the queen as he walked to the edge and looked over at the sea of people in front of him. The smile on her face was quickly replaced with absolute contempt before she adopted a neutral expression, but Will noticed it, nonetheless.

"This boy has committed crimes against the kingdom. He was found looking for forbidden texts in our city. We know he did not act alone." The king's booming voice echoed out across the square. "He has refused to name his conspirators. This is your one chance to come forward and spare his life now."

Will moved forward, pushing his way through the tight crowd. He couldn't let Rupert take the fall for his actions, he had to do something, anything. He started to raise his hand, ready to call out, when someone held onto him, covering his mouth.

"What are you doing in here, Will?" Lord Nathaniel demanded, looking down at him. He removed his hand from Will's mouth.

"Lord Nathaniel, please help him," Will begged.

"We need to get you out of here. Now!" he replied. Lord Nathaniel started pulling him away from the royal road, further into the crowd.

"Lord Nathaniel, please, you need to help him, it's my fault."

"What do you mean *your fault?*"

"I'm the one who was looking for the symbol," he replied, rubbing his wrists.

"Oh gods, you know," he replied, glancing from Will's wrists to his eyes.

"What do you mean, you know?" Will replied. "Do you know about the symbols too?"

"Seb STOP," Aylise's voice called out in the crowd.

Will and Lord Nathaniel turned towards the sound of Aylise's voice. She was pulling on Seb's sleeve as he fought to get out of her grip.

"Get off me!" Seb called out.

Seb manoeuvred out of her grip, pushing himself forward. Aylise fell backwards, colliding with the wall of a stall. Time seemed to slow down around him as Will watched Aylise fall into the stall. Her legs lifted from the stone street, and she fell over bales of hay in front of the store. A lantern swinging from a hook on a timber post fell to the ground. The hay strewn across the ground ignited around her before she even had time to stand.

"Aylise!" Will and Lord Nathaniel called at the same, time rushing towards her.

Aylise panicked as the fire ignited high around her. People scattered away, doing their best to avoid the flames. Seb stopped moving and watched helplessly as the flames encased Aylise.

Will surveyed his surroundings as he sprinted towards her. He glanced from stall to stall. Finding his opportunity, he sprinted towards a stall close to the flames.

"Move!" He pressed through the crowd, pushing people aside without a second thought.

He reached for an axe resting against a wall and climbed up the wooden crates stacked against it. From the roof of the stall, he could see the whole area around Aylise. The flames were rising higher and moving closer towards her. She looked up at him, fear radiating from her.

"I've got you!" he called out.

Will lunged for a rope that was attached to the stall, secured to a wooden beam that expanded over parts of the square. Hacking at the rope, he freed it from the roof of the stall below his feet and swung it around in front of him. He adjusted his tension on the rope, took aim and leapt off the building towards her.

As Will sailed across the top of the square, he locked eyes with his mother. She stared up at him, her eyes wide. *Focus on now*, he quickly said to himself as he swung towards the flames. As soon as his body started to rise, he leapt from the rope, pushing with all his strength towards Aylise. He brushed through the flames as he landed on the ground hard, rolling once, twice, before stopping in front of Aylise. She pulled him up and hugged him.

"Will. What do we do?" she cried, gasping for breath.

Will took in his surroundings. The flames were surrounding them on most sides. The stall next to them was still intact, but the flames were slowly making their way towards the roof of the stall. As the area around them continued to burn, people started to clear the area away, hoping to contain the burning.

"The roof. It's the only way."

Will pulled Aylise and boosted her up on top of the stall. He jumped, his outstretched hand grasping the edge of the roof. He managed to hold on and pull himself up.

"Now what?" Aylise said as the flames grew higher and closer. "I can't make that jump."

"You won't have to," he replied.

He pulled the axe free of his belt and hacked at a rope attached to the back side of the stall. It was attached to another wooden beam over the square.

"Come here, and hold onto me," Will said, panicking.

Will was starting to perspire from the heat and nerves wracking through his body. If he failed this, he could kill her.

"When I say go, jump with me, okay?" he said, securing the rope around one arm and scooping Aylise up in the other. Although he was terrified, he couldn't deny it felt nice to hold her. Aylise wrapped her arms around his body and nodded. "Go!"

Will and Aylise leapt from the roof of the stall. They sailed through the air, their feet brushing the top of the flames as they curved down towards the ground.

"Let go!" Will called as he cleared the flames and began to rise.

Aylise let go of him and Will swung his arm around, hoping to give her any extra momentum. Every muscle in his arm burned as he did. Will watched as Lord Nathaniel and Seb raced to her, scooping her up from the ground. She made it: she was safe. Will was so distracted watching Aylise that he didn't notice that he was swinging back towards the flaming stall.

He panicked as his body and the rope were engulfed in flames as he swung through. He cleared the flames, swinging higher into the sky above the stall. He slid downwards as the rope began to burn and untwine. He leapt from the rope, reaching out for a taut line. He swung the axe around it. Holding it above the line, he glided down towards the ground. Will felt the symbols on his arms before he saw them: he had burnt away part of his clothes. They were glowing so brightly it was hard to look at them.

Will let go of the axe and dropped to the ground, rolling around to put out the flames on his clothing. He had landed closer to the centre of the square, and those that were nearby gave him a wide berth as he stood up. Older citizens were gasping and pointing at Will. He glanced down at his wrists. The symbols were glowing brighter than they ever had.

Haveena and Rickard stared at him from across the square. Even from this distance, Will could feel the rage emanating from the queen as she looked at him. She stepped forward onto the landing.

"Andeux, execute the boy!" she called out, pointing towards Rupert without even a glance in his direction. Her eyes were fixed on Will.

Will hadn't even noticed that Rupert had been placed on the executioner's block. He'd been so occupied helping Aylise he had forgotten about him. Andeux raised his sword in the air and swung it down swiftly. Rupert's head landed on the stone steps, rolling several times before it stopped. Seb's scream echoed through the square. Will desperately wanted to run to him, but his own fear froze him in place.

"And bring me that boy now."

~ CHAPTER FOUR ~

Fear spread through Will's body like wildfire. As the queen looked down upon him, rage continued to burn behind her eyes. Guards started running in his direction. Andeux the executioner lunged off the landing towards him. Scared and confused, Will quickly looked around: he needed his mother, his father, Lord Nathaniel, anyone who could help him. Will found Aylise and Seb: she was safely wrapped in her father's arms. Lord Nathaniel was frantically looking from his daughter to Will. Seb was scared and confused. Will found his mother across the square, his father was crouched low and running towards him.

"Run... Go..." his mother called out to him.

Guards were moving closer to Will. People started to leave the square, running from the oncoming guards. His father was too far away, he wouldn't make it to him in time.

"Will!" screamed Aylise.

A hand wrapped around Will's arm. "Quickly, Will. Move. Now." The person began to pull him out of the square.

"Will, Will!" he heard screamed across the square.

Will looked back at Aylise and Seb as they were dragged from the square by Lord Nathaniel. Separated from his family and friends, Will suddenly felt alone and exposed. He looked up at the woman who was pulling him along, and the familiar face shocked him.

"Yana? What's going on?"

Yana was an old friend of his family. She owned a tavern in Basilium and one in Fawkeston. Although Will had never set foot in her Basilium establishment, he had spent many a day in her Fawkeston tavern when he was growing up.

"Well, the cat's out of the bag now, isn't it?" She grinned down at him as she pulled him through the streets. "Keep up, lad. We're getting you out of here."

"What do you mean?" he asked. Almost slipping as the stone ground gave way to dirt streets.

"As much as I'd love to stop and have a yarn over an ale, now's not exactly the best time, mate," she drawled. "Now, Will, listen to me." She spoke each word clearly as she ran through the streets. "Do you remember the village of Oldwell?"

Yana did not stop running as she spoke to Will. She gripped his arms tightly as they wove among the people moving away from the square. Yana darted to her left down an alleyway. Will lost his footing, but Yana pulled him up and continued running, a quick jerk right and then a rush to the left again.

"Find the boy, spread out!" The clinking of armour stomped into the hard earth, reverberating around them. Will couldn't determine which direction that shouting came from, though he could hear the clinking of armour close by. Yana quickened her movement.

"Will, do you remember the village?" She asked more urgently.

"Yes, I remember it."

The alley they were running down ended and Yana pushed on across a street full of people running away from the square. Will could see the glint of armour down the street. Yana turned sharply down an alley, then another sharp turn to the left down another side alley.

"Good, go to Oldwell, Will. Run and don't look back. Do you understand me?"

A sharp turn to the right again, Will was losing track of where they were now.

"What do you mean, go there? Why? What is going on?"

Yana pushed them out onto another street. Will lost his footing again, nearly falling to the ground. Yana pulled on his arm harder, steadying his feet. Will could hear armour moving close by again, fear and adrenaline coursing through him. They ran faster into another side alley.

"Wait," she whispered, halting and throwing him against a wall. They were tucked behind a stack of boxes, hidden from view. The clinking of armoured footsteps carried further away.

"Quite a skill set for a tavern owner, Yana," Will said between huffed breaths.

"Oh, I'm quite the talented tavern wench, dear boy." She winked at him. "Talented enough to get you out of here. Talented enough to keep you alive all these years, too." She smirked at him and looked towards the end of the alley. "Let's go," she called out, leading him along the narrow path. "Now listen, Will. You're in danger." She paused as they turned down another street. "Do as I say, go to Oldwell and wait for us there, do you hear me?"

"Danger? Why?"

"Will!" Yana raised her voice now. "Do you understand?"

"Yes, I understand."

Yana pulled them into another side alley.

"Good, run Will. And don't stop until you get there. Avoid the roads, trust your instincts." Yana turned another corner. A man stood waiting for them.

"Quickly get him out of here, they're not far behind us." The man grabbed Will's arm.

"And Will?" Will looked up into Yana's eyes and saw pride in her eyes: warmth and care that he had never seen in her before. "I promise we will explain everything to you when you get to Oldwell. Be safe." She kissed him on the head. "Don't do anything stupid. Think like a tavern wench and you'll be fine."

"Wait, you're going there too?"

"It's not the time for a yarn and an ale, boy!" she called out as she turned out of the alley, and she was gone.

"Quietly and quickly," said the man, holding Will's arm and pulling him along.

He was dressed in combat leathers and had a sword sheathed by his side. Will could hear people shouting and scrambling around them. Every now and then, a soft breeze would blow across a street, bringing the smell of salty air with it. Were they following the beach? The man weaved between streets, somehow managing to avoid any guards. They darted left, right, left, left again and then out into a street.

Weaving between people in a crowded street and rapidly moving along the huge city disorientated Will. He tried to look around for familiar landmarks, any indication of where he was, but he was well and truly lost. Large orange fireworks exploded, erupting in sound and light across the sky, followed by another, and then another. Will could almost see them clearly as they crossed a street, but was sharply pulled down another street and led into a side alley.

"Find the boy!" someone shouted close by. Armour clinked behind the shouting.

Will's companion's grip tightened on his arm as the man ran faster. They cut right again into another alley and paused.

"Who are you?" Will shadowed his companion, who held himself against the wall. Will's whole body was aching, he panted, desperately trying to catch his breath as his muscles burned. His heart raced. How did everything turn to shit so quickly?

"Let's do introductions when we're not fugitives."

"Oh, okay then," Will huffed between each word.

The companion waited until the armoured sounds faded away and began to run again.

"Don't worry, lad. We'll get you out of here."

"Thanks," Will replied, rather confused.

Will struggled to keep up with him as they darted between the crowds. Most people seemed to be staring up at the fireworks in the sky. A few were still running away though, at least they seemed to be getting further away from the square. But, with less people around, there was less cover for Will. He looked behind them down the street, his eyes darted from one side of the street to the other. No guards, yet. *Faster Will, get out of this city.*

"In here." His companion pulled Will down another alley to their left. The ocean greeted them at the end of the alley.

"Are we going there?" asked Will, pointing at the sea.

"This way," he replied gruffly.

The man pulled Will down another side street. A woman was waiting for them, hidden in the shadows. She also wore combat leathers and carried a sword at her side.

"Galea, we haven't come across any guards yet," the man said quickly. "We had a close call though, you need to be quick."

"Thanks, Finley. The tunnels are just up ahead."

"Let's move then," Finley nodded in reply.

Will's short reprieve was over. He closed his eyes and took a deep breath filling his lungs with the smell of the salty water. It had the calming effect he had hoped for.

"I'm ready," he replied.

Galea started moving up the sloping street. A door opened in front of them and a royal guard walked out into the alley. His eyes darted from Will to his companions and back. The marks on Will's wrists had faded slightly, but they still glowed distinctly.

"Look out!" Finley snipped.

"I have the boy!" the guard shouted.

Finley released Will's arm and unsheathed his sword. Galea drew a dagger from her belt and lunged at the guard. They crashed into the wall, armour and bones banging together. The sound reverberated through the alley. Galea withdrew her bloodied blade from the guard's neck and untied his scabbard after he collapsed to the ground.

"Take this, you'll need it. We have to go." She handed the sword to Will. "Keep that sword out, Finley."

The three of them moved out towards the ocean. *Okay, we are moving west along the city.* Will realised with a sigh. On the beach, a deep trench had been created in the sand. Water gushed into it from a large tunnel: the labyrinth of storm sewers that weaved underneath the city.

Will followed the tunnel line. It rose to the higher points of the city. Were they fleeing through the sewers?

"Come, Will, let's move," Galea hissed.

She moved towards the tunnel entrance, a glint of silver caught in the corner of Will's eye. Finley launched in front of them and Galea threw her arm out to stop Will. Three guards stepped out from an alleyway close to the tunnel entrance. The guards moved closer, drawing their swords as they walked.

"Drop your swords and hand the boy over," the guard in the middle called out. "Walk away from him now and we'll let you live."

"Take the boy and go!" Finley called out, not taking his eyes off the slowly advancing guards. "You know what to do."

Will felt Galea's fingers slowly grip around his arm.

"Get ready to move." She spoke in barely a whisper, never taking her eyes off the guards.

"For Arulean!" screamed Finley, charging towards the guards.

As soon as Finley charged, Galea turned and ran along the street, holding onto Will's arm as she ran.

"We found the boy. Guards, assemble. He's escaping!" one of the guards behind them called out as steel clashed with steel.

Will tried to look back but Galea pulled him into an alley. The sounds of swords clashing drowned out the next turn. Galea moved quickly through the maze of alleyways. Left, right, forward, across a dark lane, up a set of stairs, in between two buildings, down an alley, left, right and right again.

"Where. Are. We. Going. Now." Will gasped between each ragged breath as his legs burned.

Galea stopped abruptly. Will started to speak then fell silent. Armour clinked heavily in front of them. It was so loud, almost as if the guards were running right towards them.

"This way, quickly," Galea hissed, pulling him into another alleyway.

Galea opened a door and pulled Will in. They darted through the shop, pausing briefly at the front door as Galea looked up and down the street.

"Now, Will."

They ran up the street. Will followed Galea's every step. Fireworks erupted all over the city again. Will panted as they ran, his heart beating fast in his chest. He had never felt fear like this before. Why was the queen after him? Was he going to die before he got out of the city? And why Oldwell? What did Yana know? Were Aylise and Seb in danger now too? Each thought felt like a huge wave slamming him under the water, barely giving him a moment's reprieve before the next wave washed over him. *You need to stop, Will!* He told himself. *Focus on right now! Focus on what you can control right now.*

"Let's pick up the pace." He pushed the pain in his legs aside. If he wanted answers, he had to get out of the city alive.

"We don't have much further to go," Galea replied, moving faster through the city.

As they turned another corner down an alley, a man stood ready to fight, at the sight of Galea and Will, he lowered his sword.

"Thank the gods, the guards are everywhere," he said.

"Stay together?" Galea asked.

"No, they're looking for a woman and a boy now."

"That fast?" she replied.

"No matter, we separate, we know what to do," the man replied.

"Don't look back, Will. Just keep going," Galea said, smiling at Will. She turned and exited the alley.

"Come along now, we need to get you out of here."

Will followed him along. This companion didn't feel the need to hold onto Will, which he wasn't going to complain about.

"What's your name?" Will asked as they turned into another alley.

"Jon," he replied.

"Thank you, Jon."

"Anything for your parents," Jon replied, smiling softly at him.

Jon led Will out of the alley, across the street and towards another alley. He stopped at the opening. Will nearly walked into him and glanced over Jon's shoulder. Fear shuddered through Will at the sight of four guards walking towards them.

"The boy is here!" shouted one of the guards, charging towards Jon and Will.

"Quick, move," called Jon.

The city walls loomed overhead as Will and Jon kept running. A hope sparked in Will, urging him to keep going. "In here," Jon hissed.

"Search everywhere. They're close," shouted a guard close by.

Will unsheathed the sword as he ran. Jon turned into a small, mostly deserted street. The air was cold and still in the shadow of the city wall. A man stood at the end of the street, looking directly at Will.

"They're close, take him and go, I'll hold them off," Jon said to the man. He unsheathed his sword. "Go, Will."

"Where are we going?" Will asked, panicked. His body continued to ache.

"Close the gates, the boy is close. Spread out and find him," shouted someone close by.

"This way." His companion turned into a small street.

The man started to move further ahead of Will, widening the gap between them. Will followed his companion along the side of a shop. The street was littered with crates and boxes. Clinking armour grew louder. Will's heart beat faster as the sounds grew nearer.

Armoured hands wrapped around Will. Adrenaline and fear coursed through him as he looked over his shoulder at the knight who was pulling him closer. Will looked around nervously as the knight pushed him against the shop wall. "Get your hands off me."

Will could hear armour and shouting getting closer to him. The knight kicked a crate at his foot aside, exposing a sewer opening. Before he had time to even see into the dark abyss, Will was pushed through the opening.

~ CHAPTER FIVE ~

Will landed with a splash. He was in a dark chamber where the only light was from the opening above him. The knight stood over the opening looking down at Will. Instinctively, he jumped out of the ring of light into the shadows of the chamber.

I'm trapped. Panicked thoughts raced through his mind. *I'm going to die here.* Panting and scared, Will tried to look out into the dark looking for any escape. The chamber was too dark, and his eyes needed time to adjust to the swift change to the light.

Shadows moved across the light above, drawing Will's attention back to the opening. The knight was holding Will's sword in his hand.

"Stay quiet and get to Oldwell," the knight called out, tossing Will's sword into the pool of water.

Will watched the knight push the crates back over the opening. The light dimmed in the chamber, and only small pockets of light poked through the holes in the crate.

Will fell to the ground and began to shake. The adrenaline and exhaustion finally caught up with him. He was thirsty, sweaty and sore all over. He inhaled deeply, the cool air easing some of the tension. *I'm not going to die here... I'm not going to die here...* he told himself with each breath in and out. *I have to get out of here.* Will closed his eyes and continued to breathe, and his heart began to return to a normal pace. He opened his eyes after a few moments. More of the chamber was visible. He was close to a stone wall that curved up to the roof. He closed his eyes again.

Seb and Aylise. I need to find them. Aylise... I saved her, she's going to be fine. Will smiled at this thought. *It felt good when she held onto me.*

Will heard water running through the chamber. There was a current close by. A voice nearby echoed through the chamber. His thoughts stayed on Aylise. He felt like he could see her, sense her, and feel her. Was she close?

"Will... Will..." called the voice. Aylise? Was she calling to him?

Will opened his eyes and launched off the floor. He was standing in a large sewer tunnel, bare, except for the water flowing across the floor from a grated opening in front of him. There was nobody else in the room. It must have been adrenaline or the nerves playing with his mind, he told himself.

I have to get out of here. He reached for the sword glinting in the water. *Which way?* Will's companions had moved him west through the city. He had entered the city through the eastern gate and moved along the coastline towards this tunnel. He knew he was close to the city walls. *Oh, yes!* The tunnels opened out to the sea on the western peninsula of the city. He was a strong swimmer, and he thought he would be able to handle the seas swimming back to the shore. But some of the tunnels opened out to the cliffs. If he found himself in one of those tunnels, there was no way possible to land safely on the jagged rocks below.

A small opening led out of the chamber behind him. He moved through it and followed the long winding tunnel. The air was cool and still in the tunnels, and the bottom of the sewer was wet and slippery. He tried to avoid walking through the stream of water that seemed to be slowly rising. Small pockets of light broke through grates to the streets above, illuminating the way along the tunnel. Shouting voices and clinking armour crept through some of the openings, echoing through the space. At others, Will heard hushed voices and sweeping movements. Were the citizens fleeing the guards? Will quickened his pace, moving further and further along the tunnel.

"Move. Now!" someone shouted from above.

Will stopped moving, metal scraping reverberated through the tunnel somewhere behind him. A grate had been opened somewhere! He began to run, pushing his body hard. Ahead, the tunnel merged with another, Will followed the flow of the water. More metal scraping… another grate opening?

They're coming. Will's heart raced as he pushed himself through the deepening aches in his body. He was so focused on the thought of pursuers in the tunnels that he didn't feel the current of the water quickening, nor the subtle slope down. He looked backwards, scanning behind him. It was then he noticed the moss growing up the walls. Before he could react, his feet swept up into the air. He began to slide rapidly down the tunnel. He moved faster, as the tunnel grew steeper, trying desperately to reach out for a surface to hold onto.

The tunnel opened into a large chamber, where Will plummeted down to a pool of water below. He landed with a loud splash and sank down, curling up to protect himself, he prepared to hit the bottom. He bounced in the water, never hitting the bottom, water cushioning around him. He floated back to the surface. Finding his feet he stood, perplexed, in the waist-deep water.

How did that happen? Will looked up at the tunnel. He should have hit the bottom of the pool. He plunged his hand into the cool water and brushed his hands along the stone floor of the pool. There was nothing else in the water to explain what just happened.

"What in the gods' names is going on today?" Will said aloud, looking around the chamber.

Will was in a large, dark chamber. The ceiling reached up to the surface, small grates allowed light to shine into the chamber. Tunnels led away from the chamber in three directions, sealed by dark, rusted gates. The water rushing into the chamber from the tunnel Will fell through became louder as the stream of water increased into a faster torrent. The sound bounced around the large space. A large archway led into a dark open space, another tunnel dropping below. The water overflowing from the pool cascaded into the darkness. Will walked towards the edge of the pool, rising higher out of the water with each step. He carefully inched himself towards the edge of the pool, leaning over. He could hear the echo of water rushing along far below.

"Hmm, perhaps not that way," he said, dismayed at the idea. He stepped back from the edge.

"No, you certainly won't be going out that way boy," a voice called out.

Will spun around at the sound of the voice. The rusted metal gate at the back of the chamber groaned as it swung open, its hinges protesting with a harsh creak. A chill ran down his spine. The queen's executioner strode into the chamber, a smile creeping across his scarred face as he stopped at the edge of the pool. Will unsheathed his sword, but Andeux only laughed.

"Put it down, you stupid boy," Andeux wheezed. "I'll make it less painful if you do."

Will's heart pounded in his chest, adrenaline surging through his veins. His gaze darted around the chamber. Were the other gates open? Andeux circled the pool, unsheathing a bloodied axe with a slick, wet scrape. The motion stained his hands with old blood and gore. Which perfectly fit with his filthy clothing. Old, bloodied stains caught the dim light. His eyes gleamed with malice and delight. Will hesitated. Should he risk the gates? More guards could be on their way. Instead, he edged toward the large opening behind him, where the pool stretched below.

"What does the queen want with me?" Will asked, as he and Andeux slowly circled around the chamber.

"Your queen will speak with you."

"It seems like she wants my head more than my conversation," Will retorted. Andeux's malicious smile stretched from ear to ear, confirming Will's worst fears. "I'm just an ordinary boy," he said, almost pleading.

Andeux stalked Will through the chamber like a lion stalking its prey. Andeux was far too close for comfort as he slithered towards the edge of the archway. Will continued his slow shuffle away from Andeux, inching slowly towards the opposite side of the room. Perhaps he could try one of the gates? If it wouldn't open, he could run around to the gate Andeux came through.

"You are far from ordinary, boy," Andeux replied.

"But I'm nobody..." he whimpered meekly.

"Pathetic!" Andeux shouted, attempting to close the gap between them. He was now at the edge of the pool where it dropped down into the darkness.

Before Will could even think about running, a rusted metal gate groaned open, screeching metal-on-stone booming through the chamber as two guards stormed in. He spun, shifting his focus from Andeux to the new hunters in the room. Will unsheathed his sword and swung it in a defensive arc as he inched closer to the edge of the pool.

"Come to me, boy," Andeux heckled Will. "Don't make this harder on yourself." The guards began striding towards Will. He was surrounded, there wasn't anywhere left to run. "Good boy, now come here," Andeux cooed.

Will's eyes darted from Andeux to the guards as they moved closer to him. Will inched backwards, moving closer to the edge of the pool, towards the drop.

"What are you doing?" Andeux demanded, his voice louder and angrier with each word. "Don't be foolish." Andeux charged towards Will.

"Get away from me!" Will screamed out, reaching out to shove Andeux away.

Will's body began to shake as a powerful energy ignited in his chest. The energy coursed through his veins, travelling down his arms. His hands began to glow with a bright golden light. Golden energy swirled around his palms and blasted out towards Andeux. The energy raced across the chamber and connected with the centre of Andeux's chest. It lifted him off the ground and launched him into a wall at the far end of the chamber. He collapsed onto the stone floor at the edge of the pool.

Will stared down at his hands, bewildered. How did he do that? His gaze turned towards the guards, who had stopped their stalking. Will lifted his hands towards them, ready to blast them away. The energy wasn't coursing through him anymore, and he had no idea how he did it. But they didn't need to know that.

"Creature!" Andeux shouted. He pulled a dagger out of his sheath and took aim towards Will.

"Not today, little man."

Will turned and jumped over the edge of the pool, launching himself into the darkness. Will slammed into the slanted stone wall hard as water cascaded from above, pushing him faster down the wall. He tumbled down, plummeting into a pool of water below. The moment he hit the water, he was swept along the fast-moving current. The water stung his eyes as he tried to swim to the surface. He collided with a wall as his body twisted around, and he kicked for the surface. He welcomed the rush of air into his lungs.

The torrent of water relentlessly pushed him along the passage. His fingers brushed against a stone jutting out and he held tight. The muscles in his arm felt like they were ripping apart as he tried to hold on, his legs flailed around as the current tried to pull him further along the tunnel.

There was a dim light at the end of the tunnel. *The exit, but which one?* His fingers slipped over the edge of the stone and the current pulled him away towards the light. Will sped towards the exit. The sound of the water gushing out into the open air reverberated loudly around him. Whether it was the ocean, the cliffs or the beach he was about to slam into, he didn't know. *Gods help me.* A burning sensation spread through his body. Will was launched out of the tunnel and towards the cliffs below.

~ CHAPTER SIX ~

Aylise couldn't escape the screaming and shouting. Every way she turned, parents screamed as they scooped their children into their arms and fled. Guards barged through the crowds, shoving people out of their way like they were annoying insects that needed to be swatted. Aylise's heart felt like it was shattering into a thousand pieces as she watched Will flee the square. It had all happened so fast. One moment she was trying to hold Seb back, the next she was trapped in the flames and Will ran away. The queen must fear the symbols on Will's arms. Why else would she have such a visceral reaction to seeing them?

"Where are we going?" Aylise asked her father as he dragged her away from the square.

"Not now, Aylise. Just move!" he hissed.

The queen's shrill cries echoed through the city streets. Aylise looked for Seb, who was being led away by his parents, his tear-streaked face flushed. He looked at her and his bottom lip trembled uncontrollably. She could feel his devastation, while her heart broke for her friend, all she could think about was Will.

"Seb, we have to help him," she cried out.

"But how?" he sobbed.

"Did you see his parents?"

"They were…" he stammered as he tried to speak. "They were in the square."

"Quiet. Both of you!" Lord Nathaniel called out. "The three of you caused enough problems today."

Her father's reprimanding silenced Aylise. His words stung with enough implication to confirm Aylise's fear – that they had led Rupert to his death. A quick glance back at Seb confirmed he had heard her father too. *I'm sorry Rupert, I'm sorry Seb*, she thought to herself in quiet shame and guilt.

"Light the signal," her father called out.

One of her father's soldiers leapt at the command, running ahead and disappearing into the crowd. She couldn't ascertain to whom he was commanding in the chaos around them.

"What signal, father?"

"Not now, Aylise. Ana, take her," he barked through gritted teeth.

Lord Nathaniel paced ahead to his soldiers, who snapped to attention as he neared. Aylise strained to hear pieces of their hushed conversation. Though her efforts were futile with the noisy crowds moving through the city. Her mother pulled her away from her father, weaving their way out of the city.

"Focus, Aylise, we need to leave quickly," Lady Ana huffed. Her back was stiff, and her eyes wide with fear.

"Mother, what's happening to Will?" she replied.

Her mother's reply was drowned out as fireworks erupted in the sky from outside the city walls. Large orange sparks shot up into the sky and exploded out from the centre. Orange, red and gold sparks spread out from the fireworks. Aylise couldn't recall ever seeing bird-shaped fireworks before, yet there was something familiar about them. She stopped moving, lost in her own thoughts, gazing up towards the sky.

"You need to keep moving if we're going to help Will," her mother said in hushed tones.

"Why are those fireworks shaped like the marks on Will's wrist?" she replied, throwing all caution to the wind.

"I'll explain everything when we leave the city, I promise. We can't risk talking here," Ana replied, she seemed alarmed by Aylise's revelation.

The street became a shoulder to shoulder stampede as city guards moved from various alleyways and crossroads all moving in the same direction. *Hunting Will, no doubt.* Aylise looked back to find Seb, still trailing close behind.

"The fireworks," he mouthed to her, his eyes wide with understanding.

She nodded a silent reply and tapped her wrist. Seb hurriedly nodded in agreement. Another firework erupted in the sky, this one seemed closer than the previous. It was the same orange and red sparks that flew up into the sky and created the magnificent bird-like shape. Aylise recalled her father's words: *Light the signal.* Was he responsible?

"It looks just like them, doesn't it?" Seb said, moving up next to her.

"My father told his men to light the signal when he walked off," she replied.

"Quickly, Aylise, out the gate," her mother called out.

Three guards were dead on the ground in front of the gates. Blood pooled on the hard earth around them. The portcullis had been propped open by two wooden beams. They emerged through the gates into a scene of utter chaos. Her father and his soldiers were in a skirmish with city guards. Swords swung and clashed in the air, steel scraped on steel as each side attempted to wipe each other out. Lord Nathaniel cut through the guards so swiftly that each soldier barely had time to counteract her father's strikes before meeting the end of his sword.

"Mother!" gasped Aylise. She had heard the stories of her father the great warrior, but it was something else to see this side of him.

"To the carriage, now," her mother barked, pulling them over to the stables where their carriages had been left.

Another firework raced into the sky in the distance. It peaked and erupted in the same pattern. They were signals! *But who were they warning?*

Guards charged out of the city gates, running straight towards their gathered forces. They pushed and shoved the poor innocent souls trying to escape the city. The soldiers clashed with the guards, following the same rhythmic dance of bodies and swords until they fell to the ground. Seb's father unsheathed a sword and charged into the fray.

"But your father's not a soldier?" Aylise gazed at Seb, who looked as equally dumbfounded as she felt.

"Quickly get in the carriage both of you," commanded Lady Ana. Her eyes were wide, and her arms began to shake as she ushered them into the carriage.

"But what about Will?" she asked, incredulous. "Why is all of this happening?"

"Get in the carriage now!" Lady Ana barked, turning on Seb and Aylise with such ferocity, it took Aylise by surprise. "Do as I say and be quiet."

Aylise and Seb almost fell into the carriage as they were pushed through the door. Lady Ana hastily shut the door behind them.

"We need a carriage man now," Seb's mother called out, panicking.

Aylise and Seb sneaked a glance out the window to watch the rest of the skirmish. Dead men from both sides lay scattered around the ground. Though it didn't seem to be making a difference to ending the battle, more guards continued to march out of the city towards her father. One of their men ran over to the carriage.

"Get them out of here," Lady Ana commanded with all her authority. "Avoid Fawkeston. We're compromised now. Take the royal road west, go."

What did she mean compromised? Her younger sister Natalyn was at home in Fawkeston. Was the town in danger? Aylise felt helpless to untangle the threads of the unending questions swirling through her mind. And where was Will? *Oh gods, Will.*

"Keep your heads down and be quiet. I promise I'll explain everything in Oldwell," Lady Ana spoke softly through the window. "I love you," she smiled at her daughter.

"Go now," she commanded the soldier.

The carriage began to move along the road, running parallel to the city. It began to pick up speed as they gained momentum, the cabin bouncing around as the carriage sped along the road. Soon the skirmish was behind them and Aylise strained to see out the window. Though more carriages, horse riders and people on foot were following along the road.

"Did you know your father was a fighter?" Aylise asked Seb, turning around to face him.

"Not at all," he replied, bewildered. His eyes were puffy and red still.

"I think we've been deceived for quite some time," Aylise replied. All of the day's revelations wove out of the tangle in her mind.

Aylise pulled away from the window and watched Seb. He kept his face down, looking at his hands with his shoulders hunched over. Small huffs escaped his mouth as he sat with his own grief. She shuffled along the seat towards him, placing her hand over his.

"I'm sorry about Rupert," she spoke softly to him.

Seb turned towards her as tears began to stream down his face. He collapsed into her arms, his body jolting as he sobbed into her chest. Aylise felt fraught as she held him. Her guilt for her part in Rupert's death rattled her. Why did she allow it? She never should have agreed to this. Why didn't she speak to her parents? If she had, Rupert never would have died and Will wouldn't be in danger.

"I'm so scared," Seb spoke softly, looking up into her eyes.

"Our mothers wouldn't have left us if we were in danger now," she replied.

"I guess," he whispered, biting his lip and gazing at his hands. Aylise recognised his nervous tell, quietly making a mental note of it.

Another firework erupted into the sky in the distance. The same colours, the same shape, another signal. *Oh Will, we have to do something.* She couldn't escape the nagging thought. She looked out the window back towards the city. The road was full of people. Some had abandoned the road altogether and fled across fields and weaving between trees. She followed every shape closely, desperately looking for Will. The flat grassy lands started to transform into small rolling hills. Soon enough they would be shielded from the city.

She shuffled across to the other side of the carriage, peering out the window. She felt compelled to look out towards the sea. She couldn't explain why, but she couldn't take her eyes off the area. The western peninsula of the city rose up in the distance and water gushed out of the city drains into the sea below. She watched and waited, unable to explain why she couldn't avert her eyes. One of the tunnels started glowing brightly.

"Seb, what do you suppose that is?" Aylise asked, pointing towards the light?

Seb moved over and stared out the window. The glow became brighter, changing colour from white to a golden orange glow. It looked similar to the colour of the symbols on Will's arms. As the light began to dim, a shape shot out of the tunnel. *Oh gods*, it's him.

"It's Will!" she shouted, facing Seb.

They watched the shape fly out of the tunnel and fall towards the ground.

"I can't see from here," Seb said, standing in the carriage. "But those cliffs on the peninsula are lethal."

Aylise clutched the side of the carriage as she watched Will fall. But as he moved towards the earth, they travelled past a small hill, obscuring their view.

"No. Wait. It's Will!" Aylise screamed, banging on the roof of the carriage.

"Stop the carriage!" Seb joined in.

The beach and the city appeared from behind the hill. There were a few people on the beach, but as they travelled further away, it was hard to see any identifying details about them.

"Stop the carriage now," pleaded Aylise, opening the door to the carriage and looking directly to the driver.

"My Lady, please get back inside," he called out rather firmly. "My orders are to take you both to Oldwell."

"But we saw Will, we can't leave him." The driver remained silent and hurried the horses along. Aylise sat down and huffed. "Why won't anyone listen to us?"

"We're going to find him," Seb replied.

"How?" said Aylise, turning towards Seb.

Seb's lip had stopped quivering, he looked out the carriage window to the road behind them. Aylise watched him silently, taken back by the change in his demeanour. He moved across to the other side of the carriage, staring outside. The landscape on either side had changed from the windy hillside road to an open area closer to the coastline.

"We're not letting another friend die," Seb proclaimed, turning towards Aylise. He puffed his chest and held his back straight.

"What's your plan?" she replied, determined and encouraged by Seb's own bravery.

"We're jumping from the carriage," he replied matter-of-factly. "Get the driver's attention. He'll stop the carriage. That will stop our parents' carriages, we'll find Will and they'll find us."

"That's actually brilliant, Seb," Aylise glanced out the carriage. "We better move quickly, before we're too far from the city. I'll get the driver's attention, get ready to jump."

Aylise pushed open the carriage door and stepped out onto the footplate. Seb took a deep breath and followed her out. Although she could sense his apprehension, he had a spark in his eye. She believed him when he said they weren't leaving anyone else behind.

"I'm ready," Seb said, nodding at her. Aylise, smiled in return and turned towards the driver.

"Hey!" she screamed out, getting his attention. "We're not leaving him behind," she proclaimed, and jumped from the carriage.

Seb leapt from the foothold after her. They landed on the dry grass and rolled several times before they found their balance. Seb grasped for Aylise and pulled her to her feet. The carriage driver shouted, and the horses whinnied. As the carriage stopped, Aylise allowed herself a moment of glee. Seb's plan was working!

As they ran along the fields, more carriages started to move along the road, Aylise recognised her father's crest.

"The other carriage is stopping. Seb, it's working," she panted, her dress snagging on the brambles and bushes as she ran towards the beach.

As they neared the ocean, they started to run up a small hill. Aylise quickened her pace, the hopeful thought of seeing Will on the other side driving her forward. She was almost to the top when Seb jerked her arm, pulling her down. He covered her mouth with his hand as he scurried under a bush.

"Guards," Seb whispered ever so softly into her ear.

Mixed in with the sound of the waves crashing along the coastline was a soft clinking of armour. Aylise said a silent prayer to the gods as the guards crested the hill. They weren't running in their direction, thankfully. Without Seb's swift actions, they would have been seen.

"Oh no," she whispered with a heavy heart.

"They're heading towards our families," Seb gasped, finishing her sentence.

She spun to face Seb. His lip trembled, mirroring the shock that left Aylise gaping at him, her breath caught in her throat. A fresh wave of realisation crashed over them. They had put the people they loved in danger again.

"Those guards are wet," she noted, listening for signs of people moving around them.

She crawled around to the other side of the bush, and Seb followed closely behind her. At the top of the hill, they dropped out of sight, running down the other side and surveying the beach below. Mighty waves crashed along the shoreline and large rocks and outcrops jutted out into the ocean. A soft sea breeze carried a fresh and salty tang in the air. Long grasses and large healthy bushes and shrubs scatted the landscape below. The dark city walls loomed over the area. Torrents of water gushed out of the sewer tunnels dotted along the wall. Water cascaded out of the tunnel closest to the shore, plummeting down towards the cliffs. Fear coursed through Aylise, *that was the tunnel Will exited, it was the closest to the road, it had to be that tunnel.*

"Seb, what is that?" she asked, her heart pounding in her chest as she pointed to a mass on the beach.

"No, it can't be," he uttered in barely a whisper as he began to run towards the mass.

The mass became clearer as they ran closer towards it. It was a person lying face down on the sand. Their white shirt clung to their body and a large red stain pooled across their back.

"Will!" Aylise screamed, tears welling up in the corner of her eyes.

"Please no," Seb gasped, running ahead.

Seb reached the body first. Blood-stained sand surrounded the body. Aylise was shaking as she stood behind Seb, who slumped into the damp sand. *Please don't let him be dead, please.* She sent another silent prayer to the gods.

"Please don't be Will," he whispered as he turned the body over. "It's not him," he sighed. "It's not him."

Aylise sighed in a moment of reprieve before a new fear took hold. "Where's Will then?" She looked around, her eyes wandering towards the cliffs. "He might be trapped up there." She ran awkwardly through the sand.

"Aylise, don't be reckless," Seb called out. Seb wiped the dead man's hair from his face and placed his fingers across his eyelids to close them. "May you find peace in the next life," he spoke softly.

Aylise threw rational thinking aside as she attempted to scramble up the cliff face. The horrific thought of finding Will's mangled body in a crevasse both terrified her and pushed her forward. Hoping against all hope that she was wrong.

"What's that over there?" Seb called out, pointing along the beach. Aylise had climbed a few feet up the rocks when she looked back. "Look there." Seb glanced her way.

Aylise gazed along the beach. A person was running away from the city, ducking into cover and weaving around large rocks. They disappeared from view and back again as they moved. Their white shirt flapping around them. A warmth that she desperately needed spread through Aylise.

"It's him," she exhaled deeply as she jumped off the cliff side. "Quickly, we have to catch him." She began to run along the sand.

"I'm by your side," Seb replied. His determination matched her own.

Aylise was impressed with Seb's sudden bravery: his timid demeanour seemed to be left behind in Basilium. She had an inkling of the cause of his sudden change. It was lingering within the pain he tried to hide but clearly wore in his eyes. Had she not been preoccupied with Will, she would have tried to talk to him. The two eager friends ran towards Will, unaware of the guards following them, led by a balding man with a vendetta.

~CHAPTER SEVEN~

Queen Haveena watched from a large balcony in her private quarters of the castle. Basilium had quickly turned from its usual hum of activity to a quiet ghost town. The citizens of the city had fled back to their homes, shutting their doors and closing themselves off to the outside world. Those who didn't have homes in the city gathered around the inns and taverns, waiting for the gates to reopen. Those without homes at all had burrowed back to the slums, where they could disappear into the complex maze of passages, tunnels and hideouts.

Haveena's royal guards were overseeing the operation to find the boy. They controlled the city guardsmen who were combing every inch of the city for him and those that helped him escape. Her spies throughout the city had brought back whispers of conversations taking place in inns and taverns: whispers of the boy who escaped and the strange marks that appeared on his arms. Most adults in the city would have recognised the sigil if they had seen it up close, but there were only a handful of people who would know what the glowing sigil on a person's arm would mean. *Could it really be true?* they asked each other, *Maybe there is hope for Arulean after all!*

How is this possible? She wondered, *I eradicated the last remnants of magic.* She turned her gaze towards the dark grey clouds looming over the city. The first rays of sun started to shine through patches of disappearing clouds yesterday. They hadn't bothered her then, but they troubled her now.

This cannot be. She grasped onto the balcony railing so tightly that her hands started to turn white and looked down towards the square. The place was filled with so many memories, both good and bad. She had lived comfortably for the last eighteen years and that could not change now. She turned away from the city, storming back into her chambers. King Rickard sat in his large black velvet chair in their sitting room. He was still dressed in his armour and cupped his chin with his hand while he stared at the floor.

Mounted on the double-height dark walls behind him was an ostentatious painting of the king and queen. Their stern features in the dark and moody painting fitted the aesthetic of the room. A single iron chandelier hung from the black ceiling. The castle, like the rest of Arulean, had bent to Haveena and Rickard's rule. The castle had once been light and bright, sunlight bounced off the golden accents in every room. Haveena remembered it well, but she preferred how it looked now.

"Do you see what's out there?" Haveena pointed outside. "Sunlight."

"It does that from time to time. It is spring, after all," Rickard replied nonchalantly.

"Not like that, and you know it. It's the boy."

"What of him?" he glanced towards her. "He's just a peasant boy."

"Don't be so nonchalant about this. You saw the sigil and you know what that means." She paced back and forth across the room. "This boy could be our undoing."

"You're overreacting," Rickard raised his voice. "Andeux will dispose of him easily. Go and pour yourself a wine."

She flung her goblet towards Rickard. It sailed past his head, breaking into tiny pieces as it impacted with the wall.

"Don't you dare speak to me like that, Rickard. You know what that sigil means!" she screamed across the room.

Rickard marched towards her, arched his gloved hand back and slapped her across the face.

"Never." He wrapped his hands around her throat. "Speak to me like that again, Haveena." His strong fingers squeezed down on her throat. Haveena silently sent her magic in his direction, but it couldn't penetrate his own magical shield. "You got us into this mess in the first place, you stupid woman." He released her and shoved her backwards. "Had you not been so hysterical, we could have grabbed him quietly. Thanks to your theatrics, he's more than likely fled the city."

"So, you are concerned about him then." She smirked at him, relishing in the fact, then quickly spun away from him. She didn't want to give him the satisfaction of seeing the tears forming in her eyes. *Stop it, now!* she told herself, *You're stronger than this.* A knock on the door distracted her from her self-pity.

"Come in," Rickard barked.

A royal guard marched into the room, paused and bowed in their direction. "Your Graces, I have word from the general."

"And?" Rickard replied.

Queen Haveena turned towards the young guard, eager to learn the boy's fate.

"The executioner followed the boy into the tunnels. They found him in the western cistern chamber."

"Does he have him now?" Haveena asked casually, hiding her anxiety.

"No, my queen. The boy jumped down from the pools into the tunnels," the guard replied.

"From the cistern? But those tunnels lead out to the peninsula cliffs." *No one could survive that drop, unless...* "Has his body been recovered?" she asked.

"No, my queen... he... ah..." the guard paused.

"Yes?" Rickard and Haveena replied at the same time, their tone giving hints to their joint concern.

"He's escaped," the guard replied quietly.

He's alive then. Rickard was right, damn him. She paced the room as her mind wandered through every scenario imaginable.

"Where is Andeux?" she barked out.

"He is in pursuit, my queen."

"Well, the boy won't be alive for too much longer." She looked towards the guard. "Leave us!"

The guard bowed and left the chamber, as Haveena continued to pace around the room. *Stop it. Don't show your cards*, her mother's words popped into her mind. She stopped pacing. That bastard was right, she should have grabbed him quietly.

"It seems things are not going to your plan then," Rickard mocked.

"How are you so calm?" she hissed.

"I'm not bothered by the boy. Nothing or no one can hurt me. Let him come for us and I'll crush him into the under-realm."

"You better," she replied as she walked towards the balcony doors.

The sea breeze was cool and refreshing across her face, helping to simmer some of the anger brewing inside her. *She always loved it too.* Haveena looked out to her quiet city. Now that word had been received that the boy was out of the city, patrols were starting to converge back in the bailey below. *Andeux will get matters under control.* He was loyal and vicious, but could she truly trust him to get the job done? She had made great personal sacrifices to get here. She had most of Arulean under her control: she wouldn't let it all slip away now. Rickard liked to act like a tough brute, but he was worried about the boy too. He liked his position now just as much as she did. She just had to be smart and play her cards right. She adjusted her dress and turned back into her chambers.

"Rickard, my darling," she called out as she walked over to him.

~ CHAPTER EIGHT ~

Will pressed his body against the rocky inlet at the bottom of the cliff, shielding himself from view above and below him. Rocks and debris had fallen down the cliff face near him. He struggled to hear anything over the sound of the waves crashing against the rocks. Travelling along the seaside cliffs had been a risk, but it had served him well so far. There were plenty of places to hide from the roads above, but when he arrived at the next beach, he thought he should investigate whether he was far enough away from the city to travel closer to the road again.

He glanced out from the alcove and slowly started to make his way along the cliffs. The rocks were hard and jagged under his feet. He moved as fast as he could, doing his best to stay out of sight. The natural curve of the land made moving along the cliffs difficult to scout ahead. As he passed a large boulder, soft yellow sand and trees greeted him. The next beach wasn't that far ahead of him and the city had disappeared behind the cliffs. He sighed with relief that it was finally out of sight: he felt like he had been running for hours.

Would the executioner be out of the city by now? He must be, but was he still chasing after Will? He still wasn't sure how he survived the fall from the tunnels. His whole body had burned up like it was on fire as he rushed towards the opening. He had felt like he was flying, as he shot fifty feet into the air and splashed down into the ocean. He emerged quite a safe distance from the cliffs and was able to easily swim to shore.

"How did you do that?" asked a man in a white shirt, as he walked along the sand.

"No idea," he replied, giving him a curt nod, before running along the beach, not giving the man another thought.

Now Will was bone dry and his salty shirt clung to his salty body. His leather pants and shoes weren't dry yet, much to his annoyance and discomfort. Wet leather against your skin wasn't the best feeling when you were on the run. Will followed the slope of the cliffs down towards the beach. A flat valley lay between Will and the next seaside cliffs at the other end of the beach. He would be exposed from all sides once he stepped out onto the sand. There were several people down by the sand, packing up their horses. They laughed as they mounted them and started to ride along the royal road towards Basilium. *I wouldn't go there if I were you*, he thought to himself.

Will's eyes darted around the area as he moved down to the edge of the beach, hidden behind a large rock. Horses whinnied somewhere unseen, followed by the rickety sounds of a carriage travelling along a road. The noises grew louder. Was the royal road close by? He glanced out from behind the rock, catching a glimpse of the carriage moving along the valley before disappearing behind some trees. *Perhaps it would be best to stay along the cliffs for now*, he thought, terrified by the idea of being caught by the guards, and without anyone to help him.

He took a deep breath and ran out from his cover. His heart raced as he landed in the soft sand and ran as fast as his legs could carry him. His senses overloaded as he crossed the distance of the deserted beach. He heard rustling along the valley and chanced a glance sideways. There didn't seem to be anyone around him, so he focused on the end of the beach, pushing himself forward. He wove between the large rocks scattered across the beach. As he stepped forward, he sank further into the soft sand, losing his balance. He almost toppled into the sand but managed to stay upright. He paused for a moment, to take in his surroundings. From here, he could see the royal road snaking down from the cliff parallel to the beach, before turning inland. The whole area was still deserted; there wasn't another visible soul around.

Will began to run again, trying to avoid being exposed in the open for too long. He lunged behind a large rock at the end of the beach and panted heavily. He sank into the sand to catch his breath, relieved to have made it across the beach unseen. His hands shook as he wiped the sweat from his brow. There was a tension coursing through Will that felt unrelated to his physical exertion: he couldn't shake this awful feeling that he was being followed. He didn't understand how, but he could feel someone there: someone watching him.

"Focus, Will," he said to himself, trying to clear the thoughts from his mind. "Oldwell. How am I going to get there?"

Following the royal road didn't feel right anymore: he was too close to the city and the road was too commonly travelled. No doubt the royal guards would be out looking for him too. *But why? Why did she want me so badly?* Will wondered, looking at his wrists.

"You're doing these strange things to me, aren't you?" he said as he stared at his wrists.

How had that energy shot out from his hands? Has he always had the ability? And if so, why had it suddenly been triggered now? Yana knew, his mother and father knew, Lord Nathaniel knew, and the king and queen seemed to know, too. Why hadn't anyone told *him*? Was he dangerous? *No, don't do this to yourself Will*, he told himself.

"Right. Oldwell." He focused his attention on his current situation. "Haven's Rest isn't too far from here. The town can be quite busy, but there are lots of docks along the coast there. I could take a small boat," he pondered. He found talking out loud to himself easier for sorting through his thoughts. "Yes! That's it. I'll sail to Westvale beach. It's not too far to Oldwell from there."

Will leapt to his feet, emboldened by his plan. He surveyed the area around him once again. He still couldn't shake the feeling that he was being followed, but the only thing accompanying him were the seabirds resting along the rocky coastline. He looked back towards the city still hidden behind the cliffs, but he knew it was there. Turning back, he began his new journey to Haven's Rest.

The spectral form floated above the sand behind Will. It had sensed him only a few days ago. As Will's powers grew, so it grew, too. It had escaped that place. Then the boy came into the city. The sigil was clear and easy to spot even before it started glowing for everyone else to see. Once it sensed him, it stayed close, following him ever since he fled the city.

He was a resourceful boy, it was marvellous how effectively he escaped the city. He was clever too, the boy could sense it. *Oh, he'll be powerful.* The boy didn't seem to have a handle on his powers yet. No matter, he would soon, and the longer it stayed by the boy, the stronger it would grow, too. Could the boy's power bring it back to its true self? Maybe?

It followed Will as he moved around the coastline. Now that it had found him, it was going to get back what they had lost.

Will estimated that he had left Basilium approximately three hours ago. The clouds were shifting from muted grey tones to dark blueish grey. The sun would be setting soon. He couldn't escape the dread-inducing thought that he wouldn't make it to Haven's Rest before sundown. For then it would be too dark and dangerous to walk along the cliffs. Although it was his intention to wait at the edge of town for darkness to fall so he could get in and out unseen.

He climbed onto a rock, sitting high along a cliff's edge. The roof tops of the buildings in Haven's Rest were peaking over cliffs in the distance about four coves away. He sighed with relief: it seemed easy enough to get there by nightfall, if he was quick. There looked to be a small village or settlement in the next cove. Will could just make out several buildings and a dock. The roads seemed to be deserted. The royal road was inland, hidden somewhere behind the rolling hills and trees. Should he risk taking the roads again? It would certainly be faster and less treacherous for him. Though he'd travelled reasonably well so far, and the niggling fear to avoid the road kept lingering in his mind.

The quiet was broken by horses whinnying and galloping. Will flattened himself to the rock as the sounds of hooves beating against the earth grew louder, closer. He waited as the sound passed and trailed off into the distance.

He moved up slightly. No horses, no riders: he was alone again. *Right! No more thoughts of roads. The cliffs it is.*

He climbed down from the rock to continue his journey when a familiar whistling sound passed by his ear. He felt the air move around him before he saw the arrow land. He slid down the rock and swiftly moved into an alcove. Someone had found him, and judging by the rustling and rocks sliding down the cliff, they were closing in on him. He looked down to the ocean below: could he make that jump?

He shuffled along under the cover of the overhanging rock. The rustling sounded like it was all around him. His senses flared up, everything seemed heightened. He bolted out of the cover and ran along the cliffs, leaping over rocks as he moved. He followed the cliffs around to the left, revealing the bay he saw earlier. It looked like a fishing port. Perhaps it was connected to a small village nearby? It was too small to be a functional settlement for anyone, and there didn't seem to be a home in the area, so it was safe to assume it wasn't private lands. There were four buildings nestled beyond the shore and a small building connected to a dock jutting out into the bay, and a small fishing boat moored at the dock. There was space for other boats along the dock too, but Will guessed those boats must have been out for the day still. That boat could be his escape: anything to get away now. The area seemed empty from this distance, he couldn't know what or who was lurking around the corner.

Will grabbed a large rock and threw it out to sea. He heard the rock splash loudly into the water below and continued to move down the cliffs further into the bay. Another arrow whistled past him, and he spun and leapt down onto a rock below, slipping and hitting the stone hard. *Get up. Go.* He picked himself up and jumped down to the beach below, dashing behind a large rock and chancing a glance back. Andeux was standing on the rocks, his bow taught in his hand. He'd found Will.

"Shit, shit," he huffed out, as he caught his breath.

Will's senses flared up again. He could hear the movements of Andeux's tiny feet as they hit the sand, each movement clear and precise. He glanced towards the largest of the buildings at the back of the bay. He could clearly see the people hiding inside the building, their small eyes peering out from the gaps in the timber. Why were they hiding, and who else was close by? He ran out from the rock, running in a zig-zag towards the dock. He didn't need to look back to know where Andeux was. He could hear his every move, every step closer to Will. A dagger started to sail through the air behind Will. He rolled, tumbling low in the sand as the dagger sailed past him.

Will lunged for the dagger in the sand and ran behind a large sand dune. The dock was one hundred feet away. *I can make it.* Will heard sand crunching above him, so he rolled his body and swung the dagger above him. The blade opened the flesh on Andeux's outstretched hand as he lunged for Will. Andeux fell and rolled into the sand. Will moved again, rolling under a large fallen tree, careful to avoid the jagged branches coming from the trunk. Andeux followed close behind. His fingers brushed against Will, and he held on. Will lost his footing and tripped, faceplanting in the sand. When he stood back up, Andeux had drawn an arrow and was pointing it directly at his chest.

"You have nowhere to go," the executioner spat smugly, stepping backwards towards the sand dune.

Will began to weigh up his options. Dead or alive, Andeux would take him back to Basilium. He was too far away from the dock to run, and he was too exposed. Except for the people he saw hiding in the building, there didn't seem to be anyone else around. He unsheathed his sword.

"You don't scare me, little man," he called out, trying to aggravate Andeux.

"I don't care if I have to carry your limp corpse over my shoulder," Andeux laughed as he drew his bowstring back. "In fact, that makes it easier for me at this point."

Will was about to charge towards Andeux, when a flash of blue above caused him to stop. Aylise lunged over the hill, swinging a large rock above her and bringing it down on Andeux. Seb ran from around the dune, sword in hand. Seb lunged towards Andeux, who lowered the bow and swung his armoured arm into Seb's stomach, launching him out into the sand. Will bolted towards Andeux. He swiped left and right with his sword, trying his best to remember the moves his father had taught him, but Andeux was too fast and too good. A searing pain spread across Will's chest as Andeux's shoulder connected with him. The impact launched Will through the air. He crashed into the sand and his vision blurred as he stood back up. None of the sparring with his father had prepared him for this moment.

Andeux held Aylise to his body. One hand wrapped around her neck, the other holding a dagger, he smiled smugly at Will.

"Stop! No! I'll go with you!" Will screamed as his heart began to beat fast.

"I always win, little boy," Andeux snarled at him, "and I'm going to have my fun with you all now," he cooed with pleasure as he raised the blade towards Aylise.

Unbridled panic and fear coursed through Will's veins as he saw the dagger rise in the air. His body surged with the strange heat and the forceful energy.

"No, you won't," he replied vengefully.

This evil little man had caused him enough hurt and pain today. Will raised his arms out to his side as energy coursed through him. It took control of Will's body: he was merely a conduit for the power rising through him. His hands swung out in front of him and as his palms connected, a fiery energy erupted from them. It blasted him back into the air, as his world turned to black.

Seb wouldn't have believed it if he hadn't been there to see it. One moment all felt completely lost as Andeux easily subdued them, then suddenly Will's hands were glowing as the fiery blast erupted from him. Seb grabbed Aylise, holding her close as the energy wave rushed towards them. He pulled Aylise away from Andeux, who seemed to be utterly transfixed on Will. The blast sent Aylise and Seb tumbling through the sand. After the wave passed, Seb and Aylise found their feet and surveyed their surroundings.

"Oh my," Aylise mused, her hand clutched over her mouth.

Seb turned towards the large fallen tree. The executioner was wide-eyed, and blisters covered his body. Was it the fireball, or the large trunk protruding from his chest that killed him? He suddenly didn't seem as dangerous or frightening, with his arms and legs swinging in the air. *Good, he got just what he deserved. Asshole! We got him for you, Rupert.* Seb bowed his head as Rupert's wide smile drifted into his mind. Oh gods, it hurt so much. He just wanted to run back into the city and tell Rupert how sorry he was.

"Will," Seb called out, bringing his thoughts back to the now. "Where's Will?" Seb screamed, running towards the beach.

"I don't know," Aylise replied nervously, following close behind Seb, "where is he?"

"I don't know where he landed," he replied, his eyes darting from the beach to the water. "I think he went under," Seb called out as a cold shiver ran down his spine.

Fear coursed through Seb. While the port seemed deserted, the energy wave and the fighting had been quite loud. If Andeux was here, then there must be more guards not too far behind. Seb gazed towards the empty buildings nearby, where was everyone? Surely there would be someone here?

"Aylise, untie the boat, we have to go," he called out firmly.

"We can't just steal some poor fisherman's boat," she replied incredulously. "It's unladylike."

"Do you see a fisherman loitering around here right now?" he called out as he ran towards the dock. "Just untie the fucking boat," Seb snapped back and dove into the ocean.

The salt water stung his eyes, and his clothes weighed his body down as he swam through the dark waters looking for Will. He flayed his arms around him, rolling around in the depths as he felt for Will. His head started to feel light, so he pushed for the surface as his lungs craved oxygen. He filled his lungs the moment he felt the cool air on his face.

"Did you find him?" Aylise shouted, her voice barely audible over the water lapping around him.

"No," he called out, trying to keep his head above the water.

Where are you, Will? His anxiety was sky high, but he took a deep breath and dove back into the water. The further into the depths of the ocean he travelled, the harder it was to see. How was he ever going to find him? The thought was almost paralysing. His heart had already been shattered once today, he couldn't let it happen again. Seb had been so terrified all day. As a matter of fact, he'd been like that his whole life: terrified of the dangers of the world outside of his peaceful life in Fawkeston. It was different for Aylise. She was a lady, and she was protected by her station. Will never once thought about consequences until they slapped him in the face. Seb had always been the voice of reason, when he felt bold enough to speak up. He was the one to think things through before acting. But look where that had gotten him, look what it did to Rupert. But when the carriage driver refused to stop for Will. He just snapped and threw all thought and caution to the wind, Seb wasn't going to let another loved one die.

Where are you, Will? Seb thought helplessly as he swam further into the depths. A glowing light in the corner of his eye caught his attention. *There!* He pushed his body through the water. Swimming as fast as he could towards Will. He locked his arms around Will, and he kicked hard for the surface.

Seb sucked in the fresh air as he hit the surface. He pulled Will to the surface, holding his head above the water.

"Aylise, help," he called out, swimming towards the boat tied to the dock. "Help me pull him up."

Aylise held onto Will as Seb climbed up into the boat. Together, they hauled Will over the side. The three of them landed on the deck with a loud thud.

"Is he alive?" Aylise said. Turning Will to his side. "Open his mouth, is he breathing?"

"Yes, it's shallow, but he's breathing," Seb replied, panting.

"How did he not swallow any water?" Aylise asked, growing more and more frantic.

"I don't know how," Seb replied in a huff as he attempted to regulate his own breathing. "How did he shoot a fireball out of his hands?"

A thwacking on the side of the boat drew their attention. Up on the dune above the body of the executioner, a royal guard was knocking an arrow to his bow. Another was running along the beach towards them. An older man was pointing at them, at the boat. Seb guessed that must be the boat's owner.

"Get down," Seb called out, as another arrow sailed past.

Aylise dropped down, as Seb pulled the sails up on the boat. As soon as the sail locked into place, the boat started to move. *Thank the gods, there's a good wind.* He thought as another arrow sailed through the air, lodging itself in the mast above Seb's head.

The boat moved away from the dock and the guard stopped running towards them as a strong wind pulled them further and further away.

"Stay down," he called to Aylise.

"Where do we go now?" she replied.

"As far away from here as we can."

The spectre followed the boy. Memories began to come back, old rights and wrongs. Life, love, power, strength, talent, wickedness. Thoughts and feelings that were once long lost and forgotten. The boost from the surge of power on the beach was as enriching and enticing as it was addictive. The three teenagers were special, and the bond was growing stronger. How did they do it? What quest were they embarking on? Where were they going... The boy's power could give life again. The boy was the key, the boy had to stay close.

~ CHAPTER NINE ~

Will soared through the air. The sun warmed his face, and the wind whistled over his body as he weaved between the clouds. Below, a city glowed in the sunshine, its bright golden structures shining like beacons of light in the sun. *How peculiar*, Will thought. It looked just like Basilium, but without the grime, dirt and pollution. *Could it be?* He flew down towards the earth, shooting like an arrow soaring towards the city. He levelled out close towards the castle. The same pregnant woman from his dream in the forest was standing on a balcony. A wave of heat surrounded him. He aimed for her, flying as fast as he could. The flames were coming, he knew it, he could sense it. He yearned to save her. The woman began to fidget, looking back towards the castle. She ran towards the edge of the balcony as flames burst out of the castle. She held her hand out for him.

"Will!" she screamed as she was engulfed in flames. Just as their fingers intertwined, he was pulled away from her by some unseen force.

"No!" he screamed as he was pulled further and further away from her.

"Will!" a voice called out.

He searched for the source of the voice. In a blink, Basilium was gone, the woman on the balcony was gone. He was flying above snow-capped mountains, another all-too-familiar sensation coursed through him. Was he dreaming?

"Will," the voice called again.

A blonde-haired girl was flying next to him, she seemed familiar to him too. Had he dreamt of her before? He had a vague memory of flying in these mountains with her before. Her pearly white teeth glowed in the bright sky as she smiled at him. She pointed down to the mountains below, drawing Will's attention to the convoy of people riding horses along a small mountain pass. Several wagons and carriages were pulled along by horses in the middle of the convoy. They seemed familiar. But who were they?

"Come to me, Will," she called out to him, her velvety voice was soft and angelic.

"Who are you?" he asked.

She smiled at him again and dived down towards the mountains. Will was pulled after her, completely unable to control his body. He dropped faster and faster towards the mountains. He was guided along, following the girl as she weaved between the trees, ducking out of sight. A bright flame caught his eye, atop a mountain in the distance. It burned over a structure. *What is that?* he wondered.

"You'll find out soon enough," the girl called out from somewhere unseen.

Will opened his eyes. As the bright flames dispersed, they were replaced with the moon, which lit up the sky. Several dark clouds with glowing moonlit rings littered the sky. It took Will a moment to realise that he wasn't dreaming: he hadn't seen the sky this clear in years. The soft rocking came from the boat bobbing up and down in the water. He glanced around him and felt instant relief.

"Seb, Aylise," he sighed, smiling as they turned around, "you're okay."

"Will," they called in unison. Seb was at the tiller of the boat. Aylise ran along the deck and wrapped her arms around him.

"Thank the gods you're awake," Aylise cooed, brushing his hair out of his eyes.

"Where are we?" he asked, looking around the boat. "How long was I out?"

"We're sailing along the coast, I'm not sure where exactly," Seb replied. "I've been slowly making my way south until you woke." Will walked up the deck towards Seb as he continued speaking. "There was still daylight when I pulled you out of the water." Will's eyebrows raised at that. "We passed out after we set sail. I don't know what happened. I think the intensity of the day caught up with us all." Will glanced around. "I don't know how long I was out, but I've been awake for a few hours now."

"Oh," Will replied, rather shocked and confused.

"But, Will, more importantly... What's happened to you?" It was Seb's turn to sound surprised. "When did you start conjuring fireballs in your hands?" Seb asked, attempting to look neutral.

The memories came flooding back to Will like the rush of water out of the tunnel. Fleeing the castle, blasting Andeux, twice. His friends finding him, fighting Andeux.

"What happened to the executioner?" he asked.

"Your fireball. It, ah... Well, it blasted us all back," Seb said softly. "But... It impaled him." Seb's eyes twinkled ever-so-slightly as he said it.

"He's dead?" Will asked.

Seb nodded in reply. Part of Will was elated; he'd escaped the city... but he had also killed someone. It's not like the executioner was some innocent person; he was going to hurt Will. He was going to take pleasure in killing Will... but did that make it better? He wanted to kill him when the fireball shot out of him. He wanted to make him pay for what he'd done to Rupert, to Aylise, to him. Did that make him bad?

"Will, what happened to you after you left the square?" Aylise asked.

Will told them every detail about his escape from the city: how he was guided by Yana; how it seemed odd that she had a perfect escape plan in place, ready to go. That she instructed him to go to Oldwell.

"That's where our parents were sending us too," Aylise said.

Will didn't skip over the details about the chase through the tunnels, but he choked up because he didn't quite understand how the energy took over him. How it erupted from his hands.

"I almost don't believe it happened," he said.

"Well, as someone who witnessed that very power, I can safely say it was real," Seb replied.

"We saw you shoot out of the tunnel," Aylise said.

"How?" he asked.

"We were travelling along the royal road. We were looking for you when I saw the tunnel light up. Oh Will, it was so bright, I'd never seen anything like it." Aylise paused momentarily, looking into Will's eyes. "I couldn't see your face, but I could sense you, like you were calling to me. I knew it was you."

Will's cheeks flushed, thank the gods, it was dark.

"How did you do it?" Seb asked, "How did you shoot the fireball?"

"I don't know. But it wasn't like the cistern, that was different." He paused, trying to remember the moment. "I was so scared that I reached out instinctively; I just wanted to push him away. I just wanted a chance to escape, and then it just shot out of me.

"Go on," Seb said encouragingly.

"The fireball was different. I was angry, I wanted to hurt him. He killed Rupert because of me, he tried to kill me, and he tried to kill you both. Hells, he nearly got Aylise. Then it took over again." He paused, looking down at his hands. "I don't know what's happening to me, but whatever it is, it's getting stronger. I need answers and I think we're going to find them in Oldwell."

"So why is everyone sending us to Oldwell?" Seb asked.

"Your guess is as good as mine," Will shrugged, "but we need to get ourselves there. Keep a look out for Westvale."

"Why?" Seb and Aylise asked.

"It's the fastest way to Oldwell."

"Oh no, I think we passed it a long time ago," said Aylise.

"Shit," Will hissed, looking towards the shoreline. "How did we miss it?"

"We were asleep, we didn't mean to. But we were exhausted," Seb replied.

"Wait if we were all out, who was sailing the boat?" Will looked around for another person.

"No one. It was strange, Will. I hadn't ever felt so exhausted in my life. There was such a strong breeze when we left that fishing port. We were lucky actually. It got us away from those guards really quickly. As soon as we were clear of their arrow range, exhaustion just hit me. I woke up just before Westvale Beach. I can't explain how the boat didn't sail out to sea or crash ashore, but somehow, we just kept sailing."

"Oh," was all Will managed to say as his mind raced over the possibilities.

'I'm sorry, I didn't know about Westvale," Seb replied, "but now that you say it… I should have known better myself."

"It's not your fault, we just have to work out where we are," Will replied, looking towards the coastline.

Large parts of the northeastern coastline were framed by large cliffs that plunged into the sea. Large rocky islands scattered the sea close to the shoreline. Will didn't recognise the coastline. It was hard to see in the dark and there were no villages glowing along the shore: they could be anywhere. The moon shone down on a sandy beach just ahead of them.

"We need to pull in now, let's head for that cove," he called out, pointing to the beach ahead.

"Will, can you take over? You're better at this than me," Seb said, looking down at the tiller in his hand.

Will obliged and took control of the boat. As he steered the boat towards the shore, the sails snapped taut, pushing the boat faster towards the coast.

"Give me some slack on the sail," he called out.

The moon disappeared behind heavy clouds, covering them in darkness. The darkness made the journey exponentially more difficult. Seb fumbled with the sail as the boat continued to move faster towards the shore.

"Hurry up, Seb," Will called, his voice quivering with nerves.

Aylise moved over to Seb, helping him pull at the ropes attached to the sail. Will's hair flapped forward and the strong winds whistled in his ear. The boat continued to speed faster towards the coast. He felt the boat jolting before he heard the sounds of splintering wood grinding against rocks.

"Hold on to something," Will called out as he fell forward, sliding down the deck into Seb.

The boat crunched into pieces around the rocks, twisting the boat onto its side. Will, Aylise and Seb plummeted towards the dark water. Will held onto the mast, holding himself above the water. The strong current dragged his feet towards the cliffs. Seb surfaced several feet away.

"Are you okay?" Will called out.

"I'm fine," Seb called out attempting to swim towards Will. "Gods, the current's strong!"

"Where's Aylise?" he gazed out around the sinking boat.

Will let go of the mast and plunged into the water. As soon as he entered the water, the current pulled him away from the wreckage. Waves crashed against the rocks around him, masking the sound of Seb's voice. His head barely visible as they bobbed up and down with the waves. He swam towards Seb, searching around him as he dipped up and down in the sea. A small movement caught his eye at the base of the large cliffs in front of them.

"Look," Seb called out, pointing in the same direction.

"I see her," Will replied.

"I'm here," Aylise's faint voice broke through the sounds of the wind and sea as they swam towards her. "Quickly, take my hand," she called as the moon broke through the clouds, illuminating the area.

Seb clasped her shaking hand and she pulled him from the water. She spun around and pulled Will out next. He clamoured up the rocks, relieved to be on a flat surface.

"This is the second time today I've pulled you both out of the ocean," she chuckled.

"And hopefully the last," Will replied, "thanks."

"Where do we go now?" Seb asked, shivering.

They were on the edge of a cove, surrounded by tall cliffs. Waves crashed up against the rock they were standing on. When the current pulled away from the cliffs, rocky outcrops were exposed briefly before they disappeared underneath the roaring waves. Will turned his gaze upwards, a sinking feeling spreading through his body.

"We have to go up," he said, looking towards his friends. "It would be suicide to walk across this, and we don't know how long we have until the swell sweeps us away from here."

"But there has to be..." Seb started to reply.

"It's that or swim out of this cove and around to the beach," Will said matter-of-factly, "What do you want to do?"

Aylise and Seb looked from Will to each other and back. Aylise silently nodded.

"I'll go first," he said, reaching up for a handhold on the rock face.

It turned out to be rather straightforward to ascend the rock face. Smooth edges made it easier to reach for areas to hold on to, though it didn't help ease the tense feeling of being one false step away from plummeting down to death. Will had yearned for adventure for most of his life, but whatever this was, it was not quite what he had in mind. *I'm sure this would be much more thrilling if I wasn't being hunted by the most powerful people on the continent,* he told himself.

Will grasped a ledge and pulled himself onto the top of the cliff. A building stood on top of the hillside, its spires towering high into the sky.

"Give me your hand," Will called out, reaching down to pull Aylise up the last edge.

When she was safely up the rock face, he clasped Seb's arm and pulled him up. Seb's whole body shook as he collapsed on top of Will.

"I'm..." Seb began, huffing, "in no rush to do that again anytime soon. Good gods, that temple has seen better days."

"No better place to hold up," Aylise replied, as rain started to fall.

The temple was a ruin. The front doors were nowhere to be seen, leaving the front rooms exposed to the elements. Mosses and grasses grew through the cracks in the stone and large sections of roof had collapsed, roof stones littering the floor. The round central chapel remained protected from the elements, though quite a lot of the stones around the pillared statues of the gods seemed to be one gust of wind away from falling over.

"It's a shame to see such an old temple turn to ruin, it must be well over two thousand years old," Aylise spoke softly.

"I suppose that's what happens after almost twenty years with no upkeep," Seb replied.

As Will sat down on the floor in the middle of the room, the statue of the Mother seemed to be staring at him. She was the goddess of wisdom, whose knowledge and power kept balance in the world. She was the nurturer; the wise leader of the gods. To her left stood the statue of the Shield, the warrior god whose strength and might protected all of Arulean. People prayed to the Shield to give them the strength to protect their lands. They prayed for him to stay strong and deter those who would seek to harm the inhabitants of Arulean. Next to him stood the Archer, god of the hunt and the land. The Archer kept nature in balance. The statue of the Archer seemed to be deteriorating faster than the other statues. The irony wasn't lost on Will that it was the Archer's statue that mirrored the state of Arulean. On the other side of the Mother was the Maiden. She was the goddess of love. Her beauty, her ardor, and her compassion brought people together. Facing the other statues was the Guardian: the god of death. The Guardian was always represented as a cloaked figure. Some speculated the Guardian was a sweet and gentle crone, greeting you like an old friend as she carried you into the next realm. Others described the Guardian as a skeletal creature, ready to take souls away. Whatever version of the story you believed, it did not matter, for the Guardian did not discriminate. Whether you greeted them like a friend or dreaded their arrival, the Guardian arrived all the same.

Since Haveena and Rickard had captured the throne, praying at temples had become less common. It was well known that Haveena and Rickard held no reverence for the gods. Temples had become rundown, unable to maintain their upkeep without crown funds to help them. Had the gods given up on the land? It had seemed like its very essence was dying, drying up more and more each day. Surely the Archer wasn't happy about that. The wisdom and histories of the gods were slowly being wiped away... but then, where was the Shield when the Kyllarian family was wiped out? Were the gods biding their time? Had they abandoned Arulean? Or had they never truly existed in the first place? *Probably best not to wonder that in their house of worship*, he thought to himself.

"I'd say you're right there, Seb. It certainly looks run down to me," Will replied mischievously.

"Any idea where we are?" Seb asked.

"Oh gods," Will paused for a moment before continuing. "I think we just crashed into the Dragon's Jaw."

"I think you're right, Will," Aylise said looking around the room. "This temple was built above the Dragon's Jaw as a beacon for those who wished Arulean and the gods harm. They would sail close to the land and be crushed in the dragon's teeth."

"You read far too much," Will winked at her, "but what did we do to piss off the gods?" Will looked at the statues again.

"Well, we didn't die, did we?" Aylise flashed a wicked grin. "Perhaps the gods were on our side."

"So, let's try and work this out," Seb said, sitting next to Will. "You're shooting blasts of energy and fireballs. You're flying, or levitating shall we call it?" He shrugged. "What do you think brought it on? Why is it happening now?"

Will looked into Seb's dark eyes. They were red-rimmed and hollow, like a gateway into Seb's shattered soul. It had been a harrowing couple of days.

"I'm sorry you've been dragged into this." Aylise and Seb started to retort. "No, please, let me say this." Will paused, taking a moment to compose himself. "I'm so sorry about Rupert, I wasn't fair to him, and I got him killed. And now I've dragged you both into this mess."

"It's not your fault," Seb replied, tears welling in his eyes, "and you haven't dragged us into anything. We were never going to leave you behind."

"Ever since the campfire, I haven't been able to escape this strange feeling inside of me, it's burning through me constantly. It's quiet now, but it's still there... When it starts to rise up, something changes in me, it takes over my body and I can't control it."

"It's okay to be scared," Aylise replied softly.

"Thank you," Will replied. "I'm scared because I don't know what it is. But I don't think it's bad, whatever it is, I don't feel like I'm bad."

Wind and rain howled around the ruin, battering against the weak stone structures and finding its way into the inner worship room. The three of them sat huddled together, wet and cold, in the middle of the room. Will's chest started to burn again, and the feeling spread around his body.

"Come closer and hold me," he called out, pulling Seb and Aylise close and wrapping his arms around them. He could feel the warmth spreading across his body and out towards his friends.

"Oh Will," said Aylise softly, looking at him and then down at her hands on his arms. "This is remarkable."

"How long will this magical heating trick of yours work?" Seb asked.

"Do you think this is magic?" he asked.

"What else would it be?" Seb replied, looking around them as Will pondered Seb's words. "Will, do you think you could conjure a fire?" Seb asked.

"What?" Will replied.

"You did throw a fireball at the executioner." Seb paused. "I'm not asking you to throw fireballs around the room. But why don't you try lighting a fire?"

"I... could try," he replied.

Seb strode around the room, gathering pieces of timber, shards of what looked like an old door and some branches. Seb smiled, dumping the items in the middle of the room.

"We'll need some kindling to get the fire going."

"I've got that sorted too," Seb called out, walking away and coming back with a handful of dried leaf litter.

"Umm, maybe stand behind me... Please..." Will said hesitantly.

Aylise and Seb did as he asked and moved behind him. He focused on the fire inside him, feeling for that spark that seemed to live there now. He lifted his hands in front of him and pointed them towards the makeshift firepit. Will imagined a fire surging through his body, heat coursing through him and erupting from his hands.

Nothing happened.

Shocked, disappointed and slightly embarrassed, Will stared at his hands, but he could feel Aylise and Seb gazing at him with anticipation. When he finally glanced towards them, his cheeks flushed with embarrassment.

"Try again, Will." Seb smiled at him. "You can do it."

Will closed his eyes as the cold battered the chapel and the winds slithered across his body. He yearned for the fire to appear; to warm his friends and keep them safe for the night. Just like that, he felt the spark appear and fire spread through his body again, starting in his chest and coursing through him. Keeping his eyes closed, he focused on the need for fire and warmth. He thought about his interactions with Andeux, and how the surges came when he needed to protect himself. He thought of Aylise and Seb, and his urge to keep them warm.

He felt power vibrating through his body and he pushed that feeling towards his hands. An orange light appeared at his palms: a flaming ball of energy erupted from his hands and sped towards the leaves. They caught alight and a large fire roared to life. Warmth and light spread through the room as quickly as relief spread through Will. He had done it: he controlled it.

"Oh, Will," Aylise called out in amazement.

"That was the most amazing thing I have ever seen," Seb said, stunned.

Will smiled as the warmth encompassed them. These new abilities were strange and confusing, but it brought him great comfort knowing that his friends supported him, nor did they judge him. They wandered around the temple, looking for anything they could add to the flames or possibly eat. Will hadn't realised how hungry he was until he brought the fire to life.

Will rolled up his charred sleeves and held them over the fire, turning his arm around so his wrists were facing up. As the fire licked his arms, the symbols on his skin appeared. The longer he held his arms in the fire, the brighter they glowed. He stared at the symbol, studying every inch of it.

"And you truly feel nothing? No pain at all?" Seb asked.

"Nothing," Will shook his head. "I don't feel a thing at all."

"That's remarkable," Seb replied.

"We should try and get some rest," Aylise said softly. "It's late, and gods know how long it is until sunrise. Let's sleep and in the morning, we'll find food."

Will and Seb nodded at Aylise, curling up in front of the fire.

"Well, Lady Aylise, how will one cope with a stone floor as a bed?" Seb said mockingly, in a shrill voice that sounded like one of Aylise's old governesses.

"I guess this is a first for us all," she replied, snickering as she rolled over. "I don't recall either of you missing out on a bed for the night."

Will smiled at his friends and curled up into the fire, feeling its warmth. When he closed his eyes, he tried not to think about the dangerous journey to Oldwell, or what he would discover when he made it there.

It was fascinating watching the teenagers from above. Oh, how the boy is adapting to his power. He was truly amazing. More memories drifted to the surface as the boy conjured the flames. Memories of a secret discovery, a plan, an attack, could this really be? A translucent shape was beginning to form, growing stronger and stronger by the minute. The boy's power would continue to help. Trapped for so long... this feeling of freedom. The feeling had to stay. There was no going back and there was no stopping, no matter what.

~ CHAPTER TEN ~

Diffused light was shining into the room when Will woke the next morning. The door leading to the entrance of the temple was slightly ajar. He explored the room, trying to open the various doors that led out. Three of the doors led back to the main entrance hall, one of them opened to a large room with a large pile of broken timber on the floor. It was the remnants of a broken staircase that led to the upper level and into the towers. The other door led to a small room, the wall opposite the door was completely destroyed. Will stared out into the forest beyond the temple. The sky was dotted with clouds and the sun was shining. Will stepped out of the building and wandered around. Among the bare and empty trees stood tall, leafy, healthy trees. He ran his hands through a green leafy maple tree.

"It's amazing, isn't it?" Seb called out, walking towards him and holding a bundle in his arms. "Here, have some of these!" He held his hand out.

"Fae berries! My gods, where did you get these?" Will exclaimed, sinking his teeth into the largest purple berry.

The flavours exploded in his mouth, the juices quenching his thirst instantly. Gosh, when was the last time he drank some water? He had a waterskin with him, but he hadn't touched it since yesterday morning. Seb handed him a bundle of berries.

"They're all around here," Seb replied, throwing another berry in his mouth. "They taste so magical."

Aylise walked towards them from behind a shrub, carrying a bunch of berries in her hand. They sat in happy silence while they consumed their breakfast berry after berry, each bite seemed to bring Will to life.

"Take as many as you can with you," Will said.

"Way ahead of you, sleepy," Seb replied jovially.

"What time is it?" he asked, looking for the sun behind the trees.

"It's mid-morning. Sunrise was about three hours ago," Aylise chewed on another berry. "So, how are we going to get to Oldwell?" she asked.

Will looked down at the fae berries. They were only found in the Amaranthine Forest. As far as he was aware, they didn't grow anywhere else on the continent.

"I'm fairly certain Dragon's Jaw is on the edge of the Amaranthine Forest." It was hard to be certain without a map, but he mulled on it. "We have to cross the royal road to get to Oldwell from here, right?"

Aylise and Seb nodded.

"Then we have two options. We continue through the forest. It might take a bit longer and it could be hard to navigate through the unfamiliar territory, but we're more likely to remain undetected in here."

"Or?" Seb asked.

"Or we go around the edge of the forest and make our way to Korgun. From there we can take the royal road up and around to Oldwell or cut through the forest from Korgun to get there."

Seb and Aylise silently mulled over Will's proposition. The forest stretched out for miles along the hilly terrain, they could be lost in there for days, but that was the point, wasn't it? Don't be seen, don't be found.

"As much as I hate to admit it, I'd rather not be out in the open when the guards come marching down the royal road," Seb said matter-of-factly.

"It truly is the sensible option." Aylise paused. "They're less likely to find us in the forest. And we'd be less likely to be seen by any beasts."

Although beasts and creatures from the under-realm never seemed to wander too deep into the Amaranthine Forest, there had been sightings out in the open plains and smaller woods around Arulean. Their sightings had increased in recent years.

"I agree," Will replied smiling. "Through the forest then."

They agreed not to linger too long by the temple. They were, after all, on the outskirts of the forest, and the sooner they made it to Oldwell, the safer they would be. Korgun was east of Dragon's Jaw and Oldwell was north of Korgun. As long as they used the sun to travel in the right direction, they would hopefully make it to Oldwell relatively unscathed. Once they were happy with their plan and packed their berries, they set off through the forest.

They had been walking for hours through the rough terrain of the forest. The sparse trees and shrubs soon gave way to large trees standing tightly together. Thick shrubs, bushes and grasses swayed around the base of the trees, camouflaging their roots, which tangled in their clothes and snagged on their bootlaces. When they came across clearings along the way, they stopped to snack on some berries and rest. Each time, they looked for the bright spot in the sky, using the sun to navigate northeast through the forest. They were by no means experts at navigating, but they were certain they were walking in the right direction.

"Look at that," Will called out, pointing into the sky as they entered another clearing. Seb and Aylise joined Will, gazing into the crystal clear sky. "I don't think I've ever seen such a beautiful sight."

"It's spectacular," Seb called out, "isn't it?"

"And so is this." Aylise pointed towards the ground.

A brown, withered and limp shrub was swaying in the breeze. It started rustling, louder and louder. Long green shoots of grass grew out of the earth and the base of the plant started to change. The stems of the bush thickened. The brown leaves of the plant unfurled, changing colour to a vibrant green. It was like the plants had suddenly woken from a deathly sleep and were drinking heavily from the earth.

"How peculiar!" Will noted, not taking his eyes off the shrub. "You're seeing this right?"

"How is it happening?" Aylise asked, looking around the clearing.

"I have no idea," he replied, "do you hear that trickling?" His ears prickled at the sound: as it grew from a trickle to a hearty burbling.

"This way, quick!" he called out, running through the clearing.

Aylise and Seb followed him as he ran back into the thick bramble of the forest. He let his ears guide him, using the stream to navigate his way, pausing when the sounds softened and changing direction until it grew louder.

The forest opened up to a large, long dried-out riverbed. Will jumped down, running to the middle of the riverbed where a small stream flowed. He filled his flask and drank heavily from it. The water soothed the aches through his body. Aylise and Seb followed him down, filling their own flasks.

"Thank the gods, I needed that." Aylise wiped her lips.

Will sat down and drank another big gulp of water, letting the liquid hydrate his body.

"I feel like that strange shrub we saw back there," Will laughed.

"Slowly coming back to life," Seb giggled.

"I don't think it was water nourishing the plant," Aylise replied, cocking her eyebrows.

"What's that supposed to mean?" Will asked, dumbfounded.

Aylise looked at him pointedly.

"What?" he replied, throwing his hands up.

"Um, you two?" Seb tapped them on the arm. "That's odd, right?"

Will spun around. The water along the stream was starting to flow much faster, and a distant rushing sound grew closer. The water was starting to rise fast.

"Get up, now!" he shouted, pushing himself up and leaping across the stream to the opposite side of the river.

Aylise and Seb followed close behind, running away from the fast-rising water. Several Wyblings – large lizards with spiked heads that grow over two feet long – were attempting to run away from the torrent of water chasing them down the riverbed. They were swept up in the leaves, branches and debris that had settled along the dried-up riverbed. It took mere seconds for the small stream to transform into a roaring river fifty feet across. The river kept flowing past for quite some time, filled with all the debris caught in its path. Once the debris cleared, the river began to slow down to a pleasant stream you could merrily float down. Seb scooped his arms into the water, cupping his hands and bringing them to his lips.

"Did you know that the water in Arulean has always been safe to drink because all the water in the kingdoms flows from the fae lands in the Coronet Mountains?" Seb paused as Aylise drank the water too. She smiled deeply as she tasted the water.

"When magic died out, the rivers stopped running so purely," Aylise looked thoughtfully at Will. "That was the purest water I have ever drunk in Arulean."

"I don't understand your point," Will replied.

"The sun is shining in the sky, the moon was out last night," Aylise gestured towards the river. "Long dried riverbeds suddenly flow with fresh, clean water. Plants are magically coming back to life, and you start to blast fire balls from your hands. Do you truly believe that it's not all connected?"

"Are you saying this is my fault?" Will replied, unable to finish his sentence.

"Fault?" Aylise winced. "That would imply that you've done something wrong. So, no, but I do believe that you are connected to the fact that Arulean has been dying for eighteen years and now small patches of it are coming back to life."

Will gazed at Aylise, mulling over her words. If she's right, is that why the king and queen want him dead? And even if it was true, how exactly was he healing the earth? It didn't make sense. He sighed. It was frustrating to find himself with strange abilities that he didn't understand.

"I really wish my parents had told me about this sooner," Will sighed. "Everything is changing, I feel it in my gut. And I'm not sure I'm ready for that yet." There was so much more he wanted to say, but he just couldn't. "Come on, you two, let's keep moving."

They walked for hours through the dense forest, following small tracks and trails where possible, careful not to stray too far from walking north-east. They passed other streams flowing with clean drinking water, long luscious green reeds dotted the shoreline and clusters of fae berry bushes swayed their plump fruits close by. Will briefly reflected on Aylise's words but decided to give them no more thought. He had to focus on getting to Oldwell, nothing else mattered right now.

"We're going to have to stop and set up a camp soon." Will said, looking into the sky. "The sun is getting low, and I haven't seen the royal road yet."

"Stop at the next clearing then?" Aylise asked.

"Agreed." Will paused. Something had brushed against a tree close by, rustling the low-hanging branches. "Hello?" He looked towards the noise.

"What is it?" Seb asked, turning towards the tree.

"Who's there?" Will called out. "Come out."

Will's fingertips started to tingle, heat radiating from them. Relief washed through him as energy coursed through his veins. *I may not be able to control this, but it sure comes in handy.* His wrists started to burn. The sigils came to life, glowing like a lantern slowly igniting, softly at first, then lighting up every inch of the sigil. Will walked towards the tree and lunged forward, there was nothing out of the ordinary behind it. He expected to find someone or something hiding in the branches, but there was nothing hidden among the rustling leaves. He walked around the tree back towards Aylise and Seb.

A branch snapped behind him. He spun around, raising his burning hand instinctively. The fiery energy appeared, hovering in front of his palm, followed by a high-pitched scream.

"Please," a soft voice said, "I mean you no harm."

A translucent figure of a girl appeared, floating in the air. It was hard to see her at first, but the longer she floated in front of Will's outstretched hand, the more she materialised. Her hair was out and flowing down her back. Was she blonde? It was hard to see, but her hair was light and silvery, like the rest of her. Her translucent skin flushed with a small amount of colour. Her whole body seemingly corporealising, before the colour drained from her face, returning to a translucent appearance.

The girl marvelled at her body, twirling around in the air as she looked at herself. She cackled loudly like a child who had just been handed a large bowl of sweets.

"Who are you?" Will said firmly, "and with all due respect, *what* are you?"

"My name is Cara, thank you for returning me to my form. It's a pleasure to meet you, Will," she replied softly.

"How do you know my name?"

"Because I've been following you," Cara said confidently. "Since the moment I saw your sigils glowing in Basilium."

"So, it is a sigil then?" Will asked, looking down at his arms. "What does the sigil mean?"

"You don't know?" She looked bewildered. "You mean to tell me you have no understanding of them?"

Will stared at her silently.

"Oh dear, I wasn't expecting that." She paused. "Will, it's the sigil of the phoenix."

"The what?" Seb and Will asked together.

"You mean to tell me that none of you have heard of phoenixes?"

"No," Will and Seb replied.

"Well, I read the name on a book two days ago called *The Phoenix Wars of the Fourth Age*, but that's as far as I got," Will continued.

"Yes, I have," Aylise replied at the same time.

Will and Seb turned towards her, but she was looking at the spectre curiously.

"Perhaps you should set up your camp first, before it gets too dark," Cara suggested.

"Or you could tell me now," Will replied sternly. "I've had enough of people telling me..."

"I'll explain everything when you get to Oldwell," Cara interrupted him.

"What's at Oldwell?" he asked sceptically. He watched her cautiously. Did she have some inkling of where they were headed?

"That's where the lady who helped you flee the city told you to go. It's also where the three of you discussed travelling to." She paused as the three of them stared at her. "I told you, I've been following you since you appeared in Basilium."

"Will, maybe she's right, we should set up camp." Aylise looked at him sternly as she pulled him close. "She's been following you for over two days. If she wanted to hurt you, she would have." Aylise spoke softly.

"She's right," Cara replied, smiling. "Even in this form, fae have excellent hearing." She tucked her hair back, revealing her pointed ears.

"Okay," he muttered his reply. "We set up camp, then you talk," he said for everyone to hear.

Will had never met a fae, as a matter of fact, he'd never met a ghost before either. Was she a ghost?

"There's a lovely spot over there," Cara said, pointing at a spot further into the forest. "Those bushes will obscure you and your fire from view as well as providing shelter.

"We'll follow your lead then," he replied.

They followed Cara, who glided through the forest, weaving through trees until they came across two large rocks with a small opening between them. Large shrubs and bushes obscured them from view, and the rocks protected them from the elements. There were plenty of broken branches, dried leaves and grasses to get a fire going. Should he try again? He looked down at his hands.

"Don't be afraid, Will." Cara smiled at him encouragingly. "I've seen what you can do."

"But I don't know how to control it." It felt strange admitting that to a spectral being that he had just met.

"It comes naturally to you, doesn't it?" She paused, looking right into his eyes. "You don't know how to control it yet, but that will come in time. Trust your instincts and reach for that fire burning inside of you."

"You have a lot of explaining to do when I'm done," he replied, staring at her in amazement. *How did she know all this?*

Cara smiled at Will as he knelt and concentrated on the fire inside of him.

"Feel the fire, Will. Seek it out." She paused. "Can you feel it?" She waited for him to nod. "Good, feel it move through your body and guide it towards your hands." He followed her instructions, feeling the energy course through him. "Now, let it flow and release it from your hands, slowly. Let it out, slowly," Cara continued.

He pushed the energy through his body. His hands felt energised as little fireballs dribbled out of his fingers and disappeared. *That was embarrassing.*

"Keep concentrating. You can do this, Will," Cara said encouragingly.

Will pushed harder, focusing the energy as it moved through his body. It swirled in front of his palm and a stream of fire flowed from his hands, igniting the kindling. The fire slowly roared to life, much more smoothly than it had in the temple. Will smiled at Cara and turned to his friends, who were grinning from ear to ear as they sat down with him.

"Well done, Will," Cara said, her eyes warm and full of pride. "You might be new at this, but you're a fast learner."

Will sat in silence, waiting for Cara to begin speaking.

"Okay, it's time to start talking," he said after waiting in silence long enough. "What do you know about these sigils?"

"Two days ago, I felt the sigils activate on you. I'm presuming it was the first time it happened?" Cara paused, continuing only when Will nodded. "That's interesting, it normally happens when one is much younger, that could explain the surge in power." She mumbled under her breath. "Anyway, when I felt the sigil, I felt a power surge through me. A presence in me that I hadn't felt for eighteen years."

What presence?" Will asked.

"Me. I felt me, like a part of my soul came back to life." She paused, her eyes full of sorrow. "I was killed by dark magic wielded by Queen Haveena. That dark magic trapped me in a shadow realm. I couldn't move or feel any joy. I was tortured every day. I lost myself, I lost who I was, I lost my loved ones. I couldn't see the world, only darkness and decay. And there I stayed, trapped for eighteen years."

Cara paused again, her sad frown turning into a soft smile and her eyes lit up with joy.

"Then I saw your sigil burning bright and I felt a change inside of me. Something that was long lost." She paused again, Will waited with bated breath. "I couldn't describe how foreign it felt after so long. I reached for the sigil and felt a surge of power radiate through me. I held onto it tight, and it lifted me from the shadow realm. I was back in this land, weak, confused, unsure of who I was or where I belonged. But I was home."

Cara smiled softly at Will, was that pride?

"I floated around Basilium, unsure why I was brought back. But then I felt the sigil again, I felt you. I watched you save her." She gestured towards Aylise. "I saw your sigil glowing again and felt another surge of consciousness flow through me, I felt it giving me strength. So, I followed you."

"I could sense you." He looked up at her, as if all the pieces of a puzzle were suddenly falling into place. "I could feel a presence following me. I had presumed it was the guards... which, it turns out, was fairly accurate... but why didn't I see you?"

"Don't you understand? Your power, your strength is what gave me back my form."

"And that's why you're following me?" he replied, a shiver running down his spine.

"No, Will. I followed you because you are a phoenix."

"You know I don't know what phoenixes are, so why don't you tell me?"

"Aylise," Cara called out, turning her attention to Aylise. "You said you've heard of phoenixes, why don't you tell us what you know?"

Aylise seemed unsurprised that Cara knew her name, too.

"I've only heard my father mention the name in hushed tones." She looked thoughtfully at Will and Seb. "From my understanding, they're magical creatures. Fire breathing birds, imbued with powerful magic. They haven't been seen in Basilium for over one thousand years." She smiled with understanding. "When I asked my father about them, he got quite cross and made me promise never to utter the word again."

"You're right about that. The last of the firebirds left our lands before the end of the phoenix wars of the fourth age a thousand years ago." Will suddenly wished he'd read that book in the forest. "But that's not the phoenixes I am referring to," Cara said, smiling at Will again. "I'm referring to the order of warriors who are imbued with the power of said magical creatures."

Will appreciated Cara pausing, as it allowed him a small moment to comprehend what he was hearing.

"For millennia, phoenixes fought to defend Arulean from the most dangerous threats. Some phoenixes are generational. Some weaker, some stronger. And some phoenixes are the first in their bloodline born with the gift. But the one thing that always remains the same is that a phoenix's power activates when the balance of powers calls for them to rise."

"And you think I'm a phoenix because of this…" he waved his arm "Sigil?"

"Yes, you bear the sigil of the phoenix, Will, and I have seen your power. I have no doubt that you are a phoenix. One hasn't been called for over one thousand years, but the balance of power has called to you, Will."

"A tyrant has ruled over Basilium for eighteen years now. Why wasn't a phoenix called sooner? Arulean is dying, crops don't grow, rain doesn't fall, rivers dried up, the sun doesn't… oh." He stopped mid-sentence. That was true until very recently.

"I can't answer why you weren't called sooner," she said sadly. "Perhaps you're not the only one who has been called. Whatever the reason, you have been called now."

"But I wasn't called." Will didn't mean to raise his tone, but he felt like he was going around in circles. "I fell into a fire and then these appeared." He swung his wrists out. "It's as simple as that. It doesn't mean…" He sighed and slumped down on the earth.

"I know this can be hard to accept, Will. This is a lot of information to take in." Cara waited a moment and Will looked to her. "I know one thing for certain. You are a phoenix, and whether you believe it or not, Queen Haveena sees it too. She saw your sigil and now she hunts you.

Your friend died because he carried a piece of parchment with the sigil on it."

Seb fidgeted uncomfortably at the mention of Rupert.

"I'm not trying to scare you, Will. I am trying to warn you," Cara pleaded, "She will not stop hunting you down.

"Why does she want me dead?" He held his breath as he waited for Cara's response.

"I do not have the answer to that, I'm sorry." Will's heart sank at the reply. "But I know this: King Rickard and Queen Haveena wield the darkest of magic. There is only one being capable of stopping someone that dark."

"A phoenix!" Seb whispered, finishing Cara's sentence.

Will shuffled sideways, moving closer to Seb. They gave each other the same knowing look. They were in over their heads.

"Will we need to go to Oldwell. The sooner we get to my father, the sooner we are safe," Aylise spoke up, her wide-eyed expression implied she too, felt the same.

Will felt uneasy. Could he really be a phoenix? Could he trust Cara? He glanced towards her; she was watching him intently.

"Come here, Will." Cara smiled at him, waving him over. "Come stand with me." He did as she asked. "I want you to visualise your power in your mind, feel for that energy."

Will felt uncertain about her request. What did she want him to do? Although she seemed to be helpful and kind so far, he did not completely trust her yet, but she stared at him with her wide eyes full of hope. *Oh, what do I have to lose?* He thought to himself, before closing his eyes and searching for the burning feeling. It was in that moment that he realised he couldn't feel it anymore, the burning was gone. A flicker of energy ignited in his chest. He grasped it, allowing it to spread through his body. It felt different to the burning feeling he was so used to. This felt... natural.

"I feel it!" he exclaimed.

"Good, now hold onto it and open your eyes," she replied. He did as instructed. "Your powers are new, I'm going to teach you some control, okay?" He nodded in agreement. "Now focus on that energy, can you feel it in your hands?" He kept his eyes on Cara as he nodded. "Good, now bring your hands up to mine and push the energy to your palms, but don't let it out yet."

She held her hands in front of her chest, and Will placed his hands close to hers. His arms hummed with power as he drew the energy there and his sigils started to glow brightly. He could feel the power building in his hands, and a golden aura began to radiate from them.

Will looked for Seb and Aylise, their eyes were wide, and their mouths were slightly hanging open as they watched his glowing hands.

"That's it, Will." He focused on Cara again. "Now push the energy out of your hands, slowly, but focus: try to hold it close. Try to make it sit in your palms."

He willed the energy out: small sparks spat out of his hands and disappeared. He felt stupid for the smallest moment but tried not to beat himself up about it. *You can do this.* He told himself. Seb and Aylise encouraged him with a soft smile and a tilt of their heads. His hands hummed as the energy flowed out of his palms and circled around his fingers. They stayed in front of his hands.

"Excellent, Will. Now feel the power radiating from it, let that power grow, and push it out," Cara called out.

Cara glided closer to Will, a smile spread across her face as he released the energy from his hands. It rose around him in a blinding light, power humming through his body. Cara gasped and her spectral form glowed as the light filled her.

Will stepped back from her, the hairs on the back of his neck rising. What had she made him do? He backed towards Seb and Aylise, who had risen.

Cara laughed gleefully as the energy filled her, becoming brighter by the second. When the light disappeared, Cara's whole form had changed. Although she still had a spectral form, her skin was richer and more colourful, and her hair had turned a soft, iridescent golden-blonde. Her eyes were as blue as the oceans around Cyandra.

"What did you make me do?" he asked, ready to run.

"You did it! I knew you could," she smiled at him. "Thank you."

"But what did you just make me do?" he asked more firmly.

"Phoenixes have healing powers, Will." She looked down at her form. "When a spirit lingers in this world, this," she gestured down her body, "is how they should look. You healed me."

"How?"

"By removing the last remnants of the shadow realm from me." She gestured her hands out around her. "But I'm not all you healed."

Will, Seb and Aylise looked down in amazement. In a large patch around their campsite, vibrant green grass had replaced the brown brittle earth underfoot just moments ago. Clusters of shrubs with large purple flowers growing on thick stems had appeared out of the ground. Will stared in wonder at the transformation. He gazed at Cara, a different burning growing inside of him.

"Tell me everything you know," he said eagerly.

~ CHAPTER ELEVEN ~

Queen Haveena slowed her pace as she passed her guards, who stood at attention. Once she had turned the corner, she quickened her pace, almost running through the palace until she entered the gardens.

As Haveena's magic grew across the lands, syphoning the life essence out of everything it touched, everything slowly withered away to near death. But she had kept her own palace gardens healthy and thriving. Publicly it served as a reminder of her power, that she could give life and take it away just as easily. Privately, she simply loved being in her garden. When she was a young girl, her mother maintained a wonderful garden full of magical herbs and flowers. Everything had a purpose and Haveena's mother ensured that she honed her craft from a young age.

"When did it appear?" she commanded, staring into the centre of the garden.

A single thick stem with a small shrub at its base had grown in the middle of her lawns. Although the purple flower had not yet bloomed, the amaranthine flower was unmistakable.

"It appeared overnight," her advisor replied. "One of the guards brought it to my attention."

Haveena walked through the gardens, taking the stairs up the battlement, she silently sighed as she looked out over the eastern lands. Withered and dying, just as they should be. *He's getting stronger.* There was no other explanation. She glanced up at the sky, the sun beating down on the lands and several white fluffy clouds littered the sky. The dense, low-lying grey blanket that had covered Basilium was gone. How had a phoenix slipped through her fingers? How could one even be called? She had wiped out the line. Without it, others couldn't be called, could they?

Haveena and Rickard had planned the siege perfectly. They had been hiding deep underground for years, and most people had forgotten them. Dyana had forgotten them. The thought still stung all these years later, *that backstabbing bitch.* No matter, Haveena was about to get her revenge.

"I can feel the spell working." She glanced towards Rickard. His eyes gleamed with hunger. Oh, she loved how he looked at her when she was practising her magic. "It's forming."

The thief was lying lifeless in the fire, their very essence forming part of the spell that would change Haveena's world forever. The thief had outgrown their use, but had played their part well, retrieving the prophecy for her. Little did they know, they had one last part to play for her.

The last of the spell formed above the fire and Haveena held the vessel in her palms, just like the book said to. The spell swirled above the fire and snaked its way into the vessel. Haveena secured the lid on top of the vessel.

"It's ready, my love." She smiled towards Rickard. Placing the vessel safely in a box on the table.

"My beautiful, wicked witch," he cooed, as he cupped her face and kissed her passionately.

Rickard's kiss felt like lightning coursing through her. His hands glided down her back and cupped her behind. She moaned deeply into his ear.

"My Lord," someone called out, storming into the room.

Rickard held his hand out and the soldier flew across the room towards his outstretched hand. Rickard wrapped his fingers around the guard's neck and squeezed. The guard swiftly grabbed a dagger and stabbed it at Rickard's neck. The blade bounced off his magically hardened flesh without a scratch. Rickard crushed the soldier's neck, who went limp.

"Never interrupt me when I am ravishing my sweet wife!" Rickard said, without even looking at the soldier. "Now, where were we?" Rickard threw the soldier aside, leaving his lifeless body on the floor.

Rickard and Haveena had some of the best sex of their lives on the floor of the chamber. Power hummed through their veins as they took turns pleasuring each other before they made their way back to the bedroom.

"Where should we release the curse?" Haveena asked Rickard as she straddled his naked body, his shaft deep inside her.

"Release it just before we crest the last of the largest hills around Basilium," he replied, thrusting himself into her. "Release the cloud before their guards even have a chance to see us. Those idiots won't know what's going on. They're likely to think a storm is rolling in." Rickard's expression turned serious. "Are you sure the curse will work like you said?"

"Oh yes," Haveena replied, biting into his collarbone, her teeth piercing his flesh. Blood began to pool around the wound, and she licked it up and grinned at him mischievously. He grinned back at her and thrust into her hard. "The curse needs time to incubate for several months, but once it's ready, it will absolutely work, my love. None of the inhabitants of Basilium will be able to see a thing. They'll be powerless against us." She bounced up and down on his shaft and cackled.

"I fucking love you," he growled at her and spun her around onto the bed.

"Forgive my intrusion, Your Majesty, you may want to see this," a guard bowed to Haveena, snapping her out of her memories.

"See what?" she responded curtly, trying to block out the memories of happier times with Rickard.

"You asked to be informed of any unusual activity. Well, this is quite unusual," the guard replied.

"Show me."

Haveena followed the guard back through the gardens. He guided her through the castle, walking through the long corridors. The guard stopped at two large doors and pushed them open. Haveena followed him with a sense of urgency and foreboding.

In the middle of the town square stood a small tree. Branches were steadily growing along its trunk, producing vibrant green leaves. At the base of the broken statues of the Kyllarian dynasty, grasses and flowers had sprung, stretching out from the statues. Haveena seethed inside: her anger coursed through her body like a poison, eating away at every thought in her mind. *Who is this boy?*

"Where is the king?" she snapped.

"In your private chambers, Your Majesty."

"That'll be all." She walked back into the castle, stomping her feet on the stone.

Haveena walked quickly through the castle, her anger growing with each step. He was more powerful than she had anticipated. She had brushed away her concerns when she learnt that he had defeated Andeux, random bursts of power were expected with new phoenixes. But that little rat, Andeux, had failed her. He allowed a teenager to flee her city and best him on a beach. Pathetic little man. But now, she couldn't brush away her concerns about the lands. He was healing them, and that was unacceptable.

When Haveena's guards wheeled Andeux's body back into Basilium, she had been seething.

"He's no use to me anymore. Throw him into the ocean and let the sharks have a feast," she waved her hand cruelly as she barked at the guards.

Haveena continued stomping down the hallway and barged into her private chambers, swinging the doors open wide. A flick of her wrist and the doors closed themselves behind her.

"There's a tree growing in the square," she exclaimed, marching towards Rickard.

"I've seen it," he replied curtly, turning to face her.

"And you didn't think to tell me?"

"Who do you think sent the guard?"

"And have you seen the amaranthine plant growing in the garden?" she said coolly.

"There isn't?" A slight hint of concern crept through in his tone.

"Yes, Rickard, there is. It's the boy. We can't let him get any stronger." She raised her voice. "There are people gathering in the city, whispering of phoenixes."

"I'm aware, Haveena," he replied, groaning at her.

"How can you be so calm?" she hissed.

"These people are nobody, Haveena," he spoke firmly. "Let the people cling to their hope. We'll march the boy's corpse through the streets for all to see."

"We need to find him, first." She raised her voice.

"That's what I have you for," he replied, his tone sharp and condescending.

"What's that supposed to mean?"

"You'll think of something. Find a magical solution." He waved a hand, moving away from her.

"And the tree in the square?"

"Leave it there. We can't show any concern for it," he replied, walking out.

Haveena spent the remainder of her afternoon in her private altar room. The room was lined with shelves filled with ancient magical tomes, herbs, potions, and supplies for brewing concoctions. At one end of the room, her cauldron and work station were nested by the fire. She sat in the large leather chair at her desk at the other end of the room. She was searching for a way to cast a location spell without using a personal item from the subject, when a strange feeling hit her.

Her mind was buzzing, like a thousand bees were burrowing into her temples and swimming through her head. It grew so loud, she nearly screamed out in discomfort. Then clarity washed over her. *Oh, oh this is interesting, that little bitch.* She smiled and sat back in her chair, twirling her fingers around her goblet and sipping her wine slowly.

"Find the king and ready your men," she commanded her guards as she walked out of her altar room. "We're riding for the Amaranthine Forest. I know where they are."

It was hours before Rickard finally formulated his plan and began to gather their forces. Haveena would have started riding straight away and sorted out the details on the way: annoyed, frustrated and impatient to begin. It took another three or so hours before they rode out of the castle. She kicked her horse hard. Her hunt began now.

~ CHAPTER TWELVE ~

Cara quivered with shame and quickly snapped herself out of her spiralling thoughts. She couldn't let the humans see. How would they ever possibly understand? Oh, why did she let Will heal her? She never should have tricked him into doing it. This aching pain made everything feel worse. The glimmer of light and hope she felt as he healed her had been snuffed out by her guilt. She could redeem herself; it was a long road to redemption ahead, but she must if she was to embrace her fae spirit.

Darkness had well and truly settled over their campsite; the only source of light was the fire crackling. Creatures chirped, cooed and yelped in the darkness around them. Cara hovered back and forth as Will, Aylise and Seb chewed on fae berries.

"What do you three know about the under-realm?" Cara asked.

"The realm of darkness and monsters?" Seb paused for confirmation. "The gateways between our realm and the under-realm are quite weak." He looked perplexed. "For such a long time, I thought it was just a children's story. A fairytale to remind children not to stray too far from home so the big bad monsters don't take you." Will and Aylise nodded in agreement. "Until you learn the truth."

"Hmm. Indeed," Cara replied. "May I ask something else then? Have you ever heard the stories of Dakarth?"

"The great war of Arulean," Aylise said. Seb and Will turned towards her. Will was always impressed by Aylise and Seb's knowledge. "One thousand years ago, Dakarth came to Arulean with his army to wipe us out. King Leonol was the king of Arulean at the time. The war lasted years. Many people were lost defending the land, but ultimately, Dakarth fell at the fallen fortress."

"I'm impressed. I'm presuming you learnt this at home?" Cara replied.

"Aylise and I read about it one day," Seb replied.

"Before Haveena and Rickard usurped the throne, the stories were known by another name," Cara continued.

"The phoenix wars of the fourth age?" Will asked.

"Correct," Cara replied. "The fallen fortress was once known as the Fortress of the Flames. It was a stronghold for phoenix warriors and the gateway to the southern kingdoms."

"What does this have to do with the under-realm?" Will asked.

"Dakarth came to our land from the under-realm," Cara replied. "Every wonderful feeling of hope, joy, love and pleasure you feel here, does not exist in the under-realm. It's dark, foul, and full of the darkest evils. It is the natural opposite to our world. Dakarth wanted the power of our world for himself. He succeeded in opening a gateway to our realm and brought with him the darkest and nastiest of creatures found on our lands." Cara paused, ensuring she had their attention. "Dakarth succeeded in spreading darkness through Arulean. Villages, cities, and whole kingdoms fell to him. Arulean was on the brink of extinction when King Leonol and the fae-Queen Elyndra, sprang into action. They converged at the Fortress of the Flames to defend our lands. But when Dakarth blasted his way into the fortress, Queen Elyndra fell in the battle. In her dying breath, she imbued King Leonol's sword with fae magic."

"So, the king used a magically imbued sword to defeat Dakarth?" Will asked, perplexed. "I don't understand what this has to do with phoenixes?"

"King Leonol came from a long line of phoenixes. Dakarth wasn't the first being from the under-realm to come to our lands seeking glory. Every time one of these beings attacked, the phoenixes stopped them. Dakarth planned to wipe out all traces of phoenixes, but he didn't count on the power radiating from the fortress, the power in Leonol's line and the power of Queen Elyndra."

"So, it was fae magic?" Will replied, still perplexed.

"No, Will, it was phoenix power, because Queen Elyndra was also a phoenix."

"How does this all relate to me now?"

Will felt Aylise's fingers intertwine with his and hold on tight. He glanced at her, her fearful eyes staring back at him. Seb looked rather ill when he glanced his way. Will pulled Seb in closer.

"As Queen Elyndra lay dying, she had a vision. A vision so powerful it's been guarded in the Tower of Wisdom in Vandfall ever since." She paused. "Rumour says the vision involved a great power and the sigil on your wrists."

Will stopped breathing for a moment as his wrist burned with recognition.

"Lord Dakarth stopped at nothing to wipe out all trace of phoenixes, and now Queen Haveena will stop at nothing until you are dead."

Will jumped up and started to pace around the fire, startling Seb and Aylise. "But why, because apparently I'm a phoenix?" He kicked at the dirt and reined himself in. "I don't want anything from her, I'm not a threat to her. I just want to live my life," he said more calmly.

"You are a phoenix, Will. And she is the last living descendant of Lord Dakarth."

"She's what?" Will stopped pacing.

"She is indeed. And when she usurped the throne eighteen years ago, she wiped out the last living descendant of King Leonol Kyllarian. The last of the phoenixes, or so she thought."

Aylise moved towards Will, slid her arms around his waist and rested her head on his shoulders.

"We'll work this out together, I promise," she whispered, kissing him on the cheek.

His cheeks flushed at her kiss. Oh gods, he wanted to kiss her, properly. The thought gave him butterflies, but it was so thrilling and enticing too. This was his moment to say something charming and funny to woo her and sweep her off her feet. He wracked his brain.

'Thanks," he mumbled, his cheeks felt bright red.

Idiot, he thought to himself. She smiled softly and stepped away from him. *Fucking idiot.*

"Okay so our problems with the queen aren't going away anytime soon. How do we stay alive now?" Seb called out.

"Firstly, we have to get all three of you to Oldwell. As Aylise said, your parents are all waiting for you there. I'm sure they will have more answers for us," Cara said matter-of-factly. "For now, we should all rest. You must be tired.

"But I have more questions," Will countered.

"You need to rest," Cara replied.

"I need answers."

"And I don't have all the answers. But everything I have told you is true. Queen Haveena wants you dead because you are a phoenix. Phoenixes are called upon in a great time of need. Given the state of Arulean, this is a time of need. We will find all the answers, we will." She paused, drifting away from him. "But you need to rest now."

Cara drifted further away towards the edge of their camp, lifted her hands out in front of her, and began to chant in faeish. Her hands glowed a soft pink as magic swirled around their camp. When she stopped chanting, her hands faded back to their translucent colour.

"What did you just do?" Will asked.

"She cast a protection spell around us," Seb replied, looking towards Cara, "didn't you?"

"I did," Cara replied. "Nobody will be able to enter our camp tonight. Rest well."

Cara closed her eyes and stopped moving. After a time, her whole form started to glow.

"She's in a fae trance," Seb said, looking at Aylise and Will's bewildered faces. "When fae spirits linger in our world, it's how they sleep and replenish their spirit."

"How do you know all this, Seb?" Aylise asked.

"Because I read a lot more than what your father approves of," he quipped. "Your library isn't my only source of knowledge."

They continued their conversation late into the evening, dissecting the limited information they had learnt so far. Some hours after Cara had first drifted off into her trance, she awoke and waved her hands towards them, her hands glowing as she mumbled.

Will instantly felt drowsy. He looked towards Seb and Aylise who were stifling yawns. Will let his heavy body drag him down towards the fire, curling up in the warmth. He closed his eyes, and the world turned black.

Will was unimpressed when he woke the next morning to the sounds of birds chirping around the camp. Aylise and Seb stirred from their sleep not long after he did. Cara was floating around the campsite watching them.

"Why did you do that?" he asked her rather firmly.

"All three of you needed to rest, I presume you slept well." She smiled, while Will continued to silently watch her. "Oh, Will, I cast a protection spell and then put you all into a dreamless sleep for the night. I did it to protect you all," she explained curtly. "Why don't you focus less on that and look down instead."

Will glanced down in disbelief. The earth around the camp had completely changed. The grassy patch had spread further from the camp. Trees were standing tall and strong, sprouting thick branches that burst with lush greenery.

"Another example of your growing powers," Cara said, smiling. "As your powers grow, so will your impact on the land."

Could this really be all his doing? Was he really a phoenix? He wasn't stupid, he accepted that these abilities were appearing. But could he really be healing the land around them? He gazed out into the forest. He'd produced those energy blasts, the fire balls, and he gave Cara form. Now he'd woken up to the healed land around him.

Will walked away from the camp onto the dead forest floor. Dead leaves and brittle grass crunched under his feet as he walked. He placed his hand on the ground and concentrated. Reaching for the power, he channelled it through his body and slowly released it from his hands.

The earth beneath his hands rumbled with energy. A soft whistling sound radiated from the earth as it began to shift. Grass shot out of the earth, the radius expanding around him. When it hit the trunk of a tree, it slowly transformed, bringing itself back to life, from trunk to tip. Will watched as the energy moved through the brittle bark and filled with life. He witnessed the land around him transform. It was so beautiful to see, he couldn't help but smile. It was one of the most spectacular things he had ever witnessed.

"Thank you, Cara. Thank you for showing me my gifts." He smiled at her.

"And thank you for bringing me back to the light." She smiled at him in return.

"I'm a phoenix," Will whispered under his breath.

"Oh yes, you are." Her smile widened. "But you still have much to learn."

"Then let's get moving," he replied, turning towards Aylise and Seb. "Let's pack up and get ready to move on, we've got a big day ahead of us."

~ CHAPTER THIRTEEN ~

Will, Seb and Aylise were hidden behind a shrub in the forest, far enough away from the town to remain unseen. Cara slowly disappeared before their eyes, transforming herself to scout through the town unseen.

"After all that planning, we still ended up in Korgun anyway," Seb whispered.

"At least we made it here in one piece," Aylise replied.

"Quiet, both of you," Will whispered firmly.

Will felt on edge. His senses flared up and his body vibrated with phoenix energy. He wasn't concerned about the energy releasing. It wasn't desperately trying to escape, it was simply humming on the surface, ready to defend him.

"I'm back," Cara's voice whispered somewhere close. A moment later, her form materialised behind the shrubs.

"Anything to be concerned about?" Will asked.

"Local town guards. The town is busy," she smiled. "I didn't see any of the royal guards though."

Will sighed deeply. Perhaps the guards had already come through or had not yet arrived.

"Do you think it'll be safe to go in?" Seb asked hopefully. "It sure would be nice to eat a warm meal and sleep in a soft bed."

Will and Aylise stared at him, smirking to each other.

"Oh, don't give me that, Lady Aylise." She glared at Seb for using her title. "Don't tell me you wouldn't love a warm bed again."

Oh, there was no denying that. Will hadn't bathed for over two days, he'd eaten nothing but fae berries, and his back was sore.

"I would," Will spoke quietly, "but there's one problem. Did anyone bring enough money with them?"

"Now, why did you have to go and ruin a perfectly good idea?" Seb replied.

"Well, I brought gold with me, didn't you?" Aylise replied.

"Of course," Will and Seb replied. They dug into their satchels and pooled their gold, silver and coppers together.

Will still felt uncertain about wandering straight into town, even though Cara had scouted around.

"Let's follow the forest up to the edge of town, cross the royal road, and scope out the other side," Will said.

Korgun was encompassed by the forest on the western, northern and eastern sides. The royal road passed through the centre of town, making it a busy thoroughfare for travel and trade. Just like much of Arulean, Korgun showed signs of life draining from the land. Much of the flora was brown and shrivelled, although it didn't seem to be as severe in Korgun as it was in Fawkeston or other towns closer to Basilium. The town was quite simple. The buildings were made of timber structures, which was quite common for forest towns. Fawkeston had a similar look in the areas closer to the forest, though the buildings became grander and more luxurious the closer you travelled into Fawkeston's centre.

They made their way into the centre of town, searching for any sign that pointed towards the inn. Cara stayed invisible to not draw any unwanted attention to them.

"Excuse me, boys," Aylise called out smiling, as she walked towards two teenage boys huddled together. "Would you happen to know the way to the inn?"

"Which one?" said the boy with dark brown skin. "There are three in town." He smiled at his friend, nudging him with his shoulder and glancing at Seb.

"I'd prefer one that's quiet," Aylise replied, sighing. "We've travelled north from Sunscythe, and we'd truly love a peaceful evening."

"I'd recommend the Pixie's Den." He pointed down a street. "It's nice and quiet by the edge of the forest." The boy looked at Aylise. "Quite the journey from Sunscythe. How long have you been on the road?"

"Weeks." Aylise smiled in reply. "What news in the north?"

"All quiet around here," he replied, returning her smile.

"Thanks for your help, boys."

"Safe travels!" he replied, smiling at Seb.

Seb flushed and smiled in return. The two boys put their heads together and continued talking as they walked away.

Will, Aylise and Seb followed the boy's directions and wandered down a street along the eastern side of town. They found the three-story Pixie's Den in the shadows of the forest.

"Travelling from Sunscythe?" Will smirked at Aylise. "That was an excellent cover story."

"And completely common and unmemorable, hopefully." She nudged him.

A short woman greeted them from the counter as they walked into the inn.

"It'll be nine silvers for a room," she informed them warmly. "There's plenty of space for each of you. You'll have your own bathing chamber in there, too."

"Wonderful, I could do with a bath." Will smiled. "Would it be possible to have a room on the ground floor?" he asked. Aylise and Seb clocked the request but didn't pry him out in the open.

"Not a problem dear," she replied politely. "Do you need any clothes laundered while you're here?"

"As much as we would love to take you up on that offer, I'm afraid our packs were stolen from the inn at Gregaron. All we have are the clothes on our backs," Aylise replied meekly.

"Oh, my dear, that won't do. Come with me." She waved them to a room behind the counter. "Feel free to take some clothes from here.

There are always travellers coming and going and things do get left behind." She smiled at them. "Take what you need, get washed up, and bring your other clothes down here and I will get them sorted for you."

"Oh, thank you," Aylise gushed earnestly, "You are too kind."

One hour later, Will was lying down on his soft bed in the inn. His skin and hair smelled like oranges, thanks to the soap in the bathing chamber. His new clothes fit reasonably well and didn't smell of sweat, dirt, or sea water, which was a pleasant change.

"This was a wonderful idea, Seb." He smiled at Seb. "I can't remember ever enjoying a bath as much as I just did."

"Absolutely." Aylise purred from the doorway to the bathing chamber. Aylise's wet hair was braided down her back, and she had swapped her ripped dress for travelling pants and a tunic that stopped halfway down her shins. Seb and Will had opted for leather travelling pants and dark shirts. They each picked up a hooded cloak to help them blend in when out and about.

"Would you like me to stay with you while you eat?" Cara asked politely. "Otherwise, I'll patrol the town."

"I think we'll be fine alone, thanks, Cara," Will replied. "I'd feel better knowing you were patrolling the town."

"I'll come find you if I sense any danger." She smiled at them.

The inn served a rabbit and vegetable stew that evening. A deep groan escaped from Will as he slurped down the broth.

"Sorry," he said bashfully, "but that is delicious." He sighed.

"I couldn't agree more!" Seb replied, ripping a piece of bread off the loaf and dipping it into the stew before throwing it into his mouth.

True to the boy's recommendation, the inn was nice and quiet. There were four other patrons in the venue. An old man sitting by himself by the fire, and a mother and father with a small child. The innkeeper, Mary – Will found out her name when he brought their dirty clothes down – came walking over with three large goblets.

'I thought you three could do with some cheering up," Mary said, placing the goblets on the table. "One of my favourite ciders; my sister makes it just south of town."

"What do we owe you?" Will asked, smiling.

"That's on me tonight, deary. You've had a rough journey to get here." She gazed over them with a motherly smile. "I'm just glad I was able to get you lot freshened up with some clean clothes and a warm place to stay." She cupped Aylise's chin and walked away.

"Cheers to your amazing cover story." Will said quietly, raising his glass and sipping his refreshing beverage.

Once Seb had finished his meal and drank every last drop of his cider, he felt comfortably full and ready to nap. They paid Mary for their meals and retired to the room.

"Thank you, that was lovely," they farewelled the delighted Mary.

Although it was tempting to explore Korgun by night, Will decided it was best to not draw any unwanted attention to himself. Cara periodically drifted back into the room, bringing with her updates on her patrols. The town seemed to be quite social in the evenings, but there was nothing that seemed to cause any concern for Cara.

"I'm going to step out and browse the books in the hallway," Seb spoke softly, as he stepped out of the room.

Seb walked down the hallway to a small shelf with a selection of books. Above the various titles, town notices had been nailed to the wall. Seb picked up a title simply called Vandfall and sat down in a quiet reading nook off the hallway. He wasn't really there for the books, he just needed time alone with his thoughts.

"You hold a heavy burden close to your heart," Cara observed softly as she materialised in the nook. She hovered where she would remain unseen from the hallway.

"What do you mean?" Seb said, his back stiffening. *What did she know?*

"I see the pain you carry, the angst, the fear. You want them to know who you are."

Oh gods, how did she know? He had never told anyone before, he was careful to hide it whenever he could.

"I, ah. I..." Seb stuttered. He clutched onto the book tightly to disguise his shaking hands.

"You don't have to be alone, Seb, and you don't have to be afraid. They'll understand."

"How did you know?" he asked. Gods, he couldn't believe he was having this conversation. It felt terrifying, but at the same time, it was nice: freeing, almost.

"I see with more than eyes, Seb," she replied, smiling down at him and cupping her translucent hand to his face. "Everyone has their own journey and their own story to share when they are ready. Until you embrace who you truly are, you'll never reach your full potential, and you've come so far already." Cara paused and looked deep into his eyes. "You want them to know who you are. When you're ready to tell them, Will and Aylise will support you and love you."

Seb chuckled slightly as he gasped for air, a tear rolled down his cheek. His shoulders felt lighter, like Cara was lifting the burden he had been carrying.

"I do want to tell them. I want them to know me. We've stepped into a world far more dangerous than I could possibly imagine. I don't want to die without them knowing who I am." He held his head high as he looked at Cara. "Thank you for encouraging me."

"All I did was name what you already felt," she replied.

Seb sat in silence, pondering her words. It had been eating away at him since the boat capsized at Dragon's Jaw. Seb had always valued his friendship with Will and Aylise. They knew each other's deepest and darkest secrets. Well, they didn't know all of his. Gods, it was scary, sharing a part of yourself that is so personal and private. But, like he said to Cara: if he was going to put himself on the line, then he wanted his loved ones to know who he truly was.

"I'm going to speak to them," Seb said, standing up and walking down the hallway before he changed his mind. For just a small moment, it felt like the weight he had been carrying around lifted away.

"Hi..." Seb attempted to sound casual as he entered the room, but he ended up mumbling. His cheek flushed bright red, and the weight almost tried to climb back on his shoulders. He puffed his chest and shrugged it off.

"Are you okay, Seb?" Aylise asked, "What's wrong?"

"Ah, nothing," he replied, "nothing at all." *I vowed to myself not to lose anyone else I love. Well, that includes me too.*

He wasn't exactly planning this life-changing moment. No one ever really wants their life to change, but it does… these moments come. Seb shut the door and began to pace by the fire. Will began to open his mouth when he and Aylise sat down in chairs. *Be brave. Be you.* He told himself.

"Please don't speak yet," Seb asked, continuing his steps across the fireplace. "Let me say what I have to say." Pace, pace, pace, back and forth. "There's something I've been wanting to tell you for quite some time. About me…" Seb began and then paused. Not daring to look at Will and Aylise: his heart was racing and his cheeks felt like they were burning as he paced. "I don't know if you worked it out already or not, but… You know Rupert and I? We were friends, but we were more than that. We were together…" Seb glanced in their direction. "Rupert and I." Will and Aylise watched him closely. Their eyes were filled with warmth and their mouths curved into small smiles. "What I'm trying to say is, *I like men.*"

Seb wiped away the tears that began to creep down his cheeks. He looked towards the fire, missing the love that radiated from Will and Aylise.

"Please continue when you're ready, Seb," Aylise said tenderly, and with those words, Seb exhaled, and the burden of his secret fell away. He chanced a glance at Will and Aylise and felt their love for him. His heart soared.

"I've known for years, but I hadn't felt brave enough to tell you." He wiped more tears away. "Rupert and I had been friends for years, you knew that, but about six months ago, it changed, it became more, and it was nice." He continued looking towards the fire. "I wanted to tell you, but I didn't really know how." He finally turned towards Will and Aylise, "I don't want to die without you knowing this part of me; without knowing who I am. I'm not ashamed of who I am, and I don't want to hide it from you."

Will stood up and walked over towards Seb. He pulled him into a tight hug and Will closed his eyes and held on tightly.

"I love you, Seb,' Will said softly. "Thank you for telling us.' Will pulled away and smiled at Seb.

"We love you Seb, no matter who you love," Aylise said, wrapping her arms around Seb and Will.

Seb's shoulders relaxed and a spark of joy ignited in his heart and radiated through him. *Oh gods, I should have said this years ago.* He felt free, he felt lighter, and he felt loved.

"You don't seem surprised," Seb chuckled.

"Because it doesn't matter," Will said matter-of-factly. Then his eyes grew wide. "What I mean is, it doesn't matter to me who you love," he corrected himself. "You matter. You are what matters to me. Frankly, I had thought there might have been something more between the two of you, but it wasn't my story to tell. It was yours." Cara glanced across the room and winked at Seb. "But it doesn't change how I feel about you." Will rolled his eyes. "Oh gods, I'm blabbering. Sorry."

"It's fine," Seb chuckled, feeling lighter with each passing moment. "I appreciate it." He continued, smiling and pulling back from them, looking directly at them. "That was far less dramatic than I imagined." He smiled.

"I understand that," Will replied thoughtfully. "How does anyone truly know how their friends and family feel about particular matters? There are plenty of people in Arulean who want to condemn those who dare to challenge traditional expectations."

"Did you know that Arulean hasn't always been so regressive in its leadership? Before the usurping, the kingdom was quite progressive. The fae kingdom still is," Seb replied.

'Well, we might just have to pay a visit to Vandfall when we're not being hunted by the queen," Aylise said, smiling.

Against his initial judgement, Will agreed to wander around the town and enjoy the nighttime activities. He felt that Seb deserved it, after his revelations. It seemed like the majority of the town had come out to partake in activities. Cara remained close by, patrolling the city from above. When they entered the square, an eruption of sound and light greeted them. A large fire burned in the middle of town. Musicians played instruments on a stage, surrounded by people sipping their beverages at tables and benches, while others danced together in front of the band.

"This is rather pleasant, isn't it?" Will smiled, forgetting his troubles.

They wandered around the food merchants who were cooking a variety of foods over open fires. It was easy enough to ascertain who was a local and who was a passing traveller. The locals sat in large groups, greeting each other and laughing, huddled together in conversation.

The band finished their song to roaring applause from the audience. They began their next song, a lively jig that had the crowd moving out of their chairs to dance.

"Shall we all dance then?" Aylise asked, smiling.

She held her hands out, waiting for the boys to take them and then guided them towards the dancefloor. They all held hands and danced in a circle, twirling around each other and bouncing along to the tune. Will smiled and laughed as he twirled his friends around his arms. It was so carefree and wholesome: something he hadn't felt for days. With each kick of his feet, he felt the weight of his new reality slipping away. Joy and laughter filled the void left behind.

"Royal guards are coming, get off the street," Cara voiced from above.

The joy washed away from the void as his new reality came slipping right back in.

"Move now," he whispered. Swiftly walking away from the dancefloor.

He led Aylise and Seb between buildings. Ducking and weaving until they were at the edge of the forest. He pulled the hood of his cloak up, darting along the forest line. He walked straight into something hard. A person in a long black cloak turned around, holding a dagger ready to strike.

"Will! You're here." Galea looked down at him. "Thank the gods. Follow me."

Will looked at the woman who had helped him escape from Basilium. Just a little spark of hope ignited in him. Maybe they were going to be okay.

"What are you doing here?" he asked Galea, following her along until he could see the edge of town. Three royal guards were standing at the edge of the royal road.

"We're here looking for you, of course," Galea whispered quietly. "We all are."

"Who else is here?" Will asked.

"Oh!" Seb called out, pointing across to the other side of town. "What are they doing here?"

Will's heart felt as if it skipped a beat. Seb's parents – Marte and Alexander – were hidden in an alleyway on the other side of town.

"We came together to look for you," Galea said. "There's a whole patrol of us in town. We split when we saw the guards riding into town."

"Come on," Seb whispered, stepping forward.

"Seb, what are you doing?" He lunged for Seb's arm and pulled him back. "Is it safe to get over there?"

"Will, we have to get over there now," Seb replied, pleading.

Will hesitated. "Just wait a moment." He watched the three guards at the edge of town. "Come on, move away," he whispered, desperately hoping they would move further into town.

As he glanced towards Seb's parents, their eyes locked. Seb's father's eyes grew wide with panic when he saw them. Seb's mother was filled with relief as she locked eyes with Galea.

"We should get moving," said Galea softly.

Seb's mother, Marte, started pointing back towards town and moving her hand in a gesture. Galea nodded in understanding.

"Go back the way we came," whispered Galea.

"We need to move quickly, Will," Cara called out, reappearing next to them. "More guards are coming."

"I don't know what to do." Will froze in place, looking up the road and back towards Seb's parents, his breath laboured. "*I don't know what to do...*" He repeated, suddenly feeling the weight of the world on his shoulders.

"Will," Aylise called out, "let's move now."

Will's senses flared up, rooting him in place. The sound of horses whinnying and armour clanking grew louder and louder. A patrol of guards appeared on the road, riding right into town. There were at least forty soldiers. In the middle of the patrol rode King Rickard and Queen Haveena. Will stopped breathing.

Go, now, Seb's mother mouthed silently across the village.

Will stepped backwards, deeper into the shadow of the forest. He stepped on a fallen branch, resting along some low brambles. The pressure of his body weight snapped the branch in two. The sound loudly radiated around them. Horses and humans alike investigated the sound, gazing into the darkness.

"Run," Galea whispered, running through the forest.

Will followed Galea as she led them through the town. Moving as fast and as silently as he could, he could hear shouting and screaming behind him, but he dared not stop and look back. Why did he hesitate? He should have run when they had the chance. Galea led them down a street further through the town. His mind flashed back to his escape from Basilium, the parallels were not lost on him that once again he was fleeing from the queen.

"Stay close and follow me. Don't hesitate!" she called back.

Galea ran out from the building and sped across the road, weaving between people who were dashing away from the new unexpected visitors in town. Will, Aylise and Seb followed after Galea. As they neared the end of the building, several people came running from the street. They collided into each other, blocking the small space.

"Get out of the way," a large man shouted, pushing them back. "You don't want to be going out there right now."

Will, Seb and Aylise were pushed back towards the forest. They looked across the other side of town. Galea's eyes were wide with fear. Guards began moving down the royal road.

They ran along the edge of town until they were standing outside the Pixie's Den. More royal guards were moving out from the middle of the royal road and slowly making their way down the street towards the inn. A shiver ran down his spine and adrenaline coursed through his veins.

"Get your things out of the room now," Will called out as he opened the door to the inn. "We need to get out of here."

"My parents!" Seb called out. "We have to get back to them!"

"We can't, Seb. Haveena is swarming the city." Will glanced up the street to the guards slowly getting closer. "If she sees them with us, we'll put them in more danger. Please, Seb," Will pleaded. Seb and Aylise hurried through the door.

They nodded politely at Mary and marched straight into their room. Will locked the door and quickly gathered any belongings into the backpack he had taken from Mary.

"Are you both ready?" he called out to Seb and Aylise frantically.

"Yes," Aylise and Seb replied.

"Good," he replied. Opening the window. "Let's go." He threw his backpack into the forest. "This is why I asked for a ground floor room. Just in case," he said as he jumped the short distance to the ground. Aylise and Seb followed soon after.

So much for a night in a warm bed. Will sighed to himself as they ran deep into the forest.

~ CHAPTER FOURTEEN ~

Will collapsed to the ground, hitting the earth hard. His mouth was horribly parched, and his head was pounding from the dehydration. In his haste to flee the inn, he hadn't thought to refill his waterskin. They had run most of the night through the dark forest, eager to put as much distance between them and Korgun as possible.

Anger bubbled under his skin. What had happened to Marte, Alexander and Galea? Will couldn't bear to look at Seb. Once again, people that Seb cared about were potentially in danger because of him. Seb looked exhausted, he was panting heavily and lying on his back on the dry, crusty earth.

"I'm sorry, Seb," he croaked.

"This isn't your fault, Will." He coughed as he spoke.

"I shouldn't have hesitated," Will replied.

"This isn't your fault."

While Seb's words were kind and well-intended, they didn't help soothe the anger and resentment coursing through Will. He rose to his knees and began pounding on the earth with his fists.

"Why is this happening to us?" he screamed, pounding the earth with each word. "What does that fucking bitch want with me?" He ignored the throbbing pain in his hands.

As he pounded his fists into the earth, a surge of energy erupted from him, radiating around him.

"Gods damn it!" he screamed as the energy flowed out. He collapsed to the earth and began to weep.

Aylise and Seb gasped loudly, and Will felt like an impulsive idiot.

"I'm sorry," he replied. "I was having a moment."

"Thanks, we're all allowed to have a moment, but that's not what we were gasping at. Look!" Seb called out, running away from Will.

Will stood up and gazed around the forest. The area was renewed. Fresh grasses grew. Trees were thick and lush, covering them in a leafy canopy. Flowers bloomed all around the area, and Seb and Aylise were drinking heavily from a stream.

Will's mouth hung open as he took in the beauty of what his power had just created.

"It's so fresh and delicious!" Aylise called out from the stream. Will smiled as he jogged towards his friends.

Will gulped down the refreshing mountain water, each mouthful a heavenly stream washing through his body. He gasped in delight and drank again.

"I take it back, I'm not sorry about that," he said, smiling.

"Or you could have just channelled your energy, instead of having an outburst like that," Cara replied, floating above them.

"Easy for you to say, you don't need water to live."

Cara gasped, Will thought he may have offended her, but she smiled, gazing away from them. Will followed her gaze. A majestic white horse was walking towards them, bowing its head and drinking heavily from the stream. It stayed there for quite some time before moving onto the freshly transformed grass and eating away at it.

"Will, you brought the horse here," she smiled at him. "You're bringing the forest back to life."

"It's not just that horse..." Seb pointed into the forest, "Look!"

Three more horses trotted towards the stream and began drinking heavily. Will moved towards the white horse, presenting his open palm as he approached. The horse leaned into his touch, looking into his eyes, she invited him to continue patting her. He didn't understand how he knew she was female, but he knew.

"Will, do it again," Aylise smiled at him wide-eyed. "Do it again. Focus your energy and heal more of the forest."

Will looked towards Cara, almost seeking her confirmation that he could do it. She smiled at him and bowed her head. He stepped away from the horses and walked out to a dead section of the forest. He knelt down and placed both hands on the dirt.

"Focus your energy, Will. Let it out in a controlled manner."

Will searched for the power in his body: the phoenix power. Rather than rage, he yearned to make a difference, to do some good. He wanted to help the animals in the forest. He wanted to help the people that would be nourished by it. The energy rose inside of him.

"I feel it," he said softly.

"Good," Cara replied. "Now, just like I taught you, bring that energy to your hands and control it as you push it out."

Focusing on the techniques Cara taught him, he pushed the energy out through his hands and let it radiate around him. The energy came out in waves, spreading through the forest, moving further and further away from him. The forest sprung to life, responding to the waves. But, as fast as it came out, the power suddenly stopped flowing, leaving Will stumped.

"Why did it stop?" he looked towards Cara.

"Power requires energy to wield it. Energy and skill." She looked at him matter-of-factly. "Both of which you are still developing… not to mention your physical exhaustion."

"Oh, that's disappointing," he replied.

"Is it? Look what you did." She waved her arms out to the forest. "That's quite spectacular if you ask me."

Every visible inch of the forest was thriving with life. Aylise watched him, she had that look on her face that she got when she was deep in thought. What puzzle pieces was she trying to put together?

"What is it?" he asked her.

"It all makes sense, doesn't it?" She waited for an understanding that didn't come. "She's not hunting you simply because she wants to wipe out phoenixes. She's hunting you because you're the antidote to her power."

She walked towards him, sliding her hand along his bicep. His skin tingled where her hands rested, oh please don't let his cheeks be flushing.

"She's been draining the life out of Arulean for years," Aylise nudged.

"And I can bring it back," he answered, as the realisation hit him.

"Well, that part seems fairly obvious with your new abilities," Seb called out sarcastically from the stream where he was stroking the mane of a black horse.

"He doesn't have new abilities," Cara interrupted, "he was born with them. They have always been inside him."

"And my parents have always known it, too. They know I'm a..." He paused. It still felt strange to say. "I'm a phoenix. Ensuring I've avoided fire all my life, the fact that they have kept phoenixes a secret from us, the sigils on my arms." He paused. "But why? Why go to all this effort to hide it from us?"

Movement above pulled their attention from each other. Birds, butterflies, bees and other insects were flying into the forest, nesting themselves in trees, drinking from the stream and collecting pollen from the flowers. Will paused, transfixed by the animals for several moments, and for the first time in days, he had felt true glee. After all the hurt and pain the discovery of the sigils had caused, here they were doing something good.

"I think it's time we asked your parents for the answers you seek, Will." Cara floated next to him.

"Do you know how far we are from Oldwell?" he asked.

"If we ride now, we could arrive by mid-afternoon," Cara replied.

"Ride? You mean the horses?" Seb asked, confused. "Without a saddle?"

"Who said we weren't using saddles?" Cara smirked at him.

Cara began chanting in faeish and twirling her hands in front of her. With a flick of her wrist, saddles materialised on each of the horses.

"Four? Were you planning to float on top of the horse?" Will asked cheekily.

Cara flicked her wrist, and a spark of energy shot towards Will, zapping his skin hard enough to sting momentarily. Cara winked at him.

"Of course not, but we're not leaving anyone behind." She floated towards the horses, a golden-coloured horse with a long mane moved closer towards her. "The white girl likes you; you should ride her."

Will walked towards the white horse, stroking her along her neck. She turned her head and watched Will closely.

"Are you ready for the journey, girl?" he asked, lifting himself into the saddle. "Let's go, you two," he called out to Seb and Aylise.

Seb followed Will's lead, the golden-coloured horse moved from Cara to Seb. Aylise mounted the black horse.

Cara led the way, floating ahead of everyone. The riderless, red-coloured steed followed Cara's every move. Will's mare trotted along, her head raised high, like she was signalling to nature that she was proud to be his escort on this important journey.

Soon they were galloping through the trails in the forest. Relief flooded Will, soon they would be reunited with their families, and soon, they would be receiving more answers.

They had made it to the edge of the forest, almost anyway. The trees weren't as dense and there were clearly marked tracks for the horses to follow.

"Not much further to travel now," Cara called out.

"Thank the gods, because I need to rest," Seb called out.

Cara had spent much of the journey talking about the phoenix riders. The phoenixes of the history books, who were so powerful they were able to call upon the fire-breathing birds from the realm of magical creatures and ride them into battle. Phoenix upon phoenix, defending Arulean together.

"The last magical creatures left Arulean three hundred years before the phoenix wars." Cara was animated while she spoke. "Legend says the only reason Dakarth felt he had a chance at winning the war was because the phoenixes had left the land." She turned towards Will, Aylise and Seb. "I can't believe how much history you've all lost, so much of our history destroyed."

Unfortunately, Cara's memories seemed to falter the closer she came to her death.

"As I grow stronger, so will my memories," she said with pride.

Will certainly hoped that was true, any further insights into Haveena would be helpful.

Aylise trotted next to Will. Stretching across the saddle, she interlaced her fingers with his. Her touch felt like fire through Will's body, his stomach fluttered, and his cheeks began to flush.

"How are you feeling?" she asked warmly.

"I'm fine." He smiled nervously. *Say something, say something, you idiot.* "Thank you for coming to find me at the beach. I wouldn't have been able to get through this if you weren't here."

"I'll always be by your side," she squeezed his hand before pulling away to hold onto her reins, "it's where I belong." Her own cheeks flushed a soft shade of pink.

Did she just? Oh boy, wow. Does that mean she feels the same way? She did come to rescue him, so maybe she did. But then again, Seb came to his rescue too, and he didn't feel that way about Will. *Stop overthinking and say something!*

"And I belong by yours." He smiled softly at her.

He was mesmerised by her eyes and her soft smile. There was so much warmth in the way she looked at him, and (dare he say?) love.

"When we get through this, I'd like to spend some time with you, just the two of us." Her eyes lit up. Will seized on the moment, boosted by her enthusiasm. "Just two of us. Would you like to do that?" He clutched onto the reins, eagerly awaiting her response.

"Will, Aylise!" Seb shouted, looking back towards them.

"What is it?" Will asked with irritation.

"We're nearly there," said Seb, pointing ahead of them. "Oldwell. We made it."

In the distance, just visible through the leaves, was a building, then two, and three, four and more. A whole village appeared. Will exhaled. Oldwell. They would be safe now.

"Let's go then," Will called out. He and Aylise kicked their horses into a gallop. Will completely forgot about Aylise's response to his question, and she had forgotten to give it.

"Not so fast," Cara spoke firmly, as she grasped Will's reins. "You're on the run from the queen." When Will didn't react, she continued. "How do you know she not there waiting for us?"

"She doesn't know where we're going," he replied, although he doubted himself momentarily. "We've been travelling for nearly a whole day. Surely, she would have been searching Korgun all night."

"Would she?"

"I don't know, sorry." He looked down, attempting to hide his shame. "My decisions just keep putting people in danger." It was time to be sensible, before he lost anyone else he loved.

"Don't beat yourself up. You're still learning," Cara said, looking at him. "Now, tell me, what's your plan?"

He dismounted his horse and walked towards the edge of the forest. Nestled in the valley below them was Oldwell. It was surrounded by the Amaranthine Forest on all sides except for a valley to the west. From this distance, Will could see people wandering around the town, but they were too far away to recognise from here. His gaze wandered over the town, looking for Lord Nathaniel's carriages, but they were either not there, or hidden from view.

"We need to scout the village." He turned towards Cara. "And look for signs of our families. The forest keeps the town protected, but it'll disguise us too."

Cara nodded in approval.

"We don't leave the treeline until we're certain it's safe. Once we do, we'll be spotted."

"Good, Will," she agreed. "We'll follow your lead then."

Staying on their horses in case they needed to flee quickly, they slow-trotted along the edge of the forest, far enough into the treeline to be disguised. They crouched low in some long grasses and crept through them until they could see through the blades of grass, while staying out of sight.

People moved throughout the village going about their business, or so it would seem. They seemed like townspeople, wouldn't royal guards scare anyone off? Or were the guards hiding? Forcing everyone to go about their business and just sitting and waiting for Will to arrive? They could be in the forest, each step could be bringing Will closer to his death. Should they just flee now?

Will moved further into the long grasses, ducking lower and creeping closer to the town. It was much easier to see the townspeople moving around, at least those closer to this side of the forest anyway. He thought he saw a familiar-looking face, but when he tried to focus on them, they walked behind a building. *Shit!* He moved through the grasses again. The person reappeared on the other side of the building, walking towards the edge of town, looking down the valley. She was wearing a long dress and wore her hair in a plait. The woman turned back towards the town, pausing momentarily to look out to the forest, right towards Will. Tears welled in his eyes as a warmth spread through him.

"Mama!" he called out, standing and running down the hill towards her. Her eyes locked with his and she clapped her hands over her mouth.

"Darian, he's here!" she called out running towards him. "They're here!" she called out louder.

Relief coursed through Will as he ran towards his mother. The town was safe, they were finally safe. His mother would have stopped him from running to her if it wasn't. Will heard the faint words of his mother. His father emerged from the village, running towards his wife when his eyes locked on Will.

Both of his parents were safe, they made it out of Basilium together. He felt like a young child running to the safety of something warm, comfortable and familiar.

"Oh, my darling boy," Selina sobbed, as she enclosed him in a tight hug. "Oh, thank the gods you're alive." She stroked his hair.

Will collapsed into her embrace, overwhelmed and exhausted from the tension he had been carrying around for days. His father joined them, wrapping them both in his arms, tears streaming down his face.

"Are you okay? Are you hurt?" he asked, pulling away and looking over Will.

"I'm fine, I'm fine." He looked into his father's eyes. "I've never been so scared in my life." He gasped, overwhelmed with relief.

"Us too," his mother cried. "We thought we'd never see you again."

"Oh, thank the gods you're all here," his father said, looking up at Aylise and Seb riding down the hill.

"Aylise!" Lord Nathaniel's voice boomed from the village as he ran towards them. Aylise stopped by Will and leapt into her father's arms.

"Father!" Aylise cried. "Oh Father, I'm sorry."

"Aylise, it's okay, you're safe." He stroked her hair. "By the gods, you gave us a fright."

Lady Ana ran from the village, holding her skirts up as she bounced along the field, her soft voice squeaking.

All the anger and frustration he had felt towards his parents the last few days seemed inconsequential in that moment. The answers he so desperately desired from them didn't matter right now. He just wanted his mum and dad by his side, he wanted to stay hidden away from everyone who was hunting him and live in a blissful daze. Could he do that, just for a moment?

"Where are my parents?" Seb asked.

It seems, bliss had another idea.

Seb stumbled back at the words, his stomach twisting in knots as Lord Nathaniel spoke. Oh gods, he thought he was going to be sick.

"They're on a scouting mission in Korgun. They were there looking for you three." Lord Nathaniel smiled. "Don't worry, they should be back tomorrow. No one has ventured too far from here in case you arrived."

"You mean they're not back yet?" Seb's tone became fretful. "We saw them in Korgun."

"Why aren't they with you, then?" Lord Nathaniel's calm demeanour slipped.

"We were on the other side of town when Queen Haveena rode in. We had to flee." Each word was spoken with a soft hiss as Seb found it difficult to breathe.

Seb frantically looked around the village, his eyes darting from building to building, searching for his parents. He turned towards the valley. *Please, please be there.* He thought desperately, praying they would gallop down the road any moment. Did they even have horses to ride back here? Oh gods, where were they? They had to come back for him.

"Sebastian." Lord Nathaniel grasped him. "When were you in Korgun?"

Seb sat down on the earth and tried to answer Lord Nathaniel's question. But he clutched his chest and began to wheeze, gasping for air.

"Easy, boy." Lord Nathaniel crouched down. "Just breathe, son, just breathe."

"We were there last night," Aylise spoke up frantically.

Seb glanced over at Will. He was ghostly white, and his mouth hung wide open.

"We were in town when Queen Haveena and her guards rode in," Aylise continued. "We were watching from the Amaranthine Forest when we saw Marte and Alexander. They were hidden on the other side of town. We were with that woman that helped Will, Galea, right?" She looked to Will for confirmation. "We got separated."

"We tried to move around Korgun to reach them, but the guards had started fanning out around town, searching for me." Will spoke softly, his voice breaking between each word.

"Don't worry, Sebastian. Marte and Alexander are smart, they would have laid low and then gone looking for you three. They'll be back soon," Lord Nathaniel said softly.

The pain in Seb's chest intensified and his eyes began to sting. He tried to breathe, but each breath felt laboured. His vision began to blur, and then everything turned black.

~ CHAPTER FIFTEEN ~

Will refused to leave Seb's side while he slept. Lord Nathaniel had rushed Seb to a nurse, and once he came around, she brewed him a pot of sleep tea. He had been asleep for hours now.

"You young ones have been through so much," she said sweetly to him, handing him a cup of the tea as she left the room.

Her slightly patronising tone would normally irritate Will. He would be quick to point out that they're not children anymore. But after the last few days, he realised they were grossly underprepared for what was out there waiting in the world. Seb looked peaceful as he slept, so much so that it tore Will up knowing that he was the cause of Seb's heartache. He was responsible for his partner's death, and now he'd put his parents in danger. How could he ever face Seb again if something happened to Marte and Alexander?

"Perhaps you should have some tea yourself," Selina spoke to him sweetly. "My darling boy, you must be exhausted."

"I'm fine," he replied flatly.

"At least eat something then," she pleaded.

"I'm not hungry."

"This isn't your fault, Will," Darian said from the doorway.

"Yes, it is." He looked away from his parents and bit his lip. He placed his hand over Seb's. How could he ever say sorry?

Seb stirred slightly in his sleep and Will withdrew his hand instinctively. He didn't want to disturb him. He couldn't face him again just yet.

"We have a lot to talk about." He turned towards his parents.

"Yes, we do. Where would you like to begin?" Selina replied.

Will walked across the room to the fireplace and placed his arms in the flames.

"I think we should start with this." He held his arms in place until the sigil appeared. "I want you to tell me the truth about the sigil."

"How long have you known about it?" Selina asked softly.

"A few days."

"And that's why you were in Basilium?" Darian asked.

"Yes." He looked down at the glowing sigil. "We were looking for answers. We couldn't find them in Lord Nathaniel's library. So, we went looking in Basilium, and because of me, Rupert was killed." He spoke softly.

"Oh, my boy. I'm so sorry, we do have much to discuss." Darian was crestfallen as he spoke.

"Not without me," Seb said groggily from the bed.

"Seb, what are you doing up?" Will dashed to his side.

"Any word from them yet?" Seb asked hopefully.

"Not yet," Wil replied softly. "I'm sorry."

"It's okay, Will. They'll be back soon." He smiled, like he was trying to convince himself as much as Will.

"Seb," Selina said softly to him, "are you okay to walk now?"

"Yes, why?" Seb looked puzzled. "Are we going somewhere?"

"Yes, we're going to see Lord Nathaniel," Selina replied, attempting to help Seb up.

"Why?" Will asked. He prayed they weren't trying to stop the conversation already.

"Because Aylise needs to hear what we have to say, too." His mother looked deeply into his eyes.

"Where is Cara?" Will asked. "She deserves to hear this too."

When Cara first appeared in the valley, she didn't receive the warmest reception from Darian.

"What are you doing with our children?" Darian barked at her. Will was shocked by his father's open hostility.

"Keeping them alive," she said softly.

"The fae abandoned us years ago, why help us now?" Darian snapped back.

"You know why," Cara retorted, puffing her chest out.

"Darian, please. We need all the allies we can get." Lord Nathaniel attempted to calm his friend.

Will's father accepted Lord Nathaniel's position. While he didn't outwardly heckle Cara afterwards, he made his discomfort well known.

"I don't think it's necessary to bring her along, Will," his father said firmly.

"We've played by your rules, father. They didn't work," Will replied, equally as firm and stubborn. "Now we play by my rules. Cara is coming too."

Oldwell Manor was a large two-story house close to the centre of town. The guardian of Oldwell greeted Will, Seb, Selina and Darian in the foyer of the home. Though he greeted Selina and Darian like old friends.

"They're waiting for you in the sitting room," he said, guiding them through the house.

Will followed the guardian down a grand hallway. The panelling on the wall was intricate and detailed, fae artworks lined every wall. Some paintings depicted fae in ceremonial dances. Glass sculptures captured the lantern light in their intricate swirling designs, and beautiful tapestries which seemed to depict Vandfall, the fae city, adorned large walls.

Lord Nathaniel, Lady Ana and Aylise were sitting on couches by a large fireplace. Aylise was sipping tea and had a cake by her side. Lord Nathaniel and Lady Ana nursed a goblet of wine.

"Okay we're all here now, who's going to start talking?" Will said firmly.

"Would you like something to eat before we begin?" Lady Ana asked softly.

Although Will wanted to refuse, even just to prove a point, his stomach grumbled as he eyed Aylise's cake.

Selina sat down with Darian, opposite Will and Seb, as they sipped tea and ate the scrumptious lemon cake. It didn't take long for his mother's eyes to start welling with tears. The cakes and tea soon sat forgotten. Aylise joined Will and Seb on the couch, and Aylise interlocked her fingers with Will's.

"I've always..." tears streamed down Selina's face as she stumbled over her words, "*We've* always known about the sigil." She looked towards Darian, Lord Nathaniel and Lady Ana. "The four of us. We should have told you sooner, but we just wanted to protect you. We wanted you to enjoy your life. If she knew you were alive, I knew she'd stop at nothing to hunt you down."

"Queen Haveena?" he asked. Selina nodded in reply. "Because I'm a phoenix?"

"How do you know about phoenixes?" his father asked.

"I told him," Cara said, floating into the room.

"And what business was that of yours to say? Typical of the fae!" Darian glared at Cara openly.

"I did what I did to protect them." She glanced towards Will, Seb and Aylise.

"Enough fighting!" Will called out. "Please continue, mother." He looked towards Selina.

"Oh, well you know about phoenixes. So... ah..." she sighed. "What do you know about the sigil?"

"Just that it's the sigil of the phoenix," he replied.

"It is. But it's also more," Selina paused to wipe away a tear. "The sigil is for a specific line of phoenixes. That's the reason Haveena is after you."

"I don't understand," Will replied.

"My darling," Selina gasped and began to openly sob, "I'm your mother. I've raised you, I love you, and I always will." She paused, she looked rather uncomfortable. She looked down into her lap and wiped away tears. Then she raised her head to look directly into Will's eyes. "But I am not your birth mother."

Will had played out mystery after mystery, secret after secret in his mind for days. In every scenario he imagined, he was not expecting to hear that.

"What do you mean?" he replied, unable to mutter anything else as he attempted to comprehend his mother's words. "You're not my birth mother? Are you my birth father?" He turned towards his father. Darian shook his head. Both of his parents looked utterly heartbroken. He supposed they could see the devastation written all over his own face. "Then who are my birth parents?"

Selina wiped away at her tears and her lip quivered. Her pain was palpable from across the room. No matter the confusion or anxiety Will felt, it paled in comparison to the wave of emotion pouring out of his mother. Aylise clutched his hand tighter, and Seb moved closer to Will, placing his hand on Will's arm.

"Your mother and father were murdered by Rickard and Haveena eighteen years ago," she paused, inhaling deeply. "We took you and fled Basilium. I swore an oath to your mother that I would keep you safe from them." Selina bowed her head and drank deeply from her wine goblet. "Haveena and Rickard would have executed you the moment they knew you were alive, but not just because you're a phoenix. You threaten their claim to the throne." She looked directly into Will's eyes.

Will's heart pounded as he waited for his mother to continue.

"You are the only son of King Eramund and Queen Dyana Kyllarian. You're the crown prince of Arulean and the rightful heir to the throne."

Will blinked rapidly and he gazed out at nothing. Rather than a sense of clarity, his mind raced with hundreds of new questions and mysteries to unravel. He felt like he was tangled in a web of lies built around his life. Will, a prince? But how?

"You're joking, right?" Seb called out, looking towards Selina and Darian. "You're a prince?" he looked at Will. Seb's mouth hung wide open, like he was waiting for the punchline of the joke to be revealed.

"No, Sebastian, Selina is not joking." Lord Nathaniel spoke matter-of-factly. He turned towards Will, leaning forward in his chair. "I understand this is a lot to take in, and for that I am deeply sorry. We've anguished over when to tell you." Lord Nathaniel's tone became quite serious. "But from the day we pulled you out of the ashes, Ana and I swore to keep you safe too."

"I was a captain in your parents' royal guard," Darian said to Will, "I was assigned to care for your mother the day of the invasion." He paused momentarily. "Queen Dyana sensed the danger before Haveena and Rickard arrived. She knew they were coming for you. Dyana commanded me to ensure her lady-in-waiting, Selina, escaped the castle." He held his hand out for his wife's.

"Am I really not your son?" Will asked barely louder than a whisper.

"You are and always have been my son," Selina's voice broke out in a ragged sob. "I may not have given birth to you, Will, but I will always be your mother."

"Why did she kill them?" he asked.

"Your mother came from a long line of phoenixes." He was aware of that, thanks to Cara's camp-side stories, but he let his mother continue uninterrupted. "Although she came from the line, she didn't possess any power. But you did: she could feel it in her womb, and she sensed danger coming your way." She stood up and began to pace around the room. "Haveena knew too. I don't know how, but she knew. You weren't due for three weeks or so when Haveena attacked. We tried to flee together, but we got separated." Selina began to weep again. "Rickard killed your father and Haveena captured your mother. She, she, she..." His mother stumbled each time she tried to speak, pacing faster across the room. "Haveena burnt her at the stake, she burnt her alive just so she could watch the phoenix line burn out of existence.

"...Then how was I born?" Will asked, each new revelation adding to the ever-growing tangle of questions.

"When the pyre died out and the smoke settled, Haveena left everything in place. Probably as a warning for Basilium to fall in line. But also, to cause suffering to those loyal to your parents." She turned towards him, her eyes filled with warmth. "We found you in the ashes. You moved just a little in the mound and then I saw your sigils glowing. I scooped you out of the ashes and ran to Yana. She kept us safe until she found Nathaniel and Ana, they helped us leave the city. We settled in Fawkeston, where Lord Nathaniel's resources could keep you safe, until you were ready."

"I need a moment," Will said, standing up and following his mother's footsteps pacing the room as he took the information in.

"You're a survivor, Will, and you have great power inside of you. Just like the great fire birds, you were born from the ashes," Selina continued.

He continued to pace back and forth across the room. He barely had enough time to get used to the fact that he was a phoenix. This latest revelation felt too far-fetched.

"Am I really a prince?" he asked softly, still unconvinced.

"Yes, sweetheart,' Selina's tone mirrored his. "You are the rightful king of Arulean."

"A king!" he gasped. The thought made him so uncomfortable it sent a shiver down his spine. "Why didn't you tell me this years ago?"

Silence echoed through the room again. Lord Nathaniel and Lady Ana shifted in their seats uncomfortably, staying silent. Aylise and Seb's eyes followed Will around the room as he paced back and forth. Aylise tapped the seat next to her, silently inviting him to sit with her when he was ready. When he nestled in next to her, Seb moved closer too, cocooning Will. They made him feel like the same person he had always been, even as everything seemed to rapidly change around him.

"It was selfish not to." Selina rested her hands on the back of the couch. "We..." She didn't finish her sentence.

"We knew everything would change for you the moment you found out about your heritage. We wanted you to enjoy living for as long as possible," his father spoke softly, as he moved around the couch to stand next to his wife. He wrapped his arm around her and kissed her head fondly. "Ten, sixteen, eighteen. Was it now? Or never? When is the right time to completely change your child's world? To expose them to the dangers that lie ahead."

"Dangers?" Will asked. "Beyond the king and queen trying to kill me?"

"Will, you're a phoenix, and quite a powerful one, too. Add your birthright into it and the road ahead is dangerous and full of turmoil." Will's expression must have mirrored the confusion he felt at his father's words. "Will, if you knew the truth of who you were at a young age, there was every chance that others would learn the truth too. There would be those who would seek your power for their own selfish desires. Then there would be those who would happily bring the heir to the throne to the feet of the queen to curry favour. Or those who would want to use you to their own agenda and advantage."

"Isn't that what you four did?" Will didn't intend for this response to be as cold as it came across. Ana, Selina and Darian shifted uncomfortably, though Lord Nathaniel stood tall, rounding on Will.

"Would you have preferred we left you there to die?" His chest puffed out and his voice boomed with authority. "Your mother and father died so you could live. We did the best we could to honour them and ensure you stayed alive."

"I'm sorry. I didn't mean to criticise…" Will sighed. "This is a lot to process."

A knock on the sitting room door stopped all conversation.

"My lord," Lord Nathaniel's advisor bowed at the door, "the party has arrived."

"My parents!" Seb spoke up.

"Not yet," Lord Nathaniel replied, "but don't fret, we expect they'll be back tomorrow."

"Will, we'll talk more later." He gestured to the other three adults in the room. "We have a meeting to attend."

Will was still trying to untangle the strands of questions running through his mind. Crown prince! It felt strange to think about it. How did his simple life as the son of a blacksmith and a seamstress turn into something so dark?

His mind momentarily wandered into his dreams. Particularly the dreams he had been having lately, the image of the golden-haired woman on the balcony flashed to his mind. They had been in the palace in those dreams. He gasped.

"Mama?" he asked Selina softly, "did Queen Dyana have golden hair?"

"Yes, why do you ask?" Selina replied.

"No reason," Will replied, averting his eyes from his mother.

"One more question!" he called out, all eyes turned towards him. "All these revelations tonight, what do they mean for me going forward?" Out of the tangled web, this question felt the most pressing.

"That is entirely up to you," Lord Nathaniel replied compassionately, but matter-of-factly. "You can embrace your birthright and join the resistance against Haveena and Rickard's reign as Will Kyllarian. Or we can escort you to Larasgate and you can sail away to another land as the anonymous Will Tavner." Lord Nathaniel's stare weighed heavily on Will, like he was digging deep within Will's soul. "I do hope you chose the former."

"Where is the resistance?" Will asked.

"In Vandfall, we have allies there already. Natalyn is also there." Will felt like an absolute ass. He hadn't spared one thought for Aylise's younger sister Natalyn, though he was relieved to hear she was safely away from Fawkeston.

Run away and be free? Now that seemed like the first sensible idea he'd heard in days. He could sail over the southern seas to Craeland and start again, no one would know who he was. He could continue to live a happy and normal life. Maybe Aylise would go with him, too? They could start a life together; be happy and carefree. Would she want to go? Would his parents come? What about Seb? Surely it was too dangerous for them to stay here, too.

"I would like to freshen up. It's been a long day, and I need to rest..." he replied, avoiding the question.

"I'll show you where your bathing chambers are,' Lady Ana called out softly. "Go ahead, I'll catch up," she said to Lord Nathaniel.

Lady Ana escorted Will through the house, leading him upstairs, along more corridors lined with artworks and fresh-cut flowers in large glass vases. She opened a door halfway down the corridor.

"This is your room, Will." She smiled at him. "The bathing chamber is just through that door." She pointed to a door on the right side of the room. "The servants have prepared dinner for you when you're ready." She stroked his cheek delicately. "You look so much like her." She smiled, turned around and closed the door behind her.

So, Queen Dyana was the woman he dreamed about, his... birth mother. The words lingered in his mind, feeling foreign and unnatural. Then his mind wandered to the dreams where he saw her engulfed by the fire. But were they even dreams or something else? When they spoke, she seemed to be warning him. Helping him, maybe? He yearned to see her again, to talk to her, but what would he say? The sudden urge took him by surprise. It felt like a betrayal of Selina to yearn for Dyana. He needed some time alone; he needed some time to think.

Will went into the bathing chamber and walked towards the mirror resting against the wall. The bath was already full of steaming water. He smiled, grateful to the servant who had prepared the room for him. He gazed into the mirror. It was hard to reconcile the difference between the person staring back at him and the boy he had been. He looked older, warier and harder. Had a few days changed him this much? He undressed and stepped into the bath, closing his eyes before submerging himself and forgetting about the world for just a moment.

~ CHAPTER SIXTEEN ~

A vast amount of food had been set out for Will, Aylise and Seb, not that they felt any urge to complain. After another long night and day on the run, it felt good to slow down. Each bite of food filled their bellies and lifted the intense fogginess of their hunger. The bath had lifted Will's spirits, restoring some sense of calm back into his life. The orange soap he had packed from the Pixie's Den had helped with that. He made a mental note to always take soap with him when leaving home, especially if he was going to follow through with his plan: he didn't know how long a journey it was across the southern seas to Craeland.

"Are you truly sure that's what you want?" Aylise leant in towards him. "Do you really want to abandon your family? Your land?"

Neither Aylise nor Seb seemed thrilled by the idea of Will leaving for Craeland. He understood why Seb couldn't even comprehend the idea of leaving. He was so focused on his parents' safe return.

"It's not my land," Will replied stubbornly.

"But it is," she shrugged her shoulders, "by your birthright."

"Aylise," he sighed, "I understand that you've had a lifetime to accept your title and responsibilities. But I've had, oh, two hours to process that my parents lied to me for eighteen years about the fact that I'm a prince. Give me a little grace, please." He began to huff, breathing heavily. Once his heartbeat had slowly returned to normal, he buried his head in his hands. "Gods, this is a mess."

"You've had a rough couple of days. Maybe you need a good night's sleep to mull it over."

"But I don't want to endanger anyone else. I've done that enough already. And I just want to live in peace."

Aylise opened her mouth to argue but was cut off by the door swinging wide open. Either the walls to this house were thinner than Will thought, and people could not help but break up tense conversations in this house. Or it was a lucky coincidence twice in one night. Either way, Yana was standing in the doorway, smiling at Will.

"Will, my boy!" she boomed as she walked into the room, clapping Will across the back. "Thank the gods you made it, not that I had any doubt in you." She rounded on Seb and Aylise, her tone changing. "And you two, running off after him. That was a stupid move, but I'm glad to see you're safe." Her demeanour lightened up again. "We've sent the scouts to fetch the party from Korgun. Your parents should be back in no time, boy." She turned towards Seb.

"I'm here, no thanks to you," he chatted back. "You helped me escape. That was planned, right? It seemed too good to be spontaneous."

"Who said I'm not that, huh?" She winked at him mischievously. He appreciated her light-hearted nature right now. "Of course it was planned. We've had plans in place ever since we took you out of Basilium eighteen years ago." She looked at him matter-of-factly. "I always knew the queen would find out about you, and I knew you'd end up in the city at some point."

"How did you know I'd end up in the city?" he asked, perplexed.

"You're a Kyllarian, it's your home. Don't pretend you haven't always felt a draw to it."

Even though he wanted to disagree with her on principle, he couldn't deny the truth: he had always felt a fascination with that particular city. He had put it down to his desire to explore new places, but had it been something else?

"So, have you always been a tavern wench, as you so eloquently put it? Or was that a cover too?"

"Smart boy." Yana smiled at him. "I'm an assassin. A spy." She grinned wickedly. "Though clearly not a very good one, spilling my secrets now."

"Oh!" Will was both shocked by her answer and delighted by her honesty. "I wasn't expecting that."

"Taverns and inns are a great place to source information from people, boy. A few ales will loosen tongues," she replied.

"I have something for you, Will." His mother walked into the room carrying a bundle.

Selina walked to the sitting area and unfolded the bundle. She laid the leather doublet and trousers across the table. The leather was smooth and supple. It was woven with bronze and gold cord in intricate patterns. Sewn into the centre of the doublet was a coat of arms: a bird with its wings wide open. Will guessed the bird was a phoenix, because it was almost identical to the sigils that appearing on his arms, though far more detailed. It was in flight in front of a ring covered in intricate swirling patterns... fire, perhaps?

"Where did you get these?" he asked his mother.

"I made them for you." She smiled softly at him. "I can change the colours if you don't like them. They're yours now, you can do as you please with them."

Will ran his hands over the smooth leather and traced his fingers over the coat of arms, each ridge of the patterns shooting a fiery sensation through his body, like his power was calling to it.

"It's the Kyllarian family sigil, isn't it?" he asked.

"Yes, my darling," she said quietly.

"I..." he began, stepping away from the couch. "Thank you for making them, they're beautiful.' He cleared his throat and turned to look at his mother. "I won't be needing them." His mother looked surprised. "I've thought about it and I'm leaving Arulean. I'll set sail for Craeland as soon as possible."

"I beg your pardon!" Yana interjected loudly. "Like bloody hell you are."

"Stay out of it, Yana," he snapped back.

"Not going to happen." She marched towards him. "Listen boy, you can't just bugger off when things get hard. We need you."

"Says who?" he retorted.

"Says me!' Yana stepped closer, yelling in his face. "You're a fucking phoenix. The first phoenix to be called in a millennia!" She pointed in his face. "And you want to run and hide away like nothing happened?"

"It's my life, it's my choice. I've hurt enough people already!" his voice began to boom through the room. His fury and guilt rising to the surface. "I got Rupert killed, I saw it fucking happen. And now Seb's parents are in danger because I walked into a fucking town."

"And we've been fucking dying to protect you for eighteen years!" she screamed in reply, pushing her finger into him, "and more of us will continue to die in the battles ahead. We did what we did to honour your parents. I didn't realise they gave birth to a quitter." She pushed him again.

"It's not wise to put your hand on prince, Yana," he snarked back sarcastically.

"Ha!" she laughed in his face, "If you want to be my prince then start bloody acting like it."

"Stop. Please!" Selina called out. "Please stop before both of you say something you'll regret." She looked towards Will. "Of course, it is your choice to decide your own future and I will support you. But it is late, and you've had a big day. Let's discuss this tomorrow."

Selina linked her arm through Yana's, and the two of them walked out of the room, leaving the doublet and pants on the table.

"Well, that went smoothly, didn't it." Seb murmured.

"I'm going to bed. Goodnight," Will replied, walking out of the room.

Will was standing in the town square in Basilium. Six large columns lined the square, and on top of each column stood a marble figure. Men and women were draped in long coronation regalia, their long capes draping down the columns, some of them holding sceptres or swords. The others holding their hand above them reaching for the heavens.

Each figure wore a large ornate crown on their heads. These were the statues of the Kyllarian dynasty that Aylise told him about. *His* dynasty... his *family*.

The city looked different, too. Trees grew throughout the square. The streets were clean, and the buildings weren't dilapidated. The sky was clear, and the scent of springtime flowers lingered in the air. The city had a radiant golden glow about it. Will heard a familiar voice and turned towards the inn. His mother and father were standing with a crowd in front of the inn, their faces hidden behind hoods. They looked dirty and unclean in their ragged clothes. If he hadn't known them, he would have presumed they were residents in the poorest area of the slums.

"Oh, they couldn't possibly!" his mother called out. She covered her mouth with her hand, attempting to hide the shock and horror on her face.

Will followed her gaze through the square. The golden-haired woman had been tied to a stake that seemed to have been hastily built. Queen Dyana... his... his mother's heavily pregnant belly protruded out from the thin tunic draped over her. Oh gods, that was him in her belly. Queen Haveena stood at the bottom of the pyre facing Dyana, a lit torch in her hand.

"No!" Will screamed, running towards her, "Dyana, Dyana!" he called out, pushing through the crowd.

Nobody reacted to his presence as he pushed and shoved his way through the crowd. It was like he was a strange mystical apparition that no one could see or feel. Even Haveena didn't react to him calling out for Dyana as she lowered the torch to the pyre.

"No! Mother! Mother!" he screamed, reacting instinctively.

Queen Dyana turned towards him, her face fraught with anguish and fear. When she locked eyes with him, she looked just like Will. She had the same wide-eyed look that Will did when he was deep in thought. Then her eyes softened, and she smiled at him when she truly saw him. Haveena's maniacal laugh shattered the horrific silence as the flames engulfed Dyana.

"Your line dies today," Haveena snarled, smirking. "If only your bitch of a mother could see you now: you and her took everything from me."

"You sealed your fate today," Dyana replied, her tone defiant. She turned towards Will. "My darling Will, you are the future of Basilium. You are the prophesied phoenix. I love you." She smiled at him, tears began to fall down his cheeks as he watched on helplessly. "I love you, I will always love you and I will always be with you. Now fight."

The flames engulfed Queen Dyana, blasting outwards and swarming around Will. When they disappeared, only a large pile of ash remained around the pyre. Almost every person had left the square. The eerie silence was broken by Selina's sobs as she walked over to the pyre with Darian and Yana. Will watched her closely as she collapsed in front of the ash. He only saw a quick glimpse of the sigil on his little baby wrists as Selina scooped him up and carried him away.

Will's pillow was wet, and his red eyes were puffy when he woke in the morning. Witnessing Queen Dyana's death was a horror he never wanted to witness. He had seen too much death in recent days. Even though she had died years ago, it hurt to just stand there, unable to do anything to help. She was his birth mother, he accepted that much: but did she truly love him, like she said she did? Or was that his mind telling him what he wanted to hear while he slept? And if that's the case, why was she telling him to fight when he had already made his decision to flee?

Loud sobs coming from the hallway broke through Will's thoughts. He leapt out of bed and walked out of his room. Seb was knelt over on the floor, tears streaming down his face, his hands wrapped around his stomach as he howled in pain.

"Seb," Will called, running towards his friend, "what's wrong?" He leant down.

"She. Killed. Them." Each word was choked out between loud howling sobs. "She killed my parents!" he screamed.

Will fell backwards. An icy chill ran through his body as each howl broke from Seb. *Marte and Alexander are dead. Haveena killed them.* Oh gods, how much more pain could he possibly cause Seb? Will's lip quivered as the cold chill spread through him. He watched on in horror as Seb broke down. Lord Nathaniel crouched down beside Seb, his solemn, furrowed brows and down-turned lip troubled Will.

"Who else?" he asked Lord Nathaniel, who just watched him silently. "*Who else?*" he asked more pointedly.

"Half the town was slaughtered," Lord Nathaniel spoke quietly, "Galea was lucky to get out and report back." Lord Nathaniel began to speak but stopped himself.

"What else?" Will asked.

"They killed the innkeeper and hung her in the middle of the town," Aylise spoke softly.

Aylise stood by her bedroom door holding her mother, tears streaming down her face. Will slid towards Seb and pulled him close, unable to speak as Seb buried his face in Will's chest. Will wasn't sure how long he lay in silence with Seb on the floor. Was it minutes, or hours? Will couldn't find the words to express his sorrow for causing Seb more pain.

"I love you, Seb," was all he could muster when he finally found the ability to speak. "I'm so sorry, Seb. I'm so sorry," he muttered repeatedly until someone pulled him away and lifted both of them off the floor.

Will ran from the house, through the back gardens, and hid among the trees. When he felt there were no eyes to watch him, he dropped to his knees and screamed until his throat was hoarse. When he couldn't scream any longer, silence followed: an eery silence that numbed every inch of him.

"I thought this might not be the best time for you to be alone." Cara appeared close by.

"But it's what I need. Please leave me alone, Cara," he croaked out.

"Here." She lifted her hand, guiding a waterskin towards him.

"Thanks," he said, drinking deeply.

"What happened to them wasn't your fault," she said softly, sitting by him in the peculiar way a spectre sat, hovering just above the earth.

"Wasn't it?" He sounded defeated as he looked towards her. "You heard what Galea said. We were about to be discovered, so they caused a distraction."

"They saved your lives," Cara replied.

"By sacrificing their own," he sighed. "Cara, how am I meant to look at him again? How can I possibly make it up to him?" He stewed on that thought for a moment. "I've been dreaming about Queen Dyana, even before I knew she was my birth mother. But last night I saw her die in my dreams. Why did I have to watch her die?" He looked towards his hands. "My birth parents, Rupert, and now Marte, Alexander, and half of Korgun. The innkeeper Mary had no idea who I was: she simply showed us *kindness*." His lip quivered. "I don't want anyone else to die for me."

"And that's why you want to run away?" Cara asked.

"I don't want to run away," he replied, much more sharply than he intended, which surprised him, "but if I go away, it'll be better for everyone. They'll be safer."

"Do you really think Haveena will just give up because you're on another continent?" She raised her spectral eyebrow at him. "Because she won't. She won't come hunting for you, Will. She'll torture and kill every single person you care about until she forces your hand." Cara floated above him in the air. "So, if you're running away because you don't care about anyone else, then by all means, go. But if you're running away to protect everyone else, then you would do better to stay right here and fight." She floated away to leave him alone in his self-pity.

Will lifted himself from the gardens and slowly made his way to find Seb. Each step felt heavy as he attempted to find the strength to face Seb, but once he heard that Marte and Alexander's bodies had been retrieved from Korgun, he couldn't leave his friend alone.

"The master has arranged a space for them to be buried on the lawns," one of the servants told Will as he wandered through the house looking for Seb. "Your friend is with their bodies in the cellar."

"Thank you." Will replied softly, following them to Seb.

Will waited outside the room while Seb said his goodbyes to his parents. His heart ripped in two every time a sob broke from Seb on the other side of the wall. They walked in silence back to their rooms to get changed for the burial rites, his sombre demeanour turning stern.

"I don't blame you, Will," Seb said, as he pulled Will into his bedroom, "and before you even dare interrupt: you can blame yourself all you want, but I don't." He looked directly into Will's eyes. "I don't blame you. I love you, you're my best friend, and I will always stand by your side. But if you decide to go to Craeland, I'm staying here to fight." Seb lifted his chin high as tears streamed down his face. "I hope you don't go, because I don't want to lose anyone else I love. So, stay here and fight with me."

"I love you too, Seb," Will said softly.

Will left the room to change. He appreciated Seb's words, he truly did, just as he appreciated Cara's words… but he had already made up his mind. Enough people had lost their lives because of him. They would be safer without him here, wouldn't they? Or was he putting more people in danger by going? He shut his bedroom door and began to change.

After the burial, Oldwell Manor was a hive of activity. Galea and Finley arrived with friends whom they called *The Rebellion*. Galea looked exhausted and battle-worn. She had a bruise on her eye, and a split lip that had begun to scab over. Finley beamed at Will when he walked into the room. Will was glad to see that he had made it out of Basilium alive, shocked by the large cut down the middle of his cheek.

"Lucky!" Finley called out, pointing at his cheek, "another inch up and they would have taken the eye."

"You look impressive!" Yana smiled at Will when she walked into the house. "Sorry about last night, kid."

"I'm sorry too." He smiled softly back.

"But you clearly needed the pep talk." She smiled at him. "So, does this mean you're staying around?" Yana asked, pointing at the coat of arms on his chest.

Will had dressed in the clothing his mother had made. The golden Kyllarian sigil was clearly visible across his chest on the leather doublet. Each head turned around to face Will. *Oh gods, it was now or never.* He took a deep breath.

"I don't want to see anyone else I love hurt because of me," he said, standing tall. "I have a lot to learn, and I'll need your help along the way. I'm terrified of what lies ahead, but I want to stay and fight. I want to avenge them." He paused, glancing towards his mother and father. "I want to avenge my birth parents." Selina smiled softly at him, her eyes glistening. "I want to avenge Marte and Alexander, and I want to avenge Rupert," he clasped Seb's hand, "and I want to avenge every innocent soul who was murdered in Korgun... I love you, Seb."

"I love you too." He smiled. "I'm glad you're staying."

"Me too."

"So am I." Aylise smiled softly, wrapping her arms around them both. "Yana's right. This is a good look on you."

"I'm still getting used to it, but thanks," Will replied.

"Do we all start calling you Will Kyllarian now?" Aylise asked.

"Not quite yet," he replied, "being a Kyllarian will take some getting used to."

"Of course," Aylise smiled, leaning close and whispering into his ear, "but Queen Aylise Kyllarian sounds really good to me." Will's cheeks turned bright red. She smirked and walked off.

"What did she say?" Seb asked, giggling lightly.

"Boys," his father called out, waking over, "we've got to leave. Our guests are here."

"Who?" Seb and Will replied together.

"The fae royal court is arriving," his father replied, "we mustn't keep Queen Keeva waiting."

Will and Seb glanced at each other.

"After you, Your Majesty," Seb drawled, bowing ironically, "time to go meet some more royalty." Seb jogged out of the room, chuckling.

Will suddenly felt out of place in the Kyllarian coat of arms; it didn't seem appropriate to wear it anymore. He wore it to the funeral to show solidarity with Seb, his parents and the cause to defend Arulean, but it didn't seem right to dress as a Kyllarian to meet the fae royals. It was too late to change his clothing now, his mother linked his arm and walked him out of the house to go and meet the fae.

~ CHAPTER SEVENTEEN ~

Darkness had swept over Oldwell by the time the party had walked through town and entered the Amaranthine Forest. Seb followed behind Will and Selina. Lord Nathaniel wove the group through the forest, not following any visible walking trail. His torchlight led them further into the forest. Aylise and Lady Ana walked behind her husband, who had his soldiers stationed at various points along the party. Yana walked at the rear of the pack. Her sharp eyes bore into the forest.

Now that he had his thoughts to himself, Seb felt numb as he walked through the forest. Each step was empty and hollow. *Is this how grief is meant to feel?* He felt like a large piece of his heart had been cut away when he watched the axe swing down on Rupert's neck. Rupert had locked eyes with Seb and mouthed out, *"I love you,"* just before he died. And love him, he truly did. Rupert had made Seb feel more loved than he could ever have imagined. He made Seb feel brave. He made him feel alive. Seb had loved him too, more than anything. Rupert had been funny and kind, brave but sensible... handsome and gentle.

Seb knew he was different years ago. Like most boys in their early teens, puberty found him and so did his hormones. He started watching Lord Nathaniel's soldiers sparring in their training ground, focusing less on their techniques and more on their sweaty muscular bodies. The more he watched them training, the more he realised he didn't watch the female soldiers like the males. He began to find Rupert attractive soon afterwards. He pined after him for years, wishing and hoping that one day Rupert might feel the same, but never dared to ask.

Then, one fateful day six months ago, they kissed. Seb thought it was so romantic, it could be a tale for the history books. Seb was reading to Rupert when he suddenly brushed his hand along Seb's cheek. Seb blushed bright red, much harder than he ever had before.

"Sorry," Rupert blushed, "I got caught up in the moment."

This is your chance, your moment. Tell him how you feel. Seb screamed at himself internally, desperate to share how he felt. "Don't be sorry. I liked it," he mumbled out.

"You did?" Rupert asked, his cheeks brightening too.

Seb moved closer and brushed his fingers across Rupert's cheek. He wanted to run his fingers along his lips. He wanted to kiss him, but he didn't dare. "Yes." He smiled back at him.

"Is this okay?" Rupert asked, as he leaned over and interlaced his hand with Seb's.

"Yes," Seb replied softly, barely louder than a whisper, his heart pounding in his chest as sparks of lightning coursed through his body.

"Can I kiss you?" Rupert asked. Seb only managed to nod his head and grin nervously before Rupert leant over and kissed him.

Every thought, concern and worry in Seb's mind disappeared as they locked lips. Seb felt like he was floating through the clouds: like the Maiden was lifting him into the heavens and filling him with all her love. Seb leaned into the kiss, cupping his hand behind Rupert's head and pulling him closer. Rupert embraced Seb and rolled him onto his back, kissing him harder, deeper, more passionately.

"I've wanted to do that for a really long time." Rupert smiled at Seb.

"So have I," Seb replied. Rupert's eyes were shining as he leant back down and began to kiss Seb again.

If only he had been brave enough to tell his mother and father who he truly was. They died not knowing their son: not knowing that he had been happy, that he had a future planned, that he was loved. He placed one foot in front of the other and plastered the relaxed and interested look on his face. *Stay brave, don't think about it, play along and don't fall apart.* He told himself, while every moment he felt he was about to crumble into a thousand pieces. How was he truly supposed to grieve while they were on the run? He couldn't, he decided – because the moment he stopped, the wave of relentless pain would come back, and he wouldn't be able to get off the floor.

They passed a heavily wooded area. Large rocks and boulders lined the way, obscuring the track from those who were not seeking it. He followed the line through boulders and emerged on the other side. The forest was less dense on this side: moonlight bathed the area in an ethereal glow. In an open valley, torches glowed through the trees, and small glowing lights danced around the branches.

"Oh, they're not, are they?" Seb spoke softly, looking towards the little lights.

"What?" Will and Aylise asked.

"Fairies." He pointed to the trees. "We're in fae territory now." He spoke softly, allowing himself the small moment to enjoy the sight.

Dark figures wandered through the valley, casting shadows into the forest. Some wore riding leathers and long cloaks, others were dressed in full armour. A tall man strode out of the centre of the valley to greet them.

"Nathaniel." The man marched forward and embraced Lord Nathaniel. "Is it really true?"

"I'm afraid so." He turned towards their party. "We wouldn't be here if Haveena hadn't discovered his secret."

"And the boy?" the mysterious man asked, his eyes darting across the party.

"He's safe, he's here."

"Glad to hear it. Queen Keeva hasn't arrived yet."

"I suspected as much. But they're close." Nathaniel smiled. "Will, come forward." He ushered Will. "Young Will, meet Lord Roderick Lewin. Roderick, this is Will."

As Will walked forward, Seb noticed the relieved expression on Will's face. He was grateful that Lord Nathaniel hadn't finished the sentence with Tavner or Kyllarian. Will extended his hand towards the man.

"Your Highness," Roderick bowed, "it is an honour to meet you."

Will just looked at the man, his mouth half open. *Oh gods, a lord just bowed to Will while he was wearing the Kyllarian coat of arms.* Seb felt for Will, who just stared, open-mouthed, at the man.

"It's a pleasure." Will smiled softly.

"Roderick is the lord of Emerald Grove," Lord Nathaniel interjected, clapping Will on the back. "We must visit sometime." He smiled towards Roderick. "Did Jakob come with you?"

"No, I left the boy at home," Roderick replied as they walked away. Talking quietly to themselves. "She didn't!" Roderick erupted loudly, stopping to stare at Lord Nathaniel. He glanced back towards Seb and bowed his head solemnly.

Seb felt like a knife had been plunged into what remained of his heart. Will and Aylise's eyes filled with sorrow as they looked back at him. No! He couldn't do this, not now. *Stay brave, don't think about it, play along and don't fall apart.* He repeated internally.

"Come on, let's keep going," Seb said cheerfully to Will, "Your Highness." Seb nudged him in the ribs and snickered. *Yes, that's it: smile, hide it, don't think about it yet. Lock it away and keep it at bay for now. The time for grief will come soon.*

As more people came into the area, more eyes followed Will. They made him feel like a caged creature being sold at market day: buyer after buyer wandering by to inspect him.

Several soldiers walked towards Will. They glanced at his coat of arms, bowed their heads and bent the knee in front of him. Slowly, more people turned to face him and followed suit, bending the knee. Will watched on in horror, his cheeks burning and panic setting in. Where was Lord Nathaniel to step in again and help him? His eyes darted around the area searching for him. He saw Lord Nathaniel bending the knee.

"Please, no, no," he protested, finally finding his voice, "please stand up." Thank the gods, the crowd obeyed.

"A humble king," a melodic voice said softly in the dark.

All eyes turned towards the voice. A beautiful woman emerged from the forest. Her skin glowed in the moonlight, and her long, dark hair cascaded down towards her navel in soft curls. Her pointed ears poked through the strands in her hair. She wore a long, silky gown embroidered with jewels and swirling patterns. A sparkling white diadem rested on her head, shimmering as she moved into the valley.

"Your Grace, it is our honour." Lord Nathaniel bent the knee again, the crowd following his lead.

Will lowered his head and bent the knee.

"You honour me. Please stand, Your Grace." She called towards Will, holding her hand out. "Come to me."

Will walked towards the woman and suddenly felt unworthy as he placed his blacksmith's hands on her soft and delicate skin. His powers prickled his skin in recognition.

"You look so much like your mother," she said, smiling at him. He glanced towards his mother, who was still kneeling.

"Queen Dyana was a good friend of mine when she was young." She turned towards the crowd. "Please rise, my friends." She turned back to Will. "Forgive me for not properly introducing myself: it's simply wonderful to see you again. I am Queen Keeva Lorenstar, the leader of the fae kingdom of Vandfall."

See you again? he wondered. "It's an honour, Your Grace. I'm Will."

She looked at the coat of arms on his chest and then looked back into his eyes. Her striking blue eyes searched his, like she was peeling away his most protected thoughts piece by piece until she found her way into his soul. She placed her hand over his chest.

"It's okay to feel conflicted," Keeva said knowingly. "In your heart, you're Will Tavner still." She smiled softly, her voice soft and soothing. "You always will be. But you can be a Tavner and a Kyllarian at the same time, because you are both."

Selina brushed against Will, squeezing his arm gently. His father followed close behind.

"Your Grace." His mother and father bowed.

"My friends," Queen Keeva beamed at them, "while I am glad you are both safe, now is not the time for our long-overdue conversation, for I very much wish to speak with your son."

"Of course, Your Grace." Selina smiled softly.

"Come with me." Keeva led Will through the crowd.

Will followed the queen as she walked through the area. Keeva's men were moving around a large mound of black stone in the centre of the clearing. They placed stones in the pile and set torches in the soft earth around it. Some of the fae were greeting the humans like old friends who just happened to bump into each other. Others lingered with their own people, talking in hushed tones.

"There is so much you want to know." Her voice carried in the wind as they walked.

"How do you know that?"

"I don't need eyes to see all, Will." She paused to face him. "It is a great honour to be bestowed with the gifts of such extraordinary creatures. Phoenixes are powerful, and you can do wonders with your gifts... but that's not what bothers you." Her blue eyes searched him again. "You seek revenge. You're angry."

Will waited for Keeva to reprimand him. *Anger will make you sloppy. You'll make mistakes*, was what his father would say to him when they were sparring. Instead, the queen gave him an affirming nod.

"Good. Let it burn inside you. That fire for justice you feel: that's how we win." She gasped loudly, pulling away from Will. Queen Keeva grew still. Her mouth hung open as she began to weep. "Tell me everything about her." She held onto his arms firmly. "The fae spirit... Cara. Where is she?"

Will was taken back by the sudden shift in conversation. Keeva seemed shocked and tense, almost as if she was desperately waiting with bated breath for Will to speak.

"She's here somewhere," he replied.

He thought for a moment. When was the last time he saw her? She hadn't stayed as close since arriving in Oldwell. She had been with them when they buried Marte and Alexander, but where was she when the party walked into the forest?

"Aylise," he called out, "have you seen Cara?"

Aylise shook her head and looked around the group of gathered people. Will did the same thing, straining through the crowd trying to find her, she was nowhere to be seen.

"I'm not sure where she is," he said softly turning back towards the queen, "and I'm not going to insult our intelligence and pretend that you can't read my thoughts somehow. What do you want with Cara?"

"We're ready, Your Grace." One of Queen Keeva's men bowed to her.

"We'll talk more about this later." Queen Keeva's demeanour instantly switched from tense to regal and poised.

The queen walked onto the black stones in the centre of the clearing. Her commanding presence silenced all those gathered around.

"Come. Gather." She gestured towards the group. "Thank you for answering the call at such short notice."

"Is it really true?" a voice called from the crowd, "Has a phoenix been called?"

Some people in the crowd gazed towards Will. *Oh gods, they are here for me!* He probably should have worked that out sooner. He fidgeted, wanting desperately to slip away into the dark of the forest.

"Dark times have plagued our lands for too long. Our forces have weakened, and our lands die before our eyes." The queen's ethereal voice gave her speech a dramatic flair: whether that was intentional or not was lost on Will. "All hope has been lost... until now."

More heads turned in Will's direction. Selina and Darian moved by his side, followed closely by Seb and Aylise. Their presence soothed the rising anxiety and tension coursing through his veins.

"There are few who know what I am about to tell you. It was my choice to keep it from you to keep you safe," she gestured towards Will, "and to keep him safe."

Everyone in the clearing turned to face Will. He instinctively found Aylise's hand and held on tightly when their fingers interlocked.

"And who is this boy?" someone called out.

"His name is Will, and he is a phoenix."

"Does he carry the sigil?" another asked.

"I have not seen them with my eyes, but he does."

"How can you be sure?"

"Silence please," she called out, and paused rather dramatically, "Your Grace, step up here please." She gestured for Will.

He obeyed, nervously walking through the crowd. The stones hummed with power as he touched their surface, and his own power surged through his body in response.

"If you please, Andayne," Queen Keeva called out.

A young fae man walked towards Will. He appeared to be Will's age, though with fae it was always hard to be sure. This man could be twenty, two hundred, or over two thousand years old. Andayne wore a long, silver embroidered tunic, woven with jewels. His long black trousers tucked in neatly to his boots, which disappeared behind his billowing pearl-coloured cloak that draped perfectly down his muscular physique. His silver-blonde hair was braided away from his face then cascaded down his back. Andayne walked forward carrying a lantern and a small unlit torch. When he was close, he placed the torch into the lantern, igniting the flame and handing it to the queen.

"Thank you, my boy." She smiled at the fae. "A phoenix has not awakened in one thousand years. Many of you would have heard of the ritual of the flames, but only a few have ever witnessed it." Murmurs broke out in the crowd. "When a phoenix awakens, they must begin their training to master the art. To begin their training, they must participate in the ritual of the flames." Queen Keeva held the torch high in the air. "Phoenix flame, from the eternal pyre in Vandfall!" she called out, "Come forward, Will!"

Will's nerves were sky-high as he walked towards Keeva. Was she about to show the gathered crowd his sigils? That was fine, the flames had never hurt him before... but what was the ritual of the flames? *Would the ritual hurt?* Will's mind raced with questions with every step closer to Queen Keeva. Everything he had learnt about Phoenixes so far gave Will the impression that phoenix power came from the bird. Was the eternal flame from a human, like the flames that Will produced? Or were they from the bird? He made a mental note to enquire about that afterwards.

"Step into the centre of the stones. The flames cannot harm you. You know this." She spoke softly so only he could hear.

"I'm not afraid of the flames," he lied.

Five fae – including Andayne – began to walk around the stones, chanting in faeish. The queen walked off the mound and began to chant with them. The air around Will changed. Power swirled through the air: Will couldn't see it, but he could feel it. He glanced in Seb and Aylise's direction. They seemed nervous, looking from him to Selina and Darian, who didn't seem concerned at all: they looked at Will with pride.

The queen paused in front of Will and drove the torch into the earth, then continued chanting. A line of flame shot out of the torch in two directions, like a curving arrow travelling around the stones. It lit all the torches that had been placed around the stone. The fae continued chanting.

The stone beneath Will began to glow, and his power surged through his body, reacting to the magic around him. He felt it flowing around him, ebbing out from him. A bright orange glow appeared through the gaps between each rock. The fae chanted louder, each new word pulsing energy through the clearing. Orange sparks stirred around the mound, swirling from the edges towards Will's feet. The torches around the edge roared to life, erupting fiery waves towards the stones. The whole mound was engulfed in flames.

The fire danced around Will, kissing his body, when a loud screeching noise pierced the air. Will was lifted off his feet. He glanced towards the crowd, unable to contain his elation as he hovered above the stones. The gathering crowd gasped, some covering their mouths as they stepped away from the blaze. Others pointed at him, talking in hushed tones to the person standing next to them. Seb and Aylise stared at him open-mouthed. His parents still looked at him with nothing but pride. The flames seemed to energise his power. He could feel it surging through him the longer he hovered above the flames. His wrists began to glow, and he felt the sharp grasp of talons wrapping around his arms, stretching his hands wide open. He glanced behind him, expecting to see a phoenix there, but there was nothing behind him. He relaxed, letting whatever force that was there take over his body. Flames erupted from his outstretched hands and soared into the night sky. The stream of flame snaked around in the sky, forming into the shape of his sigils on his wrist.

The stones glowed even brighter, and the rumbling from the earth grew louder until a large, jagged stone rose out of the mound. It glowed bright orange. Will could feel the heat radiating from the stone. His power reacted to something inside. It felt like it was desperate to reach out of his body towards the stone. Will didn't understand his power enough to know what that meant.

Once the sparks disappeared, Will glided back down to the stones. The fire sizzled out and disappeared.

"Friends," Queen Keeva called out. "I present to you Will Kyllarian, the Phoenix King."

"Kyllarian?" "She said Kyllarian?" "It can't be…" the crowd murmured.

"We kept his presence and his identity a secret for good reason. You have seen the sigil. You have witnessed the ritual." Keeva paused for a moment. "Will Kyllarian is the son of King Eramund and Queen Dyana. He is your king."

"How is that possible?" someone from the crowd asked.

"Haveena burnt Dyana at the stake and that was her own fateful lapse in judgement, for phoenixes die in ashes, but they are also born from them. Will was born from the ashes, just like a phoenix." She smiled, turning towards Will. "We bow to you, King Will Kyllarian of Arulean."

Lord Nathaniel bent the knee, Lady Ana and his men followed. Some of the gathered party bent the knee quickly too: others looked from Will to the crowd, slightly apprehensive until they, too, knelt. His parents, Aylise and Seb had too bent the knee, the four of them beaming at him.

"Please rise," he spoke softly to the crowd. *That wasn't very regal,* he thought to himself as the crowd watched him expectantly. "My road will be long. I have much to learn and I will need advisors as we navigate this new reality." He nodded his head and turned away from the crowd.

Murmurs and chatter erupted through the crowd. *Gods, why didn't he think of anything better to say!* Had he known what was happening tonight, he might have prepared. What exactly? He couldn't say. He was positively ill-prepared for tonight's event.

A flicker of light caught Will's eye from the large stone that had grown out of the mound. There was a large crack with a faint glowing line visible along the surface. He placed his hands over the crack and at his touch, half the rock crumbled away. The inside was hollow, but resting on top of a small pile of embers was a smooth black rock. It was about the size of a small grapefruit.

"An egg," said Andayne, the silver-haired fae, "a phoenix egg." He looked to Will. "You truly are extraordinary. Well, go on, take it. It's yours now."

"This is a phoenix egg?" he asked. "A baby phoenix will hatch from this?"

"Eventually! It'll need to incubate in phoenix flame beforehand, though."

"Did you hear the screeching during the ritual?" Will asked, suddenly recalling the moment.

"I did not." He spoke softly just like Queen Keeva. "The phoenix chose you during the ritual. You really must be powerful; they don't come for every phoenix." He smiled at him knowingly. "I believe your friends are waiting for you.' He looked over Will's shoulder, smiling at Seb.

Andayne smiled as he walked away to join another silver-blonde-haired fae. Will slipped the egg into his satchel as Aylise and Seb walked to the edge of the mound.

"I'll come down," he called out. He couldn't explain why, but he wasn't ready to share the news about the phoenix egg just yet. It didn't feel like the right time.

"That was incredible to witness," Seb said in awe.

"I didn't expect to be making a speech tonight," he replied.

"But you handled that exceptionally well." Queen Keeva walked over. "I'm sorry I did not explain the ritual before we began." She gestured outwards. "But from the ritual, spectacular things begin to grow."

Will was mesmerised, flowers were blooming through the clearing, more of the colourful fae berry shrubs were coming to life. The gathered group gasped in shock, enthralled by the transformation taking place around them.

"You truly are remarkable," Andayne said, walking towards Will. "Forgive me for not formally introducing myself earlier. I'm Prince Andayne. Queen Keeva is my mother."

"It's a pleasure to meet you, I'm Will," he replied, smiling politely.

"And you, too," Andayne introduced himself to Aylise and Seb. He held his hand out for Seb and clasped his hands over Seb's. "It's a pleasure to meet you, Sebastian." He smiled as he spoke in his velvety voice.

"Likewise, and please call me Seb." He smiled softly.

"And this is my closest friend, Daemoon Torvinya." Andayne waved his friend over.

The fae Andayne was talking to earlier came striding over. He was one of the most handsome men Will had ever met. He was tall and muscular like Andayne, and his light-blonde hair shimmered in the moonlight. He smiled as he walked up to the group.

"I'm Daemoon, it's a pleasure to meet you all." His pearly white teeth shone as he smiled.

Will, Seb and Aylise introduced themselves.

"Will you two be joining us in Vandfall?" Andayne asked Seb.

"Of course! We're not leaving Will's side," Seb replied.

"I'm glad to hear you're all coming," Andayne replied, his smile wide and joyous. He turned towards Seb. "Would you like to join me on a walk around the clearing? It's quite delightful to see the forest transforming."

"Oh," Seb replied rather sheepishly, "sure."

"I should attend to some other matters," Daemoon nodded in farewell. "It's been lovely to meet you all, especially you, Will." Daemoon smiled and walked away.

Aylise gazed at Will as Andayne and Seb walked away. Gods she looked beautiful when she looked at him like that. Was it safe to bring her along this dangerous path he was heading down? It sounded like there was a war coming. Did he really want to see Aylise in the middle of such danger? But if he didn't bring her along, how would he find the strength to keep going without her?

"What's wrong?" Aylise asked him. She stroked his cheek. "You look concerned."

He ran his fingers through a piece of her copper hair, twirling it around his fingers. He loved her deeply – truly loved her – always had. She was one of his best friends, but he wanted more, and he was certain she did too.

"Hello, Will, are you listening to me? What's wrong?"

"Oh, yeah, sorry. I…" he mumbled through his incoherent sentence. *Smooth, Will.*

"I know you better than anyone. Even better than you know yourself. Say what you want to say." She held onto his hand, her eyes pleading with him.

"You do know me better." He took a breath. "But Aylise, am I putting you in danger? Is my very existence. My power. Is me being a phoenix putting your life in danger?"

Whatever she was expecting, it clearly wasn't that.

"Will, we've discussed this. Our lives would have been in danger regardless." She looked at him intently. "When I watched you flee Basilium, I couldn't bear the thought of losing you. It scared me." Tears welled in her eyes.

"I'm sorry I put you through that." he said, looking into her eyes, wiping a tear on her cheek.

"I'd do it all over again for you." she replied, pulling him closer.

"Aylise." He whispered. This was it; he could say it. He was certain she felt the same.

"Yes, Will." She whispered back, gazing deeply into his eyes.

"I…"

A piercing scream broke through the clearing.

"Royal scout in the camp!"

~ CHAPTER EIGHTEEN ~

Fear coursed through Will in a sudden wave, as people scrambled and shouted through the clearing, running towards the forest. Queen Keeva began chanting in faeish and magic pulsed from her hands, casting light through the forest.

"Stay there!" he called out to Aylise as he ran across the clearing. Three of Lord Nathaniel's soldiers ran towards Aylise, Seb nested in between them.

If war was coming, keeping those he loved safe was paramount. He leapt onto the stones. Chaos had erupted around them. Three royal guards were fleeing from the clearing, winding their way towards the path between the boulders. Five guards were clashing with Will's party.

"Stop those three!" Lord Nathaniel shouted from within the fray.

The fleeing soldiers were met with a volley of arrows, many arrows missing their marks and driving deep into the trees, but the three soldiers fell with ease.

"They're down!" someone shouted.

The soldiers clashed with the remaining royal guards, felling them swiftly. It seemed too easy. Power surged through this body, and he looked out into the forest, trusting his instincts. He ran through the clearing, leaping over dead soldiers, picking up a discarded bow and in one swift movement scooped some arrows from the quiver on a dead soldier's back. He darted up the path, weaving between the boulders. Lord Nathaniel and Prince Andayne followed close behind him.

"Something isn't right. I feel it," he said softly.

He wasn't sure if this was part of the phoenix power or something else, but he followed the feeling. He listened to the forest, blocking out the noises rumbling through the camp. The forest was silent, but what lurked in the darkness? Then he heard it: hooves pounding against the earth. The shape came into view through the darkness.

"Squire up ahead!" he called out.

He ran forward, following the sound of the hooves. Cresting a hill, his gaze followed the sound and the moonlight illuminating the area. A young rider galloped away wearing royal black.

"There!" he called out, pointing at the rider.

Will threw the arrows into the ground ahead of him. Then lifted one of them out of the earth and drew the bow. He paused for a moment, watching the boy ride away. Was that the rider's fear that Will felt? He knocked the arrow, following the movement of the rider and loosed the arrow. He watched it sail through the air and said a silent prayer for the rider before the arrow sank deep into their back. The rider fell from the horse, their body twitching until they collapsed on the earth.

It surprised Will how easily he killed the rider. While he didn't take pleasure in killing them, he didn't regret it either. Was this what it meant to be a leader? No, a ruler? Making decisions that were unpleasant, but necessary?

"I didn't know you were that good with a bow," Lord Nathaniel said, standing next to Will.

"I didn't either," Will replied.

"Your powers will continue to grow," Prince Andayne replied. "Speed, strength, agility. A phoenix can be imbued with many abilities. I wonder what else you'll reveal soon."

They ran back to the clearing. The gathering crowd was tense and on alert. Will spotted Aylise and Seb with his parents and sighed. Thank the gods, they're fine.

"You care for them deeply, don't you?" Andayne asked.

"They're my world." He smiled at Andayne.

"We need to get moving, Nathaniel. If the guards are here, she's close," Selina called out, moving towards them.

"Selina's right," Queen Keeva agreed. "We must leave for Vandfall at once."

"Will she follow us there, too?" Seb asked.

"There are powerful enchantments surrounding Vandfall. It is not easy to enter the fae kingdom uninvited," Queen Keeva replied. "Andayne?" she called out, and he moved swiftly to her side. "Take them to our convoy, their belongings are waiting there." She smiled at Will with a glint in her eye. "We're always prepared."

Andayne guided them out of the clearing, travelling a different path from which they had entered. A large herd of horses were waiting on the other side when they emerged. The horses were all white or silver, covered in shimmering champagne- or silver-coloured armour plates. Nested in the herd were the four horses Will had summoned in the forest. Fae were bustling around them, preparing the horses.

"Wait for me," a familiar voice called out.

"Cara, where have you been?" Will said, as she floated towards him.

"I felt uneasy coming to this meeting, but I could not ascertain why. But no matter – I am here now." She spoke softly, seemingly unsure of herself.

"Cara!" Andayne cried. He stared at her, his eyes wide with disbelief, his bottom lip hanging low.

"Oh, my darling girl, it is you!" Queen Keeva walked forward, tears welling in her eyes.

Will suddenly remembered the queen asking about Cara, who was looking at Andayne and Keeva uncertainly. She appeared just as confused as Will.

"Oh my," Cara spoke in hushed tones, her eyes wide as she stuttered. "I. I remember, Andayne. My brother." She looked at Andayne, tears streaming down her face. "Mama, oh Mama. I'm sorry."

Will's head was spinning.

"Had you forgotten about them?" he asked Cara softly, she nodded in reply.

Will told Keeva and Andayne the story about meeting Cara, how she had been trapped in the shadow realm and that she had been slowly putting the pieces of her memory back together.

"I didn't want to believe it until I saw you with my own eyes," Keeva said tearfully.

"You saw me in Will's thoughts?" Cara replied.

Keeva nodded in reply. "Every moment he grows stronger, his thoughts quiet."

"You were in the shadow realm for eighteen years and we did nothing." Andayne looked horrified as he spoke.

"There's nothing you could've done, Dayne," she replied, reaching out to him. "Where is Isiadelle, for I wish to see her too."

"We'll meet with her in Vandfall, are you coming home with us?" Andayne asked.

"She does not remember, my boy," Queen Keeva said sorrowfully, as tension lingered in their air.

'I think we should give you a moment," Will said quietly. Will, Aylise, Seb walked towards their horses, where their parents were attending to their own. They busied themselves, like they hadn't been eavesdropping the entire time.

"It's rather peculiar, isn't it?" Seb spoke thoughtfully. "Magic works in such mysterious ways, it's connected us to a much bigger puzzle." He glanced towards the fae royals.

Will was transfixed on Cara and Queen Keeva. He couldn't escape the nagging feeling that the answers to all his questions lay with these mysterious and powerful women. Queen Keeva knew much more than she let on.

Keeva began chanting in faeish again, moving her glowing hands over Cara. Although he couldn't hear the chant, he could feel the magic at work. Cara's whole body began to glow, as she had when Will healed the shadows away from her. When the glowing stopped, Cara clutched her spectral hands to her mouth and began to sob. What transpired between them? Why was Cara so distressed? Cara and Keeva spoke in hushed tones. Keeva's guarded poise slipped every so often: in those moments it was far too easy to see the mixture of disappointment and despair across her face. Cara's sobbing grew louder, not that Will had any baseline to compare it to, but who knew that a spectre could radiate such agony.

"I'm sorry," she wept as her form began to fade, "I'm so sorry." She spun and disappeared.

"Will," Keeva called out, she paced towards them hurriedly, she had given up trying to hide her emotions now. "We must leave at once."

"Why?" Will asked indignantly, "where did Cara go?"

"She'll be back. Mount your horse Andayne, we must go."

"Where are we going?" Will asked firmly.

"We're leaving for the Fortress of the Flames." Whether she intended to be dismissive or not, she turned from Will, fussing over her son.

"Why? Please explain yourself to me," he said firmly, "This is my life everyone is meddling in."

Flames erupted around Will's hands. Flames kissed his arms briefly, then extinguished just as easily as they erupted.

"Do not presume that you can make demands of me, Will Kyllarian," Keeva snapped at him. Aylise and Seb's eyes were wide and alert as Keeva glared at Will. "Now calm down and mount your horse. Her mannered poise returned. "I will explain everything to you there." And with that, she turned and walked away from him. Oh gods, how Will hated that phrase.

Will walked further into the forest, each step alleviating the simmering rage that burned inside him. He slumped down on a soft patch of grass. Maybe raising his voice with a queen wasn't the smartest way to handle that, but when was he finally going to receive a straight answer from anyone? A flock of colourful birds pranced along the forest floor and gathered around Will. They softly cooed at him and took flight into the sky, circling above him, cooing and chirping in unison, singing their sweet song. As they flew away, their song echoed through the forest.

The convoy was over a hundred riders strong when they set out for the fallen fortress. Cara had rallied Queen Keeva's fae and the humans together surprisingly quickly.

They rode hard through the night. Will rode silently next to Aylise, mulling over the events of the evening. The ritual, Cara's relation to the fae royals and her sudden outburst all played in his mind. Cara had avoided Will on the ride. Given she had rarely left his side in the days since she announced herself, Will found this sudden change most confusing, and he missed having her close. Seb was riding next to Prince Andayne, and they chatted animatedly during the moments when the convoy cantered along wooded areas. Will envied Prince Andayne: in the several hours since they met, he had brought a genuine smile to Seb's face, when all Will had brought him was heartache and tension for days.

"Ride up with me, Aylise!" Will called out. "I want to speak with Cara." He galloped ahead of the convey. Aylise followed closely behind.

Curious glances followed Will and Aylise as they rode. Seb and Andayne moved out of the procession after them. Cara glanced back at Will as he came closer, though the moment their eyes met, she bowed her head and began to float away.

"Cara, stop," he called out, galloping harder. "We need to talk, please."

Cara moved faster, breaking away from the convoy.

"Cara, explain it to him," Will glanced towards Andayne as the prince spoke. "We understood, I'm sure he will too."

She stopped moving and turned towards her brother. Keeping their distance from the group.

"Cara," he pleaded with her, "I don't want any more riddles. Please tell me the truth. Why are we riding for the fortress?"

Cara couldn't hide the fear on her spectral face. Cara's form had become much brighter and colourful since seeing her mother.

"You must let me explain the whole story, please," she replied flatly, though her fear and sorrow were evident.

"I'd like that," Will replied, befuddled. "Please just be honest."

"Do you recall the story of Queen Elyndra's vision during the phoenix wars?"

"Of course," Will replied.

"Some – in fact, most – visions are simply just that, a vision. A premonition into some insignificant event to come. But a rare few serve a higher purpose."

"What does that mean?" Will asked.

"Those that serve a higher purpose are prophecies. Queen Elyndra's vision was a prophecy. It was about you."

"And what does this prophecy say?" Will asked.

"No one knows. After a prophecy is spoken, it is sealed and protected in the Tower of Wisdom. Only the guardians have access to them."

"But if Elyndra died in the war, who took record of the prophecy?"

"Her daughter, my mother," Cara said quickly, before Will could interrupt again, "but she cannot tell us what my grandmother saw either. When a fae passes the prophecy to the guardians and it is sealed, they lose all memory of it. It's an ancient magic that protects those with the knowledge. Only the guardians and those to whom the prophecies refer can read them."

Cara paused; her lip quivered as she gazed into his eyes, like she was desperately reading the expression on Will's face. Will felt a pang of guilt, but he craved answers more.

"Please, Cara," Will pleaded.

"Haveena wanted the prophecy," she sighed, and her shoulders slumped. Will, Aylise and Seb were frozen in place, enthralled in Cara's every word. "She knew of its existence, but she would never be able to access Vandfall to retrieve it herself." She began to cry. "I was on an important diplomatic visit to Gregaron. Whether she knew I was there or not, I don't know, but I suspect she must have. That kind of magic takes immense preparation." Cara began to openly weep. "She entranced me, Will. She clawed her dark magic into my mind. I couldn't control it; she trapped me under her power. I killed my people and did atrocious things under her control. I stole the prophecy from the tower of wisdom, and I gave it to her at the fallen fortress."

Aylise and Seb gasped loudly. Will felt numb as he tried to untangle the threads of the revelation, but slowly the pieces fell into place.

"And does she know what the prophecy contains?"

"Yes, she does." Cara kept her eyes down. "She thinks her magic opened it, she's that arrogant. It's partially true, but I think she could read it because the prophecy is about her, too."

"All of your memories are back now, aren't they? Your mother brought them back?" Will waited for Cara to continue talking, but she simply bowed her head. "What is it that causes you such pain that you've been avoiding me?"

"Will, whatever is written in that prophecy caused Haveena to curse Basilium and murder your parents." She turned away. "I'm the reason they're dead."

A fire burned through Will as the realisation sank in. Was he allowed to feel angry about the murder of two people he didn't know? It wasn't the first time he'd felt like that. Selina and Darian – the parents who had loved and raised him – had also loved Eramund and Dyana. Did he feel the same? When he dreamt of her, he yearned for her. When he watched her burn at the stake, it tore his heart in two. That wasn't indifference, but was it love? Was it Cara's fault? No, it couldn't be, he didn't believe in his heart that it was. She looked so pained as she watched him. She was bewitched, Haveena had bewitched her. The fire raged through him, each new thought fuelling the intensity. There was a common thread through each strand of trouble in Will's life. Haveena, and he wanted revenge.

"I don't blame you, Cara." He spoke quite deliberately and calmly, so she heard every sincere word. "You were bewitched, you had no control over your actions, she took that away from you. Haveena has taken enough away from all of us." He looked towards Seb.

"Forgive me!" she cried.

"There's nothing to forgive," he replied softly.

"After she read the prophecy, I became a liability to her. She killed me. She drove a dagger into my stomach… drained my life force. Then she threw me into the fire in the ritual chamber deep in the fallen fortress. That's when I was transported to the shadow realm. She never wanted me to share what I know. She wanted to keep me locked away." She wiped a tear from her eye. "But now…"

"We march for the fortress to read the prophecy." Will finished her sentence. "Let's not dwell on this anymore. You need to forgive yourself, Cara." He gazed at her fondly. "Let's move out, people!" Will called out. Andayne and Seb galloped ahead to rejoin the convoy. Cara smiled softly at him and floated away. He held Aylise's hand in his, "We do this together?"

"Always" she replied, smiling so deeply at him, he felt his heart leap with joy.

~ CHAPTER NINETEEN ~

Queen Haveena brushed her fingers across her cheek – which still stung from the force of Rickard's fist – as she watched his men comb through each building in Oldwell. She had argued against stalling in town, but he rarely listened to her, why would he start now?

"It's the middle of the night and not a lantern is lit. They're gone, Rickard," she spat. His response was his fist to her face.

Haveena drew her gaze towards the forest: her scouts had yet to return with word. She had been so close to him in Korgun, the others had sacrificed themselves as a distraction. How close was she now? Rickard had wasted precious time searching through Korgun, and the boy was long gone by the time Rickard finished his search. Haveena would have left the townspeople as they were, but not Rickard, he had to show his might. His rage simmered more and more as he left each dwelling. He left the bodies of each citizen bruised, broken and lifeless on the streets for all to see.

Haveena ripped a flower from a bush, her anger fuelled by the way they fluttered in the moonlight. The flower withered, the petals curling into themselves and turning a shade of dark brown before the entire stem disintegrated in her hand. The Amaranthine Forest was coming back to life; her power throughout Arulean was crumbling.

Her mother, Margarith, would be furious with both her and Rickard if she was still alive. Margarith hated failure of any sort. A perfectionist through and through, Haveena could still hear her shrill, acidic voice when she would scold her. Her mother had always been tough on her, teaching her the importance of honing her witchcraft and taking care of the family. She loved Haveena too, as tough as she could be, she was also loving. Not the sweet and warm nonsense that kids thought they needed. No, she loved Haveena by honing her into a powerful weapon.

Margarith was attracted to power and those who wielded it lethally. After Margarith had been betrayed by Dyana's father, King Galen Kyllarian and his wife Maeve. She had instilled their right to seek their revenge on those who would do them harm. Haveena had been a teenager at the time, growing more and more powerful by the day. She would never admit it now, but at the time, Dyana's betrayal had hurt her deeply.

When Haveena met Rickard, Margarith was thrilled with the match. Haveena had had her fair share of suitors knocking on her door, desperate to tap into the power of Lord Dakarth's bloodline... of Margarith's bloodline. Of course, the history of their bloodline was not widely known when she was younger – only those adept in the dark arts knew – Haveena had been enamoured by Rickard when she met him. He was tall, muscular, handsome and (most importantly) powerful. Already, he was building quite a strong magical skill set, but that wasn't the thing Haveena loved about him most. She loved the fact that he didn't know about her lineage when they first met.

"What's a beauty like you doing in a hovel like this?" he asked her, sliding up to her at some shithole inn at Ravenrock. The clientele were the kind of lowlife traders, thieves, assassins for hire and the occasional under-realm deviant that you would expect to see in these parts of town.

"Does that line ever work for you?" she asked, turning around to face him. She was instantly drawn to his chiselled cheeks, dark smouldering eyes and his dark brown hair. *Well, shit.* She had suddenly become one of those cliché idiot girls that you read about in the books. Gushing over a tall, dark and handsome man.

"It does, actually," he replied, his smouldering eyes doing wonders to her, as was his charming smile, "but it usually only works with the idiots. It's a great way to weed them out to find the goods."

"And how's that working out for you?" she replied, unable to hide her grin.

"Can I buy you a drink?" he replied.

"Sure," she smiled at him.

"Then it's working out great so far," he replied, winking. "I'm Rickard. What's your name?"

"I'm Havi," she replied, using a nickname she hadn't heard in a long time.

She wasn't ready to give away her name just yet. Usually, men knew her name already, lapping up to her like slobbering dogs. Or, when she finally introduced herself and they recognised her name, they suddenly became far more interested in her, going from eager for a quick fuck behind the back of the inn to suddenly wanting to sweep her off her feet and marry her. It was revolting. No, she kept her true identity a secret from Rickard at first. When she finally told him her full name, he reacted as she would have hoped.

"You didn't have to hide it from me, but I'm glad you felt comfortable telling me. My own family comes from the under-realm. Nothing noble like your bloodline, but my family has done well. It becomes obnoxious when you're trying to make your way in the world." He smiled warmly at her.

"Oh, I agree," she replied, falling madly in love with him.

When she finally told her mother she had met Rickard and that they were madly in love, she was thrilled.

"You are our future, Haveena. You are the future of Dakarth's bloodline," she replied, beaming. "Oh, this is a wonderful match, my dear." His family is well off and he's brimming with power," Margarith cackled, "One day, you will be as powerful as I." Her mother liked to tell her this regularly, cupping her face lovingly and showering her with kisses. Her mother was best at showering her with love, while also being cunning and swift.

Rickard's wealth helped take Haveena and Margarith out of the simple life they had been leading after Galen and Maeve had left them with nothing. Haveena would make her mother proud.

"Your Grace," one of her guards called out behind her, pulling her out of her stroll down memory lane, "we've found the scouts. Their bodies were…"

"Any sign of the boy?" she cut him off. "Or the other traitors?" She didn't bother to face the guard.

"No, Your Grace."

"That'll be all then," she dismissed the guard, who retreated quickly.

Haveena admired the boy for his resilience, the town was well positioned for a hideout. The long valley gave anyone hiding out a swift advantage. Had the boy seen her coming down the valley when he made his escape, or was he long gone before then? It was simple enough to flee into the forest from the town: a pursuer would be none the wiser to anyone fleeing *en masse*. She realised that she'd have to start playing the game carefully going forward. She couldn't allow him to grow any stronger. She couldn't allow a phoenix, let alone a Kyllarian phoenix to amass any more support in Arulean. She had suspected there may have been a connection to the Kyllarians when she saw his sigil. But her fears were confirmed when she read the woman's mind in Korgun. As she drained the woman's life, her own fears for her son and his royal best friend confirmed Haveena's own fear. How had Dyana's son survived?

"Excuse me, Your Majesty?" called a voice she recognised.

"Yes, Sir Jarrack?" she replied, spinning to face her most loyal guard.

"May I speak freely?"

"Of course."

"King Rickard is wasting time we don't have. The boy is gone, the town is deserted."

"I'm glad," she smiled with delight, "that I'm not the only one who sees that."

"We need to leave soon," Jarrack stiffened. "If Dyana's son grows much stronger, we're in trouble."

"You figured it out?"

"That sigil brought us to Basilium eighteen years ago. He's about the right age, too." He gazed at her longingly. "And I saw a change in your mannerisms in Korgun, that's when I knew."

"Nothing gets past you, does it, Sir Jarrack Bromley." She brushed her fingers across his cheek. "Can you pry your men away from my idiot husband and get us out of this dump?"

"Anything for you, my queen." He smiled at her. "Where are we going?"

"I'll get back to you on that," she smiled.

"Yes, my queen." He bowed and left her.

Haveena waited until she was alone before screaming into her hands. How did Dyana do it? Did she help the boy survive? Or was it his own doing? She was so enraged that Dyana had deceived her, that Lord Nathaniel had deceived her.

"I should have taken him out years ago," she hissed to herself, but having the Lord of the crown lands and his loyal subjects under the thumb had come in handy.

What would Dyana do? Haveena wondered. *She would seek the safety and security of Vandfall and the fae. Would he do the same?* Oh, but she didn't actually need to think about that to know what he was going to do, did she?

Haveena closed her eyes and felt for her magic, finding that thread in her mind. When she located it, she concentrated on it, opening her mind and seeing all. Her brilliant discovery in the castle had come in handy so far. *Oh, the fae are with them now. Of course, it's why they came to Oldwell. Shit, he's advancing, and he has help now.* Oh, her mind pulled on a new thread, panic coursing through her and a shiver ran down her spine.

"She's not!" she whispered. "Oh gods, the prophecy." She began to panic. "Dyana, you stupid bitch." She screamed out, running towards Jarrack.

"Jarrack, mount up!" she snipped. "We're riding for the Fortress of the Flames."

"The fortress, my queen?" he replied, not hiding the alarm in his tone.

"Yes!" she replied, equally alarmed. "He's looking for the prophecy."

"Move out," he shouted towards his men. "I will stop him, My queen." He emphasised each word as he spoke, his eyes dark and full of malice.

Haveena smiled at the devotion seeping out of Jarrack. He would do anything for her. That was the kind of devotion she used to receive from Rickard. Years ago, he would have done anything for her. She had loved Rickard before the crown changed him, as both their powers grew in different directions, Rickard lost his interest in her. That's when he transformed into the brute he was now. He could have kept some of his other powers, had he not been so focused on syphoning his power into that shield of his. All so he could look like the most intimidating and brutish man on the battlefield. She could tolerate him until she found a way to get rid of him, but first, she must stop the boy from stepping foot in the fortress.

"Rickard!" Haveena shouted, deciding his wrath was worth the risk. He turned towards her, glaring. "The boy is on the move to the fortress, our fortress. We'll have the upper hand. I'm leaving now, get your men moving or stay behind." She kept her head high and her back straight as she spoke.

Rickard walked towards her, each step slow, angry and deliberate. His eyes twitched with rage. She glared back at him, she was powerful too, and she wasn't going to let him push her around anymore. He stopped moving, his eyes gazing up and down her. His mouth lifted into a smirk.

"Move out, men!" he shouted, turning away from her.

Haveena mounted her horse and trotted over to Sir Jarrack, who was already on horseback and overseeing his soldiers.

"Let's move, Jarrack," she smiled at him.

"I'll be by your side every step of the way," he replied.

Haveena kicked her horse and galloped fast out of the valley towards the royal road. The journey to the fortress would take at least two full days of riding, but she would not stop. Filled with purpose, she would ensure the prophecy remained unfulfilled. The boy was playing in her territory now. She knew that fortress better than anyone, and she would ensnare him in the place she called home for such a long time.

~ CHAPTER TWENTY ~

Will and the convoy had been riding for two days. The white mare and Will had bonded deeply on their long and winding journey through the Amaranthine Forest. The mare responded to each pull of the reins quickly, almost responding instinctively to Will's desires. Will cared for her deeply in return, resting her when she required a break and ensuring that she and other horses stopped to eat and drink in the luscious forest. After each break, the rejuvenated horses made up for lost time, galloping like a synchronised horde through tight and narrow paths out of the forest.

After leaving the ritual site, the convoy rested for a few hours before daybreak. Seb was already awake when Will woke with the sunrise. Seb had changed into leathers during the night. Embossed on his doublet was the sigil of House Kyllarian. Will gazed at the sigil, his smile from ear to ear.

"I've never had a family sigil to fight for," Seb said wistfully, then stood tall and proud with his chest puffed out. "You and Aylise are the only family I have left. You're the only place I have to call home," he said proudly.

"The sigil looks good on you," Will smiled, "you're my best friend, Seb, you'll always have a home with me."

"I'll be by your side 'til the end," Seb replied.

"You'll always have a home in my kingdom, too," Prince Andayne said, smiling at him.

"Oh," Seb blushed at Prince Andayne, "thank you, that's very kind." He smiled softly at the prince.

Will and the convoy rode through the forest for as long as possible, using the forest to mask their movements through the kingdom. Once they had travelled far enough south, they left the forest and rode hard west towards the fortress. They passed rolling hills and tree-lined valleys until a stone structure emerged in the distance.

"So that's it, then?" Seb asked Prince Andayne as they rode closer to the ruins. "That's the fallen fortress?"

Large stone pillars lay in broken pieces across the earth. Mounds of broken rock and old, rotting timber were built up around the only structure left standing, a small section of a tower.

"It truly is a ruin, isn't it," Will said. "I thought there would be more of it."

"Thousands of years ago, people believed that this fortress was imbued with magical power," Seb mused. "It was said to be covered in glossy black stone."

Will dismounted from his horse and slowly began to walk towards the ruins. His power woke, sending pulses through his body. It was reacting to something in the area, responding to a power close by... the prophecy, perhaps?

"Cara, you said there were ruins below?" Will asked.

"There are," she replied, floating towards him. "Follow me, please."

Seb and Aylise dismounted their horses, Prince Andayne, Selina, Darian, Lord Nathaniel and Lady Ana followed close behind.

"Is everyone coming with us?" Will asked.

"If you want us to, of course we are," Selina answered warmly.

"Of course. I think we all need to know." Will nodded and turned back towards the ruins. He didn't want to keep secrets from anyone. "Everyone, follow Cara."

"Set up a patrol," Lord Nathaniel ordered his guards, "and prepare a camp. We don't know how long we'll be."

Cara moved between the mounds of fallen stone, away from the tower. Some of the mounds were twenty feet high, some were smaller. Each mound of rubble was so tightly packed that Will began to wonder where the entrance to the fortress was. Would they have to climb the rubble?

"Over the years, the earth swallowed the fortress," Cara said matter-of-factly as she floated along. "Most of it remains intact below the earth," she said, turning to Will, "This place holds more secrets than we know."

Cara moved towards a small stone wall that was still standing. The earth sloped upwards towards the wall. Large stones and boulders were scattered around the wall.

"Some of those secrets will reveal themselves to you... If only you know where to look," Cara said, floating up towards two large boulders.

Will walked towards her. Tucked away behind the boulders was a small opening leading into the earth. A small amount of light touched the opening before leading into darkness.

"Are you sure you want to go in there, Will?" his mother asked him, holding him tightly.

"I... No, we need answers. There's no turning back now, mother," he replied, walking into the opening.

The ground dropped below Will's feet as he moved into the dark tunnel. He paused part way into the opening, allowing his eyes to adjust to the dark. The tunnel was narrow, large rocks jutted out from the walls, making the journey through the tight space uncomfortable. The tunnel continued for a short distance and opened into a large corridor. When Will landed on the stone floor, the sound echoed along the dark space. A torch flickered down the corridor.

"Someone's here," Will whispered to Seb as he moved down from the tunnel.

"Oh gods," Seb replied, darting behind a pillar.

"What's wrong?" Andayne asked, as he and Aylise moved into the corridor.

Seb pointed towards the torch at the end of the corridor.

"Don't fret about that," Andayne smiled, patting Seb on the shoulder. "The torches are eternal phoenix flames. The magic still held, even when the fortress fell into ruin," Andayne marvelled.

"Really?" Aylise asked, walking towards the torch. "I was curious about the phoenix flame during the ritual. The flame comes from the bird?"

"It does indeed, and not just any phoenix. The myth says the flame was gifted by the ancient legendary phoenixes. All the sacred locations are lit by the same phoenix flame."

"Sacred locations?" Aylise asked.

"Ancient phoenix strongholds. This fortress is one of them." Andayne turned towards Will, watching him as he spoke. "The strongholds housed phoenixes: the humans and the birds, together. There could be hundreds of phoenixes across the continent at any given time." He paused. "Once the phoenixes stopped hatching, Arulean lost its first line of defence. As their power diminished, the under-realm grew bolder. Dakarth came to Arulean, and the phoenix wars began. The fortress has been a ruin since. The temple of the flames on the Jean Islands was the last to turn to ruin."

Darian, Selina, Nathaniel and Ana moved into the corridor, Cara floated in behind them. Andayne looked thoughtfully down the corridor – which split off in two directions – he closed his eyes and inhaled deeply. Will sensed power radiating from Andayne. It was strong, just like his mother's.

"This way," Andayne said, opening his eyes and moving down the corridor.

Will followed Andayne, the only light coming from the torches held in brackets along the walls. The corridor ended with a narrow spiral staircase and one by one they walked deeper into the depths of the ruin. Andayne stopped at the bottom of the stairs and turned to face Will.

"You know a phoenix hasn't risen in these lands for over one thousand years. Whatever we find in these ruins will set you on a path that there's no coming back from." Andayne looked at him intently. "Are you ready for that?"

Will moved from the top step into the corridor, Aylise stepped down next to him.

"I guess I have to be ready for it, don't I?" he replied flatly, "I don't particularly have much of a choice."

"But you did, you wanted to leave," Andayne replied.

"I changed my mind," Will said archly, "is it not understandable that I may have wanted an easier way out?" He held his head up high. "But I'm here now."

Andayne gazed at Will searchingly.

"You're ready, Will Kyllarian," he replied. It was a statement, not a question.

"You're going to need me," called a voice from the stairs.

Daemoon Torvinya, the fae Will met at the ritual, walked down the stairs. He swept into the room gracefully, gazing warmly at Will.

"I mean no offence." Will ensured he smiled in an attempt not to sound passive-aggressive. "But why do we need you?"

"Because I am a guardian at the Tower of Wisdom," Daemoon smiled. "If all else fails, I can read the prophecy."

"But if the prophecy is about me, I thought I could read it?"

"That's true, but the prophecy has been read, and it's no longer here. We're using our magic to piece together the traces of the magic left behind by the prophecy. Once we do so, I have no doubt that you would have been able to read it. But nothing is certain with magic, so I'm the backup plan."

"I don't fully understand how that works," Will replied with a chuckle, "but I'm glad you're here."

Aylise grasped his hand, interlocking her fingers around his.

"How are you doing?" Aylise smiled at him, squeezing his hand.

Will felt ablaze with her touch, did she know how great she made him feel? In among the chaos that had become his life, she was his constant calming presence. Whatever they discovered about this prophecy, he knew his life was about to change: for better or worse, he couldn't say. All day, Seb's words had been playing in his mind... Seb didn't want to die without them knowing who he was. Well, maybe it wasn't the best timing, but his life was about to change, and there was one thing he desperately desired to do before it did. A wooden door behind Aylise was ajar.

"Can we have a private word?" His urgent tone hid his nerves as he spoke gently to Aylise.

"Of course," she replied, looking rather perplexed.

"We'll be back in a moment," he called out to the group as he led Aylise into the room.

The room was barren, one of the walls was crumbling away, but a small amount of light managed to break through the rubble, casting shadows through the room. Clouds of dirt and dust danced through the light as they moved into the room. There was an archway on the opposite end of the room, which was blocked by large amounts of rubble and stone.

"What are we doing, Will?" Aylise asked, closing the door behind her.

"Please come here," he replied, walking into the light. He took a deep breath and reached for her hands. "I know this is strange timing, but I need to tell you this before we read this prophecy... before our lives change. I need to tell you something and I need you to hear it while I'm still the same Will. The boy you have known since birth. The boy you grew up with. The boy whose life has been changing." He smiled at her nervously as she held his gaze, she looked hopeful, giving Will the extra courage he needed. "I always thought that this would never be able to work, that you wouldn't feel the same. You're a lady, I'm a blacksmith's son."

"Who happens to be a prince," she interjected, blushing slightly.

"But that's not the reason I'm saying this. I'm saying this because whether you're a lady, or I'm a prince, or a phoenix, or just the simple son of a blacksmith." He took a deep breath to calm his nerves, "Aylise, I love you. I loved you when I was a young boy. I've loved you as we've grown up. I love you as a blacksmith's son and I love you as a prince, a phoenix or whatever I am. I loved you before I even knew what love was."

Aylise's eyes twinkled and her lips turned upward.

"I don't want to die. I don't want to leave this world or leave our old lives behind without ever telling you how I feel, what if I never get the chance to…" Will stopped speaking as Aylise placed her fingers on his lips.

Aylise cradled his face in her hands and kissed him passionately. When his lips met hers, fire exploded through his body, not his power, or maybe it was? He couldn't tell, but every inch of him burned with passion and desire as her lips met his. He placed his hands across her back and pulled her closer. Kissing her deeply. With each kiss, he fell even deeper in love with her.

"I love you too, Will. I have always loved you. I love you as Will Tavner, and I love you as Will Kyllarian. And I love you as Will the blacksmith's son." Aylise pulled away from him, looking deeply into his eyes. "I told you I would be by your side, and I meant it. I love you, and I'll be by your side until my last breath."

He pulled her closer and kissed her again. She leaned in, accepting his kiss. She ran her fingers through his hair and his whole body lit up, tingling from head to toe. Did she feel the same too?

"I'm yours forever," he whispered.

Aylise kissed him passionately. His body responded to hers, their bodies moving together. His body felt like it was burning, yearning for her as much as his heart did. He wanted to stay like this forever.

"Not that we want to interrupt you, but we really must continue on!" Seb called out from the corridor.

"We'll be out in a moment," Will replied, blushing at Aylise.

Aylise lifted Will's hand and held it against her cheek.

"Whatever we find in that room," Aylise kissed his hand gently, "whatever the prophecy says, we'll face it together."

"I'll be by your side until the end," he replied. His heart fluttered as they walked out of the room.

"It's about time," Seb quipped at them, beaming with delight. "Those doors are ancient, and you weren't exactly being quiet."

Will and Aylise's parents were beaming at them. His cheeks flushed red at the sight of their delighted faces.

"Let's not delay any longer," Will blustered. "After you, Prince Andayne."

"My friends call me Dayne," he replied warmly.

"Does that mean we're friends now?" Will replied jovially.

"I believe so," he replied, winking.

"Well then, after you, Dayne," Seb replied, smiling.

Dayne led Will further into the depths of the fortress, each step carrying them deeper into the earth. The air grew still and colder the further they travelled down. Each member of the party silently walked through the fortress. To Will, it felt like he was marching towards a destiny he had no control over.

At the bottom of another staircase, Will stepped into the corridor and clutched his chest. The air felt strange down here, it twisted around Will, pulling at him.

"What's wrong?" Seb asked, concerned. Aylise moved to his other side.

"Don't you feel that?"

"Feel what?" Seb and Aylise replied.

"I feel it too," Dayne volunteered.

Voices called to Will from behind a door at the end of the hallway. He felt the pull of the room, *the pull of power.*

"Cara," Dayne called out, "we're here."

"Are you sure you want everyone to come in with you?" she asked Will as she floated towards the door.

"Yes," he replied quickly as he walked towards the door, his stomach twisting in knots with nerves. Will felt like his whole body had been in a state of change the last few days, leading to this moment.

As Cara pushed the door open, the air around him grew heavier. The pull of the room grew stronger, louder. He took a deep breath and walked inside.

Will stepped beneath the arching canopy, torches bathing the room in golden light. Large columns lined the walls of the room and an obscenely large altar with a stone ring around the edge stood in the centre of the room. A skeleton was draped over the ring, its legs hanging over the edge. Cara hovered towards the skeleton.

"That looks human," Will called out, moving closer to the body. The room no longer called to him. Was it because he had entered?

"It's fae," Cara replied.

"Oh, Cara… it's yours…" Dayne whispered, turning towards Cara. "I can feel it."

"I know. I feel it too," she groaned with grief as she hovered her hands over the bones, "When I handed Haveena the prophecy, she killed me to invoke an ancient magic, dark magic."

"The black curse," Dayne and Daemoon muttered in unison, barely above a whisper.

"Yes," she nodded sombrely.

"What does the black curse do?" Seb asked.

"The black curse is one of the darkest magics known. It can blanket a whole city: anyone inside is helpless, trapped, disorientated… the smoke and fire choke everything. But the caster chooses who the curse affects."

"So, you can lead an entire army right into a city and guarantee your victory," Will observed.

"The odds are very much in your favour, yes," Cara countered. "The black curse is truly heinous because it requires the taking of a life, and a curse that dark demands a life of light."

"A fae life," Will replied softly. "Your life. She used you for the prophecy and then used you for the curse. I'm so sorry, Cara."

"So that's how she did it." Darian gazed around the room, as if looking back in time. "All these years left wondering how they could wipe us out like that. Of course, she had to use magic."

"It's time to summon the prophecy." Cara turned towards Will. "Can you feel the presence?"

Will closed his eyes, feeling for the magic in the room. The air moved around him, his power seeking out any presence in the room. He felt it by the altar: a power lingered there.

"I feel it." He looked at Cara. "What do I have to do?"

"I need a drop or two of your blood to start the magic. Daemoon, a blade please."

"Would you like to do it? Or do you want me to?" Daemoon asked, holding the dagger out.

"I'll do it," he replied, holding his hand out for the dagger.

Voices whispered to Will as the dagger's hilt touched his skin. The air in the room pulled him towards the altar, calling to him. Fire burned through his body, begging to escape.

"Just a prick of the finger will suffice, Will." Cara called, turning towards her bones.

Cara reached out for her skull. As her hands connected with the bones, they disintegrated into dust. The rest of her body followed suit, falling to the earth.

"Goodbye. Rest easy, now," she whispered.

Will pricked his finger with the blade, wincing slightly as the sharp metal pierced his flesh and blood rushed to the surface of his skin.

Cara, Andayne and Daemoon began to chant in Faeish, swirling their arms in a beautiful dance of magic. Cara's bone dust lifted into the air, also swirling around the room. Daemoon's hands glowed with purple-blue energy. Cara's glowed a soft pink and Andayne's glowed with a teal and turquoise energy. The room changed colour: orange glowing magic circled the room and pooled into the altar. Will felt the pull of the magic in the altar, calling to him. Cara, Andayne and Daemoon's chanting grew louder.

Will's blood lifted from his finger and floated towards Cara's open hands. The fire inside Will erupted from his hands, covering his arms in flames. The flames swirled towards the altar, setting the area ablaze, a great fire roaring to the ceiling. Cara's hands vibrated, her spectral form becoming more solid as the magic around the room intensified. Air swirled around the room, creating a vortex around everyone standing in the room. Will's blood and Cara's bones swirled around the fire together, faster and faster, then shot into the flames. The flames lifted away from the earth, swirling into a ball in the middle of the altar.

"What is that inside it?" he asked, looking at Cara.

"It's a phoenix egg," she replied, smiling.

Black and smooth, the egg was glowing brightly as the flames disappeared. The egg began to shake, small cracks and bumps appearing along the surface before smashing into tiny pieces floating above the altar. As a piece of parchment appeared in between the broken shards of the egg, the shards began to move, falling into the parchment. Will didn't need to see the small details to understand what was happening. The pieces of the egg were forming words on the parchment. Even without the small whispers or the pull of magic forces around him, he knew the egg had formed the words of the prophecy. He held his hand above him, and felt his body burn with energy as the parchment landed in his hands.

~ CHAPTER TWENTY-ONE ~

*When the last flame dies, and the phoenixes fall and darkness reigns
unchallenged. A child of royal blood shall rise. Awakened by the flames, they
will possess the greatest power of the phoenix and end the tyranny of
darkness for eternity.*

Will's gaze remained transfixed on the parchment. His heart
was beating so loudly, he felt like it might burst from his
chest. He read the words again and again, hoping with
each repeated read, he might understand it more. His eyes glanced over
the bottom line again. *"They will possess the greatest power of the phoenix
and end the tyranny of darkness for eternity."* That was why Haveena
hunted him so ferociously, wasn't it? She feared him.

A spark ignited in Will, it was comfortable and familiar, spreading
warmth and power through him. A soft tickling brushed across his
skin as he felt feathers wrapping around his body. He turned towards
Aylise, seeking her comfort, but she was gone: the room was empty.
Shadows flickered in the fiery light around him. Orange and red wings
wrapped around his body, encompassing him completely. He tried to
turn around to see the bird, but he couldn't move. He was frozen in

place. The wings curled into him, sending flames rushing towards his fast-beating heart.

"Aylise," he called out to the empty space. He waited for a response but was greeted by silence. "Aylise!" he screamed.

"Will!" a voice called back in reply.

Will opened his eyes as Aylise was shaking him, her blue eyes wide with concern. Seb stood beside her, his face dripping with sweat and his mouth wide open. His parents watched him curiously.

"Will, are you alright?" Aylise asked.

"I..." he began, confused, "I'm not sure what just happened."

"It called to you, didn't it?" Dayne looked awestruck. "The phoenix called to you."

"I think so," he replied, wiping his brow. "I've never felt a fire like that inside me before," he confessed.

"It's okay, Will. That's normal." Dayne spoke to him calmly. "It'll pass soon." He smiled at Will. "You have the prophecy?" Will nodded. "Would you like some of us to step out and give you some privacy?"

"No, thank you. I'm happy to share what's written."

Will read the prophecy to the group. Selina gasped audibly as her brow furrowed.

"What does this mean for my son?" Selina turned her gaze towards the fae.

"I will answer your question, Selina," Daemoon responded warmly, "but first... Will, do you understand what is written?"

"Haveena and Rickard, they're the reign of darkness." Everyone in the room was watching Will as he spoke. "A child of royal blood. That's me." It still felt odd saying that aloud. "What does *Greatest power of the phoenix* mean?"

"I believe it refers to legendary phoenixes." Dayne paused, waiting for an understanding from Will. "They're especially powerful." He continued when it was evident that Will didn't know what a legendary phoenix was. "There hasn't been a true legendary phoenix for a long time, even long before the phoenix wars." Dayne stepped closer to Will, his expression hardened and serious. "Legendary phoenixes are imbued with every power a phoenix can possess. I've seen your abilities manifesting, Will. I believe you could be a legendary phoenix."

"Powerful?" he scoffed, "I can barely control the flames or the energy blasts coming out of me." Doubt began to cloud Will's mind.

"Your power has not yet manifested completely."

"How can you be certain, Dayne?"

"Phoenix abilities are a lot like fae abilities. They manifest when we are very young." Lightning danced around Dayne's fingertips. "Small at first... a lightning bolt here and there. Then, as we learn to control our abilities, the power increases." He looked at Will kindly. "It will take time, but you will learn, too."

The parchment weighed heavily in Will's hand; it plagued him with doubt. How did a simple boy from a small village find himself clutching a prophecy which rested the fate of the world on him?

"I said I was ready for whatever was behind this door, but this is a lot to take in," he said, waving the parchment in front of him.

"You won't be alone," Dayne's reply was gentle and compassionate.

"I'm sorry, Will, this is our fault," his mother offered gently. "We tried so hard to protect you... To shelter you from Rickard and Haveena. We wanted you to have a normal life. We tried our best to train you where we could, without drawing too much attention to you. If we'd known about the prophecy, we might have done things differently."

"The only people who knew the contents of the prophecy are dead, apart from Haveena and Rickard." Will glanced towards Cara. "No offence." He smiled apologetically.

"But we could have done better," Selina cried. "We should have sent you to Vandfall years ago, you would have been safer there. You could have honed your abilities sooner."

"They only appeared one week ago." He walked over to Selina and wrapped his arms around her, holding her tightly.

"That raises another question," Daemoon interjected. "You're quite old to only have your powers manifesting now. As I understand, the sigil appeared when he was a baby?" Daemoon turned towards Selina.

"The day he was born," Darian replied.

"Very curious indeed. We should discuss that with Queen Keeva." Daemoon turned towards Dayne.

"Indeed, I have theories as to why they manifested so late. But nothing certain," Dayne replied.

"As do I," Daemoon replied.

While Will was curious about their theories, he was also tiring. Between the ritual, riding to the fortress and performing the magic in the chamber, he needed something to eat, some water and a good rest. The other members of the party looked exhausted too.

"Is there anything else we can learn here in the fortress?" Will asked Dayne.

"No, you have the prophecy. There's nothing else," Dayne replied.

"Then we should get above ground and rest," Will replied.

"We need to get to Vandfall and start your training as soon as possible," Dayne said matter-of-factly.

"Perhaps," Lord Nathaniel called out, stepping forward. "It would be best if we set up camp here this evening. It's late in the day, and there is shelter here already."

"I disagree, Lord Nathaniel," Cara spoke up. "We shouldn't linger here. Queen Haveena has been mere steps behind us this whole time."

"How would they know we're here?" Selina asked.

"How did they know we were at Korgun or Oldwell?" Cara replied. "Spies, scouts, intuition or magic, she found a way. Trust me, we should move on."

"Will, the decision is yours," Lord Nathaniel said gravely. Will looked from Seb to Aylise. Seb looked exhausted, like he was one moment away from passing out.

"What do you want to do?" Will asked, turning his gaze towards Aylise.

"I'm tired," she replied, stepping towards him. "Let's rest tonight, and we can leave for Vandfall in the morning."

"It's settled, then." He glanced away from Cara. "We'll set up camp here tonight."

"I'll make sure everything is in order," Lord Nathaniel said, turning and walking out of the room.

"I'll check the perimeter," Cara snapped, floating out of the room through a wall.

"You know why she feels uncomfortable here, don't you?" Seb asked, turning his gaze towards the altar.

Will followed Seb's gaze, his heart sank as he looked down at Cara's bone dust.

"Oh," he ran his fingers through his hair. "That was daft of me." He looked towards Seb. "Should I go after her?

"Perhaps you should give her a moment, and go find her later," Seb replied encouragingly.

"How am I ever going to be a good leader?" He bowed his head. "I keep blundering my way through this," he sighed.

Will needed time to think and he needed to breathe some fresh air. He tucked the prophecy into his satchel and left the underground chamber.

Aylise and Will sat atop the last-standing tower of the fortress, their feet dangling from the edge, watching the camp below. From this height, the damage to the fortress was unmissable, large stone walls protruded from the earth in every direction. Those stones protected the inner bailey from collapsing completely and they also kept the inner areas safe from prying eyes. It was only from this vantage that the structures and rooms that remained above ground could be seen.

Aylise held onto Will's hand as they watched her father's soldiers setting up their camp in the valley below. They made camp in the middle of the fortress grounds, surrounded by large stones and boulders. Passing travellers would struggle to see their camp from the roads. On the other side of the tower, the sea breeze carried the smell of salt in the air, and waves crashed against the sandy beach at the bottom of the cliffs. Aylise felt happy being here with him. She knew how much being close to the ocean calmed Will.

Even in the heightened state everyone felt around the camp, Aylise couldn't help feeling calm and content by Will's side. Her smile beamed from ear to ear and her heart filled with joy. Why did she ever doubt herself? Why did she ever hold back from truly showing how she felt about Will? Not that she had been subtle lately, but she had been when she was younger. She used to panic that her father would never approve of the match. The daughter of a lord did not traditionally marry a blacksmith's son, no matter how desperately she may have wanted to. Now she saw the way her father looked at her and Will and she couldn't help but wonder. Was his title the reason her father approved of the match? She was sure it helped. Lords and ladies were always looking for the best match for their families and what better match than the king, not that his title mattered to Aylise at all.

Aylise was about twelve years old when she realised that her feelings for Will were far deeper than just the love she felt for her best friend. She had grown up with him and Seb. The trio of best friends that had big plans for their futures, but one day he smiled at her and her knees buckled so much she thought she might collapse into a heap. She started to notice the sparkle in his green eyes, how his mischievous behaviour was balanced by his caring and nurturing nature. Then when she was fourteen, she watched him swimming at the beach. Her eyes grew wide as his smooth muscular body bounced around in the waves. She became hot and flustered. She could barely think of anything else on the way home. If only she hadn't kept her feelings quite so secret for such a long time.

"I used to think my fondness for the ocean came from my father because of his upbringing, but I guess I was wrong," Will said softly to Aylise and rested his head on her shoulder, pulling her from her memories. "Maybe it still does come from him. It's not always about blood, right?"

"Our bloodlines don't define any of us," Aylise replied, leaning into him. "It's the people we surround ourselves with and our choices that truly define who we are."

"I hope I'm making the right choices," he replied. He looked like he was deep in thought again. Lost in his own mind. "Maybe I should have spoken to my parents when I first discovered the sigil. If I had, Rupert wouldn't have died, and Marte and Alexander would be here."

"And yet, they could have died anyway," she replied softly, pulling Will into a hug. "Even if life had taken a different pathway, the destination may have been the same regardless. Death comes for us all."

"I love you," he whispered to her, "thank you for being here." Her heart filled with warmth.

"It's spectacular up here, isn't it?" Seb mused, marching up the stairs.

Dayne followed close behind him. They sat down next to Will and Aylise in the silent serenity of the tower, watching a flock of seabirds flying close by.

"How are you feeling, Seb?" Will turned towards his friend.

"I'm fine," Seb replied, clasping Will's hand. "It's lovely to be back near the ocean again, isn't it?"

"Yes, but sadly, I don't think we'll be taking any leisurely swims for quite some time," Will said.

"Why not?" Dayne replied, standing up.

"Now?" Aylise replied.

"Yeah," Dayne replied, "we are camping here for the night."

"You know what?" Will replied, smiling, "You're a genius, Andayne Lorenstar."

"I know," he smiled in return. "Follow me, then." Dayne winked at Seb.

"Can Seb and I meet you down there?" Aylise asked. "I'd like a private moment with my friend."

"Are you okay?" Will asked her.

"Of course," she replied softly, "I just need a minute." She blew him a kiss.

Will smiled at her and walked down from the tower with Dayne. Seb shuffled closer to Aylise.

"Is everything okay?" Seb asked.

"I was going to ask you the same question," she replied. Seb was silent for a moment. "What's going on, Seb?"

"I can't," he began, as tears formed in his eyes. "I can't or it'll hurt too much. Please don't make me talk about it."

"Oh darling." Aylise wrapped her arms around him, holding him closely.

"I just have to put that fake smile on my face and keep going." Seb managed to hold back his tears. "If I don't, it'll hurt too much. So, I keep a happy smile on my face for Will, so he stops blaming himself. Flirt with the prince who likes me, to stop the pain and emptiness I feel."

His lip trembled as he spoke. "Because when I don't, when I'm left with my own thoughts… my pain just wants to swallow me whole." He looked down at his hands. "How did you know?"

"Because I know you, Seb Estermont," Aylise said softly.

"I can barely find the strength to move every day. The hole in my heart hurts, it hurts to breathe, Aylise. What did I do to deserve this? My lover and my parents gone, in a matter of days."

"You're allowed to grieve, Seb. No one would judge you for that."

"But there's too much at stake right now. I can't expect everyone to carry around my burden too."

"Will already does, because he cares about you, too," Aylise replied.

"The least I can do is ease that tension," Seb replied, "I need to block it out and forget about it for now." A tear streamed down his cheek. "Please Aylise, it's the only thing holding me together right now."

"Oh Seb. What can I do to help?" she replied.

"Please take me down to the beach." He wiped his tear from his cheek, locking his emotions away where they couldn't hurt anyone, except him.

Dayne knew his way through the fortress quite well. Aylise and Seb met them at the bottom of the tower and then Dayne led them into the depths of the fortress. He ushered them through a hidden passage behind a wall panel.

"I'm pleasantly surprised it still opens," Dayne said jovially as he walked through the opening.

The passage was dark and tight. They had to walk in single file down the stairs. Dayne led the way down the passage, with his fae eyesight, the dark was no concern for him. Though he encouraged Will to conjure a fireball to assist the humans down the path. It was surprisingly easy to control, and it became quite useful as they descended lower into the passage.

Light began to shine through the passage and then opened into a small sea cave. Will leapt down onto the soft sand, water lapping around his boots. At the end of the cave, a sliver of light broke through the dark rocky walls. Dayne slipped through the crack, Aylise and Seb following behind him.

Will felt light and carefree as he slipped through the gap in the rocks and walked out onto the soft sandy beach. Large black stone pieces from the fortress lay scattered around the beach, some pieces closer to the water, others resting against the cliff edges. The waves were softly breaking against the sand, each wash of the breaking water tempting every inch of Will to jump in.

"Shall we?" Andayne smiled at Seb.

Andayne undid the clasp of his robes, sliding it effortlessly off his shoulders and draping it over a rock. He removed his tunic and his shirt. His muscular body was smooth and firm. His skin looked like silk over each ripple and curve of his body. He removed his boots and leather trousers, leaving only his undergarments on and ran into the water.

"Are you coming?" he called out.

Even though he called out to the three of them, he hadn't taken his eyes off Seb. Will might have been blind to see the way Aylise looked at him, or perhaps he couldn't truly believe it. But he could clearly see the way Dayne looked at Seb – his eyes lit up whenever Seb was close. Did Seb feel the same way? Seb enjoyed Dayne's company, that was evident, was there more to it, or was Dayne a welcome distraction from the loss of Rupert and his parents? Or perhaps it was both.

"Are *you* coming, Will?" Aylise called out. Will stared wide-eyed at her.

Aylise had undressed, removing her tunic, leather pants and shirt. She was naked from the waist up, her bare breasts peeking through the strands of her copper hair. Will resisted adjusting the growing mass in his pants.

"Oh, ah..." he stumbled, barely able to form a single word, let alone a sentence.

"Haha," she giggled at him. "Those two prefer the company of men, darling. The only man here interested in these is you." She smiled playfully. "Unless this makes you uncomfortable?" She ran her hands along her body, her smile deep and longing.

"I have never been more turned on in my life," he smiled back, biting his lip.

Will yearned to explore more of her body. Would it be terrible to slip back into the cave and explore every part of her right now?

"Come and join me, then!" She ran towards the water.

His heart skipped a beat. *I guess it isn't back to the cave right now.* He undressed quickly, praying that his manhood would soften. When it didn't, he tried his best to hide his semi-erection as he fumbled his way down to the ocean. He almost lost his footing, but somehow managed to stop himself from face-planting into the sand. *Get a hold of yourself,* he thought as he hit the water.

The temperature in the water was pleasant. Will dove into the waves. The saltwater washing over him felt like it was cleansing away his troubles. His body submitted to the ocean. Drifting along the surface made him feel like the old Will; the carefree boy whose troubles could be swept away with a simple swim. Will Tavner or Will Kyllarian, it didn't matter right now.

"Feel better?" Aylise asked him as he swam away from the shore towards her.

"Much better," he replied. His shaft began to stiffen as Aylise gestured for him to come closer, smiling mischievously at him.

She wrapped her arms around his shoulders and slid her body against his. She curled her legs around his waist and kissed him, as her breasts rubbed against his bare chest. Will's body surged with energy as they connected. Every inch of his body that touched her sparked with heat. He gave in to her touch, submitting to her every desire. As her body pressed against his, his shaft grew in his undergarments.

"I've wanted to do this with you for such a long time." She smiled at him as she kissed him deeper. "You seem to be enjoying this," she whispered to him, her eyes boring into his.

Will panted with delight, unable to find the words to describe how truly wonderful he felt. With each ragged breath, he smiled wider.

Seb laughed nearby, causing Aylise to slide off Will. Dayne had launched at Seb, tackling him into the water. When they emerged, they laughed and joked with each other. Whether Dayne was a distraction or not, it was nice to see Seb smiling again.

"Do you think that Seb is…" Will asked Aylise quietly.

"Ignoring his grief?" Aylise finished his sentence. "Yes, Will." Aylise cupped his face. "He's heartbroken and he just needs some time to heal."

Will and Aylise continued their intense underwater dance of flesh on flesh, lips on lips. Each of them moaning furiously as they explored each other.

"Perhaps, if you felt up to it, we might continue this later?" Will asked rather bashfully. "Somewhere more private?" He smiled optimistically.

Aylise bit into her lip as she smiled at him, every inch of her seemed utterly turned on by his suggestion. "Sure," she leaned forward, whispering into his ear.

"I think that's a wonderful idea too," Seb called out, his grin wide and wickedly mischievous. "I couldn't say that we approve of this display of affection."

"I'm the heir to the throne, Seb," Will replied cheekily, raising his eyebrows. "I don't need your approval." Although he laughed along with Seb's joke, he could just see the jovial mask Seb had plastered on his face drop to reveal the pain behind his eyes.

The four of them took a stroll along the sand in their wet undergarments. Exploring the coastline and enjoying the sunshine on their faces. Then they submerged themselves back in the water as the afternoon heat increased.

"We should head back up," Dayne called as the afternoon crept on, and the sun began to sit low in the sky. "It'll be dark soon."
When Will and Aylise left the water together, there was only one thing on Will's mind.

~ CHAPTER TWENTY-TWO ~

I love magic! Will thought as he walked into his tent. A steaming bathtub sat in the corner, the water was warm to touch. A selection of soaps and lotions were sitting on a table next to it.

"Just a simple something I had conjured up for everyone." Dayne winked at Will. "I heard you were fond of a tub."

"Thank you, Seb." He turned and bowed to Dayne. "And thank you, Prince Andayne."

While Will had been enjoying a leisurely afternoon at the beach, the convoy had hurried around the camp, ensuring everyone would be comfortable for the evening. Fresh game had been hunted, and fresh edible plants had been foraged. The cooks had transformed the collected items into a rich stew. Fresh bread was baked, and cider and mead had been served. It was a delightful evening. Daemoon joined Will, Seb, Aylise and Dayne at a table with Selina, Darian, Ana and Nathaniel. Queen Keeva had left earlier in the day.

"Why don't we go and take a bath together?" Will whispered into Aylise's ear when they had finished eating.

'Yes," was all she managed to whisper back before they linked hands and walked away from the table. A brief glance back calmed Will. Lord Nathaniel was beaming as Will and Aylise walked away together.

Perhaps it was a match they intended all along. *Thank the gods their tents aren't close.* Will thought as they walked away.

Will had offered Aylise a private moment to undress and get into the tub, not wanting her to feel pressured to bare her naked self in front of him.

"You're a true gentleman, Will Kyllarian." She smiled at him, and bit her lip again. "But tonight, I'm not going to be a lady." She winked at him and removed her clothes.

Her naked body was stunning. Every curve of her was utter perfection, and his eyes worshipped every inch of her. His groin stirred in his pants, unable to resist the temptation of the perfect woman standing before him. Aylise ran her hands across his chest as she walked to the bath.

"Your turn." She kissed him as she stepped into the bath and sunk into the water.

Will undressed, desperately trying to control his rising erection as he removed his clothes. Aylise's eyes widened as he removed his pants. Was she looking at him with the same desire he felt for her?

Until this moment, Will thought there was no possible way to make a bath any better. However, enjoying a bath with a person that you are madly in love with certainly made the whole experience exponentially more wonderful. Aylise washed Will's hair, rubbing lotions along his scalp. Each stroke of her fingers shot fiery bursts of desire down his body. Will returned the favour. Running his hands through her hair and lathering the potions through each strand, he washed away the built-up dirt and salt water. She responded to his touch by leaning in and kissing him. When their lips touched, it awakened something deep inside his heart. He wanted her. He had yearned for her – desired her – for years. Whatever she wanted from him was hers.

They stayed in the bath, kissing and washing the salt water off each other. Her soapy hands glided across his body. *Gods, who knew bathing could be so hot.*

"Will," she spoke softly, "wash my chest, please." She moved closer to him.

He lathered his hands in lotion and brushed them across her breasts. His cock stiffened as his hands cupped her breasts and she moaned with pleasure. Every soft breath that escaped her perfect mouth fuelled him onwards. She reached down into the water, wrapping her fingers around his shaft and stroking it. Fire spread through him uncontrollably. He leaned forward to kiss her, her open mouth inviting him in. He kissed her neck, kissing a trail down towards her breasts. Her hand remained around his rock hard erection, stroking him as his lips made his way along her breast. He stayed down there working his tongue over her nipples, her gasps and moans spurring him on, each stroke of his tongue had her gripping his shaft harder.

"Take me to bed," she moaned, her head lulling back in the bath.

Oh, gods. Aylise's thoughts shouted through her mind as Will worked his tongue down her body. They really should have stopped playing coy about their desire for each other and told each other how they felt a long time ago. Aylise would never forget this day, the day when he finally said the words. Had she sensed it before? The way he spoke to her, looked at her, and cared for her was different to the way most men looked at her. They looked at her like a prize or an object. Will had never done that, he had always looked at her with admiration and care. Sometimes she had wondered if he looked at her like that because they had always been friends, but she was wrong. Oh gods, the way he worked her nipples told her she was wrong. The way his girthy cock reacted to her hand grasping it told her she was wrong. Will desired her as much as she desired him.

A spasm of pleasure shot through her body. She clutched the sheets as her body fluttered with delight. Will had been working his tongue between her legs so well she felt like she was on fire. *Had he been with girls before?* She wondered. Could anyone be this good their first time? If he had, why hadn't he ever told her? *Because you don't tell the girl you're in love with that you've fucked another girl.* Her first time was with Lord Lewin's son Jakob the previous year, when they were visiting Fawkeston. Jakob and Aylise had spent the evening flirting over summer wine from Cyandra, when one thing led to another. It wasn't anything serious, just two drunk and hormonal young people with desires. Another spasm shot up her body, pulling her back into the now.

"I want you to fuck me, please, Will," she moaned softly.

"Are you sure?" he replied, panting as he moved up her body, his eyes meeting hers.

Gods, he looks beautiful. Sweat covered his brow, and his eyes looked hungry and full of desire.

"Yes," she replied, kissing him. "I want you to fuck me, Will Kyllarian."

"Oh!" he replied, almost purring to her, "I'm going to make love to you, Aylise Rotherwell." He kissed her again.

Aylise's heart raced as she gazed into Will's eyes. He looked at her with such tenderness that she forgot the nerves wracking through her body. That simple look transformed them into a burning desire. Will manoeuvred himself into her slowly and gently, opening her inch by inch.

It was uncomfortable at first. Perhaps it showed on her face, because Will adjusted his motion.

"I'm sorry." He spoke softly. "Is that better?" he asked, slowing down and gliding himself in and out of her.

"Yes," she called out, "Oh, Will, yes!" She threw her head back, every inch of her coming alive. She had never felt this good in her life.

They continued in a rhythm of desire, love and passion. One moment they were like hungry beasts craving their next prey. The next, they were slowly moving together, savouring every moment of their sweet, passionate encounter. Even in his wildest moments, Will was sweet with her, regularly ensuring she was comfortable and enjoying herself.

Aylise moaned into Will's ear as she climaxed, his last thrust into her finally sending her body over the edge. Warmth flooded her whole body. He climaxed with her, his guttural moan rumbled through her, though he didn't look away.

Flames appeared in his eyes, circling around his irises like a ring of fire. When they finished climaxing, he collapsed next to her, kissing her cheek softly, panting on the bed.

"That was incredible," he said, turning towards her, "Are you okay?"

"Your eyes!" She held his face and looked deeper into them. "Go and look at your eyes."

Will walked over to the mirror: his eyes grew wider as he looked at his reflection. Aylise walked towards him, not bothering to cover herself up, and placed her hands over his shoulders.

"Another manifestation of your powers, perhaps?" she suggested.

"Maybe," he replied as the flames subsided, "but let's not dwell on that right now." He smiled at her. "I'd rather go back and lie in bed with you longer."

With that charming smile of his, Aylise allowed Will to lead her back to bed. She didn't bother taking herself back to her own tent, preferring to spend the night with Will in sweet joy and bliss.

Will woke to the news that riders were making their way into the camp. The first morning light was barely breaking when Prince Andayne came marching into his tent.

"What is it, Dayne?" he asked, checking to make sure Aylise and he were appropriately covered by the bedding.

"Riders heading this way," he replied, not giving any sign of panic, though his tone was neither casual nor relaxed.

"Friend or foe?" Will asked.

"Not sure yet."

"We'll get dressed now," Will replied. Dayne turned and left the tent as quickly as he had entered.

Lord Nathaniel ushered Will, Aylise and Seb up to the top of the tower. Archers were stationed along the battlements, bows at the ready.

"Who is it, father?" Aylise asked.

"We're not sure yet," Lord Nathaniel replied. "Scouts spotted movement by the forest."

Will gazed out over the camp. Soldiers, both human and fae, were darting around, forming defensive formations around the camp. Shouts reverberated from below, horses were being mounted, and swords were being unsheathed. A dozen riders galloped into the middle of the camp. The rider in front elegantly dismounted from their horse and swiftly moved towards Prince Dayne and Daemoon. Will recognised Queen Keeva among the riders, but there was also a familiarity to the rider speaking to Dayne. Will couldn't quite work out how, as it was hard to see clearly from this distance, but something familiar sparked in him.

Dayne pointed towards the tower, towards Will and his friends. The fae rider and Queen Keeva glanced towards them. Queen Keeva began to levitate, Prince Dayne and the rider following closely behind her. The sight was spectacular to witness. One moment they were standing in the middle of the camp, the next they spread their arms wide and floated, rather quickly, through the air.

"Will, this is my twin sister, Crown Princess Isiadelle," he said hurriedly, "I'm sorry there's no time for proper introductions." His panicked look matched his voice. "My sister brings word that we have to leave immediately."

"Why?" he replied, looking from Dayne to Isiadelle.

There was certainly something familiar about her, the way she flew through the air, her blonde hair billowing in the wind, the elegance in the way she moved. Realisation washed over him.

"I've dreamt about you," he blurted out before he could stop himself, "We were flying together over a temple in the mountains." *I really should stop talking.* "That's peculiar." He looked at her, puzzled.

"Prophetic?" Isiadelle seemingly asked herself, or was she asking Will? She placed her hand on his temple. "Dayne was right, you are rather extraordinary," she replied, smiling at him.

Will glanced sideways at Aylise. Her eyes were narrowed, and her lips were pursed as she watched Isiadelle interact with Will. *Shit,* perhaps blurting out that you dreamt about another woman was not ideal in front of the woman you love.

"There are more pressing matters," Dayne cut in urgently. "We need to leave now. Queen Haveena is coming."

Will's heart started to pound against his chest, and adrenaline began to course through his veins. *She is coming; Haveena is coming.* He had to get those he loved to safety. No one else was going to die for him.

"Lord Nathaniel, get them out of here now," he shouted, gesturing towards Aylise and Seb.

"We're not leaving you here," Aylise replied.

"It's too late, anyway." Seb's voice shook as he pointed towards the forest. "She's already here."

~ CHAPTER TWENTY-THREE ~

Queen Haveena was hovering above the air at the crest of a hill. Green energy swirled around her as her long black cape billowed in the wind. Her grin was wide and gleeful as she locked eyes with Will.

"Lord Nathaniel, kindly have your guards escort my mother, Lady Ana, Seb and Aylise away from here now," Will commanded.

Images flashed through Will's mind: Queen Dyana standing on the palace balcony as the castle around her burned. A pregnant Dyana burning at the stake. Haveena ordering Andeux to murder Rupert. Fire ignited through him.

"I am the heir to the throne," he proclaimed in a booming voice that was new to all of them. He pointed towards Haveena. "She murdered my family and has terrorised our kingdom long enough." The fire spread through him. "Her reign ends today."

He locked eyes with Haveena. "I'm coming for you." Somehow, even from this distance, he knew she could hear him. He began to walk down the stairs.

"No, Will!" Selina sobbed, "You can't. Stay here, you're too important."

"You must respect my command," he spoke firmly, but kindly. "Get away from here now." He turned towards Dayne, Isiadelle and Keeva. "I would appreciate your help down there."

"We stand with you," Isiadelle nodded at him.

Power coursed through Will in response to the threat rising around them.

"Let's go!" Will called out as Haveena and her army began to ride towards their camp, King Rickard leading the charge.

"Take a deep breath and steady yourself," Isiadelle said to him, her eyes glowing.

Isiadelle began to hover in the air, Dayne and Keeva following close behind. Will's body left the tower, hovering above the air. A force pulled him along, guiding him behind the fae royal over the edge of the tower towards the earth below.

He landed in the middle of the camp. Most of their soldiers had left, having already made their way to the edge of the camp, ready for the onslaught of attackers coming their way.

"That was much faster than running down the stairs. Thanks." He smirked at the royals.

He willed his powers to the surface as he ran through the camp. He thought about Dyana, Selina, Aylise, Seb and his father, who was somewhere at the edge of the camp. His power fuelled through his body, surging from head to toe, pulsing at the edge of his skin.

"Your eyes," Isiadelle called out beside him. "You are indeed special, Will Kyllarian."

"My eyes? Have the flames returned?" he asked her. Isiadelle raised her brows and dipped her head knowingly. He felt his power pushing through him, ready to release. Flames began to appear around his hands, spreading across his whole body until he was wholly aflame. "Move aside!" he called out, running towards the soldiers at the front line.

The soldiers did as he commanded, though he was intelligent enough to realise it wasn't because of his birth title, and more to do with the fact that nobody wanted to be close to a flaming man.

"Will!" Darian called out. "What are you doing here?"

"Stay back, father." He looked towards Haveena and Rickard. "This is my fight."

Haveena hovered above her army, her mask of confidence slipped for just a moment when she locked eyes on Will's flaming form. *Good, be afraid.* Will thought, hoping that through some phoenix magic, she could hear him.

Will held onto the image of those he loved, letting the rage burn brightly through him. He waited for the power to gather around his hands, until it was so ferocious that he knew it was time. Large fireballs exploded from his hands, hurtling towards the incoming soldiers. Their horses flew through the air, their burning bodies crashing into other soldiers. Will let his instincts take control, sending fireball after fireball into the path of the incoming horde. Dozens of Haveena and Rickard's soldiers fell, their burning corpses littering the field. A fireball connected with King Rickard's chest, but merely disappeared, leaving him unscathed and unbothered by the attack. Will's mind wandered back to the vision he had by the campfire, when he first saw the attack on Basilium. None of King Eramund's attacks had damaged Rickard, now Will's own fireball left him unscathed. What kind of magic did Rickard have? Did nothing hurt him?

"Impressive, boy!" Haveena called out sarcastically. She held glowing green fingers to her throat and her voice boomed across the field. "Your power wasn't enough to save your mother, and it won't be enough to save you either, this time," she snarled across the field.

Haveena flicked her wrists and conjured green flames in her hands. She hurtled the fire towards Will. He instinctively lifted his hands above his head. The fire stream shattered into hundreds of tiny sparks above him. A wall of energy radiated from Will, shielding him from the fire.

"Will, get back!" Dayne shouted from close by.

"This is my fight! I'm not leaving!" he replied.

"I'm not asking you to. Just move!" Dayne pointed to the fae floating behind them.

Dayne hovered and joined Princess Isiadelle, who was leading a formation of fae. Magic surged through the air. It smelt like the sparks of a fire, mixed with the tang of freshly cut grass and the smell of incoming rain in a summer storm. The pressure around Will dropped as lightning gathered around the fae's hands and eyes while they floated towards the oncoming army. The air began to change, mists appeared in the air, swirling together, like lovers intertwined in a dance. The smell of a summer storm intensified as large grey clouds formed above them, bringing loud rumbles with claps of thunder. Moments later, the skies opened. Large strikes of lightning erupted in the sky, striking the earth and blasting Haveena's army apart. Haveena flicked her wrists above her, and a green shield formed around her and Rickard, shielding them and those close to them from the strikes. Lord Nathaniel and his army collided with the royal guards, steel clashing with steel as each side battled to destroy their enemy.

Will continued to send fire balls into the oncoming army as waves of soldiers charged towards him. Darian fought next to him, felling down soldier after soldier that charged towards Will. Will focused on his power bursting through his body, trusting it to protect him and those he loved. Prince Dayne and Princess Isiadelle were fighting close by, blueish light erupting around them each time they surged a lightning strike through the enemy. Their fae blades slashed through the armour of each soldier that confronted them. They were masters of their craft, easily using their magic in one hand and their blade in the other.

Haveena fought back equally as strongly as Will and the fae powers combined. Her fiery green waves of destruction destroyed everything in their path. Will focused on parrying her, his powers reacting to every strike of her flaming power. Even in the heightened moments of the attack, he couldn't help but wonder what kind of power she had. Granted, he hadn't seen that many magics at all. But it was odd to see that her green flames were almost a mirror to his power, but every now and then, her hands swirled with green magic similar to the fae magic.

Rickard was locked in a battle with Queen Keeva. She was blasting lightning at him in a continuous stream from her hand. In her other hand, a stream of magic was hurtling towards him too. He deflected the magics, allowing them to hit his chest, but he was struggling to move closer towards her, towards the battle. Keeva was the only thing stopping him from getting closer to harming their side, and she was only just holding him back. He moved closer inch by inch. His power frightened Will: how did someone get that much strength, power and invulnerability? Was it dark magic?

Haveena screamed at him as he deflected another blow from her. His power was reacting to his every thought and intention… or was *it* guiding *him*? Was he simply the vessel being led by the incredible surge of power coursing through him? Fire and heat raged through his body as he hurtled a fireball towards Haveena. She disappeared, blinking in a puff of green flames as the fireball sailed into her soldiers, burning them to a crisp of ash and bone.

"Impressive!" she called out from behind him. "You're growing stronger," she growled. However, she looked far from impressed. She looked incensed.

He hurtled another fireball towards her, and she blinked, disappearing again before it connected with her.

"You're focusing too much on your rage," she mocked menacingly, raising her green, glowing arms above her head.

He turned and threw himself to the ground and felt the heat of her fireball as it sailed above his head. She moved behind a tent in the camp. Will pulled himself up and ran after her, darting from tent to tent seeking her. When he found her, he threw another fireball her way. She waved it away easily and blinked away.

"You're getting sloppier," she called out from a boulder, "A talented phoenix would have hit me by now." Like a cat playing with a mouse, she was enjoying toying with him.

"I may not be able to stop *you* yet, but I'm making a good dent on your army," he countered steadily, hurling another fireball at her.

Will ran away from the camp, returning to the thick of the battle. He launched fireball, energy ball, fireball and energy ball into the fray, felling soldier after soldier. When several royal guards charged towards him, he crossed his arms over his body and threw his arms out instinctively: a torrent of energy blasted across the field. The soldiers charging him were hurled back; most of them did not get back up.

Darian was clashing with Rickard in the middle of the soldiers. Rickard had gained the advantage over Darian. Will's body tensed, to see that his father's excellent form hadn't managed to stop Rickard. None of his father's strikes pierced Rickard's armour, yet he deflected an attack from Rickard and punched him in the face with his armoured hand, right between the eyes. It was the only time Will had seen something penetrate Rickard's seemingly unbreakable shield, but then Will's senses flared and his whole body wracked with nerves as he watched Rickard gain on his father. The false king swung his sword, breaking through Darian's shoulder armour. Darian's guttural grunt echoed across the field as he dropped his sword and stumbled backwards.

"No!" Will shouted, running towards Rickard. "Get away from him!"

"It's your turn next, boy," Rickard taunted him, "but I'll take daddy first."

Will gave into his power and let instinct take full control of his body. Energy coursed through him and, like a wave roaring in the ocean, a pulse of energy erupted from him. It passed through Lord Nathaniel's soldiers and the fae without so much as ruffling a hair on their heads. But when the blast hit Rickard, it sent him launching into the air. Somewhere behind him, a woman screamed the false king's name. Haveena! Her voice was tinged with fear and panic as Will's power broke through Rickard's shields. Will focused on the fire burning inside him and all over his body as he prepared to hurl a stream of fire at the king.

"Stop Will, or I'll kill her," Haveena's voice boomed across the field.

Will froze and the flames retreated into his body as he turned towards Haveena. She was standing on the black stone edge of the fortress. Aylise's hands were magically bound in front of her and the false queen had her hands wrapped around Aylise's throat. Aylise's eyes were liquid with fear.

"Stop!" he screamed, panic and bile rising through his body. The flames retreated further into his body. Though his power hummed at the surface. "If you want me, take me. But let her go."

"Will, no!" Aylise cried.

Haveena squeezed on Aylise's throat, her magic surging around her fingers.

The fire in Will rose to the surface, his power guiding him. He trusted it. Were the power and his instincts one now? His power surged out towards Rickard on the ground. Holding him in place with a shield of energy.

"Just let her go, Haveena," he tried to speak calmly, doing his best to control the panic coursing through him. "Just release her, and you, Rickard and I can leave here. Let her go and I'm yours."

The armies surged and wrenched around them, completely unaware of the predicament Will and Aylise now found themselves in. Royal guards rushed towards Will, and Darian stepped in between Will and the soldiers, ready to battle.

"Please," he pleaded, "Your Grace," he added, attempting to appeal to her ego. "Please, just let her go." Tears began to well in his eyes, though he willed them away. He couldn't lose his focus yet.

Haveena smiled down at Will as Aylise began to weep and her whole body shivered uncontrollably. Haveena drew a dagger from her clothing and hovered it in front of Aylise's chest. Aylise struggled against Haveena's grasp. Will began to shake, every hair on his body standing on end. He felt utterly helpless: one false move could be catastrophic.

"No, no, please," Aylise trembled.

"Free my husband now," Haveena called out, glaring at Will. Will didn't move. "Now, or she dies!" Will didn't move.

Will continued to shake with unadulterated fear. He cried out, his gasps guttural and deep as he lowered his hand, releasing the energy force holding Rickard down. The moment Rickard was free, he picked up his sword and watched his wife.

"Good boy," Haveena mocked, "you stupid idiot."

Haveena swung the knife around and plunged it into Aylise's back. Aylise's scream echoed through the field as the knife protruded through her chest.

"No!" Will screamed out as he ran towards Aylise.

Rickard lunged for Will, swiping his sword in Will's path. The tip grazed across Will's chest, slicing through his leather doublet. Haveena disappeared from Aylise's side and Aylise fell in slow motion, stumbling and collapsing. In that moment, he desired nothing more than to be by her side. A new sensation of power swept over Will, surging through his body. In his next step, he was lifted from the ground and a moment later, Will appeared instantly at Aylise's side. She collapsed into his arms.

"Will," she whimpered out softly as the colour drained from her face.

"No, no, no," he cried out, panicking as tears began to stream down his face uncontrollably.

Blood began to flow from his doublet, pooling in the open wound on Aylise's chest. Will sobbed and shook as he tried to stem her blood loss by compressing his bloodied hand on her wound. He used his free arm to hold onto her, but she was sagging and drooping against him.

"Haveena…" Aylise called out softly, looking wide-eyed behind Will.

A pulse of energy blasted out from Will in every direction. Though he couldn't see it, he felt his power connect with the queen, launching her backwards.

"Healing. I have healing powers," he gasped as he held his shaking hand over her wound. In his panic and weakened state, his power was quiet, unresponsive. "Ahh," he gasped, "it's not working."

"Will…" Aylise cried softly.

"Fae have magic, right?" he cried, tears streaming down his face. "Dayne! Dayne! Help!" he stammered out between ragged, uncontrollable breaths.

Fear and pain coursed through Will as he watched the life slowly drain from Aylise. He held his shaking hands on Aylise as his blood – his energy – continued to pour all over them. No one came to his aid; he felt utterly alone and useless. Blood continued to flow from Aylise's wounds, and Will's own wound began to sting, their blood transforming his hands into a dark red mess.

"Please Aylise, no…" he sobbed, tears flowing with each ragged breath. "I love you, please don't go." He wept as he tried with all his strength to heal her.

"Don't let me go…" she whispered. "Will, look at me." Her voice grew softer with each word. "I love you, yesterday was the best day of my life. I'll miss you."

"Andayne!" Will bellowed, his voice booming across the camp. "Andayne! Help me!"

Andayne locked eyes with Will. His eyes grew wide and wild with panic as he noticed the severity of the situation. Andayne flew across the field towards them, landing softly close by.

"I love you," she choked through the words. "I'm by your side..."

Aylise stopped moving and her body became limp, sagging in Will's arms.

"No. No. No." he cried, throwing his head back and screaming into the air.

Seb watched in horror. Haveena had appeared on the tower as they began their escape from the fortress. In that instant, she held Aylise and disappeared just as quickly. Seb sobbed openly as he raced towards his friends: another gut-wrenching blow to Seb's already fragile emotional state. Dayne was pushed back from Will as energy pulsed from him and the pooling blood around them began to glow. Seb trembled uncontrollably as Will and Aylise began to rise into the air. He lunged for Dayne and dragged him away as heat and energy began to swirl around the hovering pair.

"Dayne, what's happening?" he asked between sobs. "Aylise... is she?" he couldn't finish the sentence. Dayne pulled him close and hugged him as he wept.

"She's gone. I'm sorry, Seb," he replied in ragged breaths.

"What's happening?" Seb asked, sobbing.

"He's awakened," Dayne replied, stroking Seb's back. "The rise of the phoenix begins."

"But what do we do?" Seb cried. "We have to save them."

Will and Aylise's bodies were carried into the sky, surrounded by the fiery energy swirling around them in a display of spectacular magic. Will's scream pierced the air around them. Will seemed to be struggling as his arms were flung out by his side. Energy coursed through Will and Aylise, passing through their bodies. It swirled into and from them from all directions. Aylise's head lulled to the side as her limp body rose higher and higher into the sky. Somewhere close by, Lady Ana's scream reverberated on the stone, her grief coursing through the camp. It seemed all eyes were on Will and Aylise as heat and energy pulsed around them. Aylise's body began to float back down, like a feather softly falling from the sky. She was surrounded by a ball of radiant light that howled like a gust of wind blowing through an open valley. Dayne ran towards her, catching her body and carefully placing her on the stone. Will continued to float in the air, his arms wide as energy coursed in and out of his body. His screams were just audible over the torrent of sound whipping around him.

As Seb collapsed next to Aylise, he broke into a guttural sob. Her eyes were open and lifeless, the sparkle that twinkled in her eye had been snuffed out. Will's body floating in the sky reflected off her eyes. Blood continued to pour from the wound in her chest and she was pale and limp. All life had been drained from her.

"Please," Seb sobbed as he looked down at Aylise's lifeless body. "Please do something. Dayne," he cried, clutching her lifeless hand. "Help her please."

"I wish I could," Dayne replied, "but I don't have the power to bring back the dead."

"Aylise." Seb closed Aylise's eyes and kissed her head. "Thank you for being my friend."

Will screamed in the air. A bright light swirled around him, and he erupted in flames. They started in his chest and ignited across his whole body.

The fire coursing through Will was unlike anything he had ever felt before. The stone below him glowed, obscuring his vision. He struggled to keep his eyes on Aylise as she drifted back to the ground. Orange and red swirling colours shimmered around the entire fortress. His arms had felt like they were being pulled apart, like a door being forced open by hidden chains. He struggled against the feeling, desperately trying to hold onto the love he had just lost.

He heard voices screaming around him as the flames encompassed him. Queen Dyana and King Eramund appeared in the light, smiling at him.

"You are a legendary phoenix, Will Kyllarian." She looked at him with pride. "Your destiny is about to begin."

A bird screeched nearby. It appeared behind the light, soaring through the air with its orange and red feathers billowing in the wind. It landed on his back. Wrapping it's wings around him and then unfolding them widely, mirroring Will's own stance.

A weight clamped around his shins and calves, then another along his thighs. His arms grew heavy as a golden armour began to form along his body. If he hadn't been witnessing it happen, he would never have believed it. His body felt alight with fire as a presence awakened inside of him. It was stronger, confident and determined. In a moment of clarity and understanding, the last of the armour formed around his body, and one final burst of fire erupted from him, showering the camp with sparks. The phoenix inside of him had risen. It was powerful. It was angry. It wanted revenge.

~ CHAPTER TWENTY-FOUR ~

Will didn't need a mirror to know that flames burned in a ring around his eyes, heightening his senses. Royal guards were advancing on Lord Nathaniel's forces: *his* forces, *his* people, *his* army to protect. Will flew towards the ground, flames burning at his fingers. As he drew closer, he sent a continuous torrent of flames soaring towards his enemies. His forces who were caught in the fire were left unscathed and untouched by the hot flames, simply because he willed it so. Each royal guard caught in the flames blew away in a pile of ash.

Will soared back into the air, flying around the field, ready to dive into another sweep. Haveena, Rickard and a small contingent of their soldiers had retreated from the battle. Will shot down from the air towards them, sending another torrent of flames in their direction. He slammed into the earth, sending a shockwave of flames in every direction.

"We have to go now," Haveena squeaked to her men, retreating backwards from Will.

Will unsheathed his sword and cut through the soldiers easily, slicing through them in one fell swoop. He blasted several soldiers with a flick of his wrist. Behind them, Rickard and two of the royal guard were retreating on horseback.

Will launched into the air, soaring high above the battlefield. He unleashed his rage towards Haveena. As the torrent of flame hurtled towards her, green flames erupted around her. Haveena, Rickard and their two soldiers blinked in a swirl of green and did not return.

Will screamed in anger, flying high above the battlefield. He watched the scene below. Flames had ignited around the fortress. Soldiers, both friend and foe, were fleeing and fighting as they moved away from the flaming ruins.

Will eyed a troop of royal guards and seethed with rage. With a clench of his fist, he rained fire on the soldiers, showering them in waves of burning hot flames. Will felt complete satisfaction as each soldier left nothing but a mound of ash and burning grass behind. As more soldiers retreated, wave after wave of flame pulsed out of him, each wave charged by the anger inside him.

He felt strange, empty, almost like he was depleting himself with each stream of fire that burnt the camp to ash. He'd never felt this much power in his life. He needed help.

"Andayne..." he called weakly.

As the anger inside him subsided, his vision began to blur. He plummeted downwards, losing consciousness just before his body slammed into the flaming earth.

~ CHAPTER TWENTY-FIVE ~

Queen Haveena marched down the hallways of Basilium Castle towards the throne room. Guards, courtiers, advisors and servants moved behind closed doors, averted their eyes, or darted down hallways the moment they laid eyes on her. Each stomp of her foot echoed along the dark hallway. Haveena could sense Rickard and Sir Jarrack marching quietly behind her, though she did not have it in her to slow her pace and walk with them.

"Get out. Now!" Haveena screamed as guards opened the doors to the throne room.

Everyone in the room scurried away. Like mice sensing a predator in their midst, they darted through doorways or walked along the perimeter of the room, hidden in the darkness as they slipped outside. Haveena screamed repeatedly as she paced across the room. She summoned her power and began blasting artworks, vases, statues and sculptures. Anything in her way was shattered into dust. She had hoped that each impact might help ease her growing frustrations, but it wasn't having the desired effect. She turned towards the doors as Rickard and Sir Jarrack walked into the room.

"Three hundred men, Rickard!" she screamed, her body burning with rage. "Three hundred, and now we have two left."

"You're at fault, you idiot woman." He marched towards her as he spoke, fury in his eyes. "You were the one who demanded we march on them."

"Had you not been a stubborn arse and marched when I suggested, we wouldn't be in this predicament," she bellowed, not backing down from her rage. "We would have had the element of surprise, instead, that fae bitch beat us there."

King Rickard struck Haveena across the cheek with the back of his clenched hand. The impact burned with pain, but this was nothing out of the ordinary for her. When he hit her, she would usually sob and apologise for speaking out of turn, hoping to ease his anger, but not anymore. She'd had enough of her tyrannical idiot husband. All he had left was his strength and his shield. Everything else she loved about him had slowly died away in the last eighteen years.

"Hit me all you like," she said, lifting her head towards him confidently. "It won't change the fact that your reluctance to listen to a woman killed our men."

When his fist connected with her stomach, the force sent her flying through the air. Her body slammed into the stone floor and her vision blurred as her head impacted the stone. Haveena cupped her head, only to confirm that it was indeed hot and sticky. When she saw her bloodied fingers, she seethed with hatred.

"My fault?" he barked across the room. "We wouldn't be in this predicament at all if you had just chopped Dyana's fucking head off like I suggested." Haveena gasped. "You had to show off and revel in the irony of burning her at the stake." Rickard glared at her. "Well done. You murdered your sister, and the boy survived."

"She wasn't my sister," Haveena snapped back.

"Fool yourself all you want, Haveena, but I know just as much as you do that you're bitter that your relationship with her fizzled out. But I suppose it was always going to, after what your mother did."

"Don't you dare bring up my mother," Haveena snapped back. "She was the greatest of us."

"Then what a shame you turned out the way you did," Rickard spat venomously. "Pining for the love of your half-sister. That's what made burning her even more satisfying for you." Rickard shrugged and smirked at her. "Well, it certainly backfired on you, didn't it."

The truth of his words stung like a thousand wasps jabbing at her body repeatedly. It was her idea to burn Dyana, her sister, at the stake. What better way to torment Dyana, but with the very element that her family line had been immune to. Had Dyana been called as a phoenix, it never would have worked.

"It hurts, doesn't it?" Rickard growled at her. "Once again, I'll pick up the pieces of your mess." Rickard paced towards her. "Now get out of my throne room before I throw you out, you stupid woman."

Haveena glared at her husband and slowly walked out of a side passage. As soon as she slammed the door shut, she ran as fast as she could from the throne room. Once she was alone, she placed her hands over her throbbing head wound and chanted, waiting for her magic to stitch her broken skin and seal the wound. Then she moved onto her red, raw cheek and stomach. The magic soothed the sharp, constant aches, but it couldn't heal the sting from Rickard's words, which hurt more than his fist, not that she would ever admit that to anyone. She should have just chopped Dyana's head off. The boy would have died with her, but how was she to know?

You should have known better. Margarith's voice echoed in her mind. *I raised you to be smarter than this, my dear.*

You raised me to be ruthless. She replied to herself.

Haveena walked towards her gardens, striding tall and proud along the corridors. When she was a child wandering these very halls with Dyana, the gardens had always been one of her favourite places in the palace. Dyana's face appeared in her mind's eye. The adult Dyana, the queen. She was kind, beautiful and compassionate. She was loved by her subjects: any one of them would have willingly laid down their life to protect their queen. Oh, how Haveena had hated her to the core. She was the false ruler: the throne didn't belong to her, it was always meant to be Haveena's throne.

Haveena stepped into the light of the gardens. Her roses crawled up the stone wall. Soft pink and red scented flowers bloomed from thick green stems. Haveena and Dyana had always loved the rose garden. Nothing had made them happier than picking roses together to place on the dinner table later that evening. They would carry their bunches and wander up to the battlements to smell the salty sea air and feel its soft caress across their cheeks. The garden seemed to have grown even more in the last few days. The grasses were greener, flowers bloomed from every garden bed, and the trees were the most voluminous they had looked in years. Bees flew from flower to flower, collecting pollen then zooming between the small birds that danced around from tree to tree, singing their sweet melodic tunes to each other. The amaranthine plant in the middle of the garden had grown much larger than the last time Haveena stood here. The large flower in the middle of the plant had bloomed, its large purple petals opened towards the sun.

As Haveena stared at the flower, her mind wandered back to times when she was young and carefree. She and Dyana loved wandering through an amaranthine plantation outside the walls of Basilium.

"Why do you have to go, Dyana?" twelve-year-old Haveena called out to eleven-year-old Dyana as they walked hand in hand through the field.

"My father says that the Aruleans must see their future ruler throughout the lands," Dyana scoffed and rolled her eyes. "I don't want to go, but I have to."

"I'll miss you, Dya." Haveena looked to the ground.

"You too, Havi." Dyana smiled at her and pulled her into a hug.

The two friends made a pact to only ever use their special nickname with each other when they were alone: it was theirs to treasure and keep secret.

"Did you see how big the flowers are getting now, Havi?" Dyana asked, looking up at the flowers.

"It's been a great season for them," Haveena replied, smelling the blooms as she passed them.

"Do you believe the stories about the flowers having magical properties?" Dyana asked, tilting her head towards the sea and smiling.

"Mama says it's not true." Haveena cupped the flower between her fingers. "But I feel magic in them."

"Can you, really?" Dyana asked, her eyes watched Haveena excitedly.

"Sometimes." She paused, not letting go of the flower. "It's like I can feel the power humming in the pistils. Sometimes I feel it calling to me, like I can absorb the magic. But I don't really know what that means." Haveena sounded so young, innocent and full of wonder.

"I think it means you're destined to be powerful," Dyana replied, smiling at her.

"Ha, I'm sure Mama would be thrilled," Haveena laughed, rolling her eyes. "Do you want to go for a swim before the day is gone?" Haveena asked her best friend, knowing exactly what would make her happy. She loved taking care of Dyana.

"Oh yes," Dyana squealed, "Yes. Yes. Yes." She was brimming with excitement.

"Haveena!" a shrill voice called out in the plantation. Haveena's mother Margarith walked through the flowers towards the girls. "Come Haveena, we must go," she snapped.

Her mother pulled her way as voices began to call for Princess Dyana.

Haveena's mind drifted from that happy day in the field to another memory. Basilium had fallen, Eramund was dead, and Dyana stood before her behind the bars of a cell in the dungeon.

"Haveena. Please don't do this to my child," Dyana pleaded, as tears streamed down her face.

Haveena watched her coldly. Standing tall and silent as Dyana cried, shackled and dirty, in the cell. Dyana had brought this on herself: she was the one who turned her back on their friendship, the one who had thrown it away.

"Please," Dyana begged, "we were best friends, we were sisters." Dyana cried. "Regardless of what your mother did."

"Don't you blame her, your father betrayed her and then your mother had us cast out," Haveena replied bitterly.

Margarith was going to be so proud of her. She was about to do what her mother had set out to do a long time ago. She was going to avenge what Galen and Maeve did to their family. She was going to wipe out the Kyllarian line.

When Haveena lit the flames around the pyre, she watched in satisfaction as they began to dance around Dyana's body, revelling in her own wicked irony. Burning the last living line of phoenixes to death was genius, or so she thought. Reliving the memory, she hadn't noticed Dyana snapping her head into the crowd and smiling. But she saw him now. The boy was standing there, watching his mother die. How was he here now, fully grown as he was in the present day? She glanced towards Dyana's belly, where the baby boy was still growing. *He's dream-walking here. He is too powerful.* Dyana glanced towards one of the shops in the square and smiled. Haveena hadn't seen it when she was here eighteen years ago. *Uh-oh.* Realisation almost slapped her in the face. She wasn't thinking about a memory, she was dream-walking here too, though she was wide awake. Simply thinking about memories. *Another interesting development in my power,* she thought gleefully. Using the moment to her advantage, she followed Dyana's gaze and saw her standing in the doorway. Selina had changed out of her gown and was wearing everyday commoner clothing, completely unremarkable and unrecognisable, not that Haveena would have recognised her eighteen years ago anyway. Dyana glanced from Selina to her heavily pregnant belly and smiled. It was relief: Dyana was smiling with relief.

"Protect him," Dyana mouthed softly into the crowd.

Anyone who saw it may have simply thought of the moment as a mother pleading for the life of their child, but Haveena knew differently now. Dyana knew he would live. Dyana saw her son watching on in horror. Dyana glanced towards Selina, who nodded solemnly in reply, even as her bottom lip quivered slightly.

When Dyana turned to ash, Haveena watched the pyre and waited. A barely perceptible movement came from within the pile of ash.

Haveena opened her eyes back in the garden. Her magic radiated in a circle around her: she was dripping in sweat, a small patch of blackened earth and dead bushes surrounded her, drained of life by her power.

Dyana knew the boy would live, and she ensured that he would survive. Haveena had been so consumed by her victory that she missed the small moments completely. It had all happened right under her nose, and Haveena was none the wiser. *"You're being sloppy,"* her mother would have chastised. Did Dyana know about the prophecy? *Awakened by the flames*, did Dyana know?

A single tear fell down Haveena's cheek. It pained her to think about it, but a part of her had always regretted killing Dyana from the moment her body turned to ash. Dyana had been her best friend growing up; her only friend. She had been so fuelled with rage and hatred for her heritage – her birthright and justice for her mother – that it blinded her. All her plans had backfired anyway, she murdered her one friend, and the prophecy was still fulfilled. No, not all backfired. She had her crown!

"I'm sorry, Dyana," she whispered, stroking the leaves of the amaranthine plant. "I'm so sorry."

"Are you alright, my queen?" a voice called out.

"Sir Jarrack," she replied, wiping the tear from her cheek. "Yes, I'm fine."

"I hate seeing him hit you," he said, turning her head to the side and stroking her cheek gently.

"I'm not fond of it either." She paused, looking into Jarrack's eyes. "He's right though. I am to blame. The boy survived because of me."

"But had he listened to you from the start, we could have been waiting at the fortress for them."

"It wouldn't matter anyway." She smiled at him softly. "Rickard doesn't like being wrong."

"Perhaps it's time that we did something about that?" he replied suggestively.

Haveena's senses flared, sensing a change in the air. Her power answered its call. "What are you suggesting, Jarrack?"

"He's nothing without you." He gazed into her eyes as he spoke. "He's an idiot warlord: a simple man with a simple agenda." He cupped her cheek in his hand. "Your power is incredible. It was your power that got him the throne, and your power that kept him on the throne, and your power that kept us alive today." Jarrack glanced behind him. "Besides, you saw how the boy's father broke the shield, didn't you?"

"Yes, I did." She smiled. Oh, nothing got past Jarrack. "But..." She began.

"No buts." He cupped her other cheek with his free hand. "You are the most incredible and beautiful woman I have ever met."

Haveena looked into his eyes. Her power pulsing from her body, seeping out of her hands.

"See, my all-powerful queen." He smiled. "We don't need the king."

Haveena moved forward, her lips meeting Jarrack's. He accepted her kiss, mouth meeting mouth with passion. He moved his hands down her body, pulling her closer. Haveena responded by undoing his belt and letting his breeches fall to the ground. Jarrack stepped back, gazing into her eyes. His mouth twitched as he tried to contain his smile while she unbuttoned her dress and revealed her naked body.

"Kiss me again, Jarrack." She spoke softly as she moved closer.

"Yes, my queen," he replied in a deep growl.

"Call me Haveena when you make love to me," she whispered.

"Yes, Haveena," he said obediently, lifting her into the air and kissing her.

Haveena smiled at Jarrack as she adjusted her dress. The sex with Jarrack was amazing: she hadn't taken a lover like that in a long time, and it was worth the wait. He was passionate, tender and caring, but rough and hard at the same time. He groaned deeply and loudly as she bit into his chest and cackled, and she licked the blood from his wound. A flash of memory raced through her mind: a memory of her and Rickard's wild sex in the fortress, the night she made the curse. She smiled to herself at the memory, everything forming in her mind. Another deep and thick thrust from Jarrack pulled her back to the present. She growled softly, smiling at her own wickedness.

Her plan had worked perfectly. She had deeply secured his loyalty, and he was ready to work the court for her.

"The plan is a good one," he said matter-of-factly, "but we will need somewhere to meet safely."

"Here, of course," she replied. "We only meet in this garden."

"Is it not too exposed?"

"Not at all," she smirked. "I cast a spell on this garden years ago. No one loyal to my husband can step foot in here; they are repelled by it."

"Seriously?" he cocked his head as he replied.

"You seem uncertain," she replied, nudging him playfully. "Now go, Sir Jarrack. We must keep up appearances."

"My queen," he bowed and left the gardens.

Haveena walked through the gardens, smiling to herself. A spark of power and joy that she hadn't felt for far too long radiated from her. She had the extra muscle she needed now, in Jarrack. It had never been hard for Haveena to attract men, but she didn't need his lust: she needed his loyalty. She chuckled. *Men are so simple.* Jarrack even thinks he thought of the plan himself. She gazed at the amaranthine plant again. Although she knew what she had to do, she couldn't help but see Dyana's face again. She appeared brightly in her mind's eye.

"He can't live, Dyana," she spoke coldly. "Not while he stands in my way."

She grasped the amaranthine flower in her hand and summoned her power. The magic surged from the plant, feeding into her. The stem began to lose its colour, shrivelling up and turning brown before it disintegrated into dust.

Haveena walked away from the gardens towards the next phase of her plan and her next ascension.

"Get ready, mother, I'll show you how truly powerful I am," she said aloud, smiling to herself.

~ CHAPTER TWENTY-SIX ~

The sounds of a wagon rattling along a track brought Will out of his slumber and back into reality. As soon as he opened his eyes, he remembered the heart-breaking moment he saw the life drain from Aylise.

"Where is she?" Will cried out when he woke up. "Where is Aylise."

Will called her name again, sitting up in the wagon. They were moving along a trail: a large convoy was moving in two columns through the forest. Darian was riding close by, Selina by his side. Prince Dayne was visible by his silver-blonde hair, he was several riders ahead of Will. His friend Daemoon was riding by his side. He gazed back and forth along the convoy, Aylise's copper hair and smiling face were nowhere to be seen. Pain tore through his heart.

"Will," Seb called out next to him, his eyes red and puffy, and his face riddled with sorrow.

Will's lip began to quiver, and every inch of his body shattered as the painful truth came crashing wave after wave. Was this what a broken heart felt like? Aylise had died in his arms, she had bled out while he watched. He was powerless to help the woman he loved so dearly. Every wave of emotion that Will had been holding in for days boiled to the surface. He wept, allowing the tears to stream down his face as he sobbed uncontrollably. It became hard to breathe as the pain seared through his body. Seb shuffled along the wagon and pulled Will into a hug. Tears were streaming down Seb's face, too. They held each other tightly, consumed by their grief. Soldiers nearby began to react to them, slumping their shoulders as their mournful wails shattered the rhythmic, thumping sounds of hooves on dirt. Selina and Darian watched the boys from a distance, giving them the space to have their private moment of mourning. Will wasn't sure how long he held his friend in his arms and cried: was it several minutes? Hours? Eternity? Did time even exist anymore?

"It hurts, Will. I tried to be brave. I tried to block out the pain. For her. For you. For everyone," Seb wailed between ragged sobs, gasping for air. "I thought if I pushed all the pain away and pretended everything was okay, that we would get through it. But... But she's gone. We lost her," Seb wailed.

Will held his friend close. It was the only way he could comfort Seb. His heart was too shattered to speak, so he just cried and held on. All he could think about was her. He failed her, he failed everyone, his power failed her.

"Where is she?" he asked Seb between ragged breaths when he finally found his voice. "I need to see her."

Seb wiped his eyes and froze. His lip quivered and his hands began to shake. His mournful demeanour crumbling.

"Oh gods, what now?" Will asked, wiping tears from his eyes while he watched Seb closely. "Seb, where is she?" Seb stared back at Will, tears streaming from his eyes. "Stop the wagon!" Will yelled, his own tears stopping as dread took over. "Seb, where's Aylise?" he asked, his voice hoarse and ragged.

The wagon came to a halt and murmurs and chatter broke the silence of the forest. Will paid no attention to the convoy: his gaze remained on Seb. Will shook while he waited with bated breath for Seb to speak.

"I'm sorry, Will," Seb began. Dayne walked towards the wagon and placed his hand on Seb's shoulder, his own eyes pained. "When you fell from the sky... When you hit the ground... Fire erupted from you." Seb sighed and Will's lip began to quiver again. "The whole area went up in flames. Our camp, the fortress, the bodies lying around. The whole fortress was glowing. I've never seen anything like it." He paused and looked up at Will. "The earth collapsed into the fortress below. We tried everything we could to reach her, but we couldn't. She went down with the fortress."

"You left her there!" Will howled with sorrow. Collapsing to his knees. "Go back!" he screamed. "Turn back! Turn back! Turn back!" he howled each word, the sounds grating along his throat.

"We can't, darling," Selina called from the side of the wagon.

"She's dead because of me!" he cried, gasping for air between sobs. "I did this. I did this to everyone."

"No, she's dead because of Haveena," Selina replied angrily. "Everything is because of Haveena."

Will reared his head back and screamed, his howling echoing through the forest. The heat rose through his body, sorrow, anger and heartbreak surging with his power. He lifted his hands into the air and let the turrets of fire release from his body. Wave after wave of fire poured from him until he collapsed on the wagon and began to cry again.

"Will, I'm so sorry." Dayne spoke in a crestfallen, hollow tone. Up close, Dayne's hair was dirty and wild. Ash, blood and dirt covered his face and armour.

"What happened today, Dayne?" Will asked numbly.

"My sister had a vision of Haveena at the fortress..."

"Yes, I remember that," Will interrupted him. He felt like an empty shell.

"I'm sorry," Dayne replied with sympathetic eyes. "Remember how I told you that your powers were still awakening?" Will nodded. "Well, to put it quite frankly, they're awake now."

Will did feel different, and it wasn't just his unwavering grief that had shattered his whole body, it was something else. His senses felt heightened. His power wasn't bursting to escape him, but he felt it there. He nodded to Andayne.

"You have completed your bond with your power." Dayne looked at him with compassion. "You saved us all, Will. We won that battle because of you."

"But we lost Aylise," Will struggled to speak. "Why did the fortress glow?" he asked in a husky whisper.

"Your blood pooled on the stones. The fortress of the flames was constructed with obsidian – at least that's how humans refer to it, but the fae know it for its true name – phoenix stone. Because of who you are, the stone reacted to the power in your blood." Andayne spoke softly and looked sadly at Will. "All over Arulean, temples, altars and fortresses will have felt the power of your arrival."

Will slumped in the wagon, his only thoughts on his shattered heart and his lost love. Just another victim of the destiny that Will never wanted but had now become such a large part of his life.

"Lord Nathaniel and Lady Ana tried their best." Dayne gazed into his eyes compassionately, his brow furrowed.

Will looked for Lord Nathaniel and Lady Ana. Even from this distance, their grief mirrored his own, their eyes were hollow and red. As Lady Ana looked at Will, her lips quivered, and she wrapped her arms tightly around her body, almost like she was trying to stop herself from falling apart.

Will leapt from the wagon and walked towards the leaders of Fawkeston. Lord Nathaniel and Lady Ana pulled him close. Will sobbed, and he held Lady Ana, his heart shattering as the tears flowed freely.

"I'm sorry," he gasped between ragged sobs. "I'm so sorry."

Lady Ana gasped and choked between sobs. She didn't respond verbally but squeezed tighter. Her ragged breaths reverberated from Will's neck, travelling to the very depth of his heart. Lord Nathaniel's arms wrapped around the two of them, and there they stayed in their grief. Crying and holding each other together in hope that they wouldn't shatter apart, like their hearts already had.

"We will avenge her. We will avenge them all!" Lord Nathaniel sobbed.

Did Will want to avenge Aylise? Of course he did, but that desire had backfired before. It was vengeance that fuelled him at the fortress. It was fear that fuelled him in Korgun. And it had been his own arrogance and recklessness that had fuelled him in Basilium.

"No," he said firmly, looking at Lord Nathaniel, "that's not the answer. Vengeance will only lead to more suffering and pain. Aylise wanted me to rise above my own vengeance. My own guilt. My own pride. She would want that for you, too." Lord Nathaniel's eyes softened. "It's not vengeance we seek. It's justice." He looked towards the convoy. "Justice for Aylise, justice for Marte, Alexander, Rupert, King Eramund, Queen Dyana and all who have fallen because of Haveena and Rickard. We'll fight for them all, because we all deserve a better tomorrow."

"We'll be right by your side," Cara said softly, drifting towards him.

"Indeed, we will." Prince Dayne called out from Seb's side.

"Where is your sister?" Will asked Dayne. He gazed around the convoy: both the princess and her mother were nowhere to be seen on the trail.

"They've gone ahead. We'll meet them in Vandfall."

"And what awaits us in Vandfall?" Will asked.

"Your training, most importantly," Dayne replied, "but first we need to rest and grieve. Vandfall will be your safe haven." Will's befuddlement must have shown on his face, because Dayne continued, "Remember, old magic protects Vandfall. Only those who are welcome may enter."

"Oh yes," Will replied, weakly smiling.

"Yes, Will," Cara replied, "we can finally rest easy and stop running."

Will sighed. It would be nice to stop running – to breathe, to cry, to hold everyone and everything he loved dearly – and just be. Most importantly, there would be somewhere safe for his family and friends: sanctuary from the dangers and destruction that came with being in his proximity.

In the distance, a faint orange glow painted the horizon. The sun was still high in the sky. If it wasn't a sunset, it could only be one other thing. The fortress was still glowing. They were not yet deep in the Amaranthine Forest.

"How far away from Vandfall are we?" he asked Andayne.

"About one full day's ride at our current pace."

"Okay, pay attention everyone," he called out, formulating his plan as he spoke. When he had the convoy's attention, he continued, "We're leaving as fast as we can. Everyone who isn't on horseback, saddle up," he called out, his voice calm but firm. "The longer we remain here, the greater the danger. We ride hard for Vandfall now."

The convoy sprang into action, preparing wagons, mounting horses and strapping down supplies in saddles.

"Seb, where are our horses?" he asked, his brow furrowed. "Did they make it through the battle?"

"They did," Seb replied warmly. The horses slowly began to trot over towards Will and Seb, like they were responding to Will's every thought.

Will ran his hands along his white mare's muzzle and climbed into her saddle. "It's good to see you." He patted her neck.

Will felt a warmth dissimilar to how his power felt when it burned through him. It was coming from his side. He rummaged through his satchel where he had left the phoenix egg. He was surprised to find that the shiny black egg was still intact, though faint glowing lines had begun to appear across its surface. The egg was hot: was it producing its own heat? He secured the egg in his satchel and nodded towards Dayne.

"Take us to our new home, Prince Andayne."

Andayne led the convoy through the forest. His horse quickly moved out of a canter and into a gallop. Will glanced back towards the glow in the distance and closed his eyes. He saw Aylise's soft smile, the way she looked at him, the way she made him feel like he was the luckiest person in the world, like the gods had bestowed such luck upon him to have been loved by her. He felt like she was somewhere there calling to him, his heart yearned for her, it pulled him towards her.

"Goodbye," he whispered softly towards the glow, "I will always love you." He turned towards Seb, his dearest friend left in the world. "It's going to be a long road ahead, Seb. I've caused you so much pain, loss, and grief already..."

"Will. My heart may be shattered into thousands of tiny pieces." Seb sounded defeated, emotionally deflated and exhausted. "I need time to grieve: I can't put a façade up any longer. Like I said, hiding from the pain and blocking it out doesn't help anymore. But you did not cause me this pain."

"Still, I understand if you don't want to…" Will interjected.

"I'll be by your side until the end," Seb replied, cutting Will off before he could say what lingered in his mind.

Aylise and Seb said the same thing to him along this journey. What he didn't realise at the time was that the end can be many places. For Aylise, her end was today: that thought tore shreds through his heart. For Will, *by your side until the end* meant a long time from now, together, old and happy: not the end of life before they even had the chance to live it together.

Will galloped beside Seb, their horses moving beat to beat along the forest road. Will took comfort in knowing that he was not alone.

Andayne galloped at the head of the convoy, determined to ensure Will, Seb and the travelling party made it safely to Vandfall. Andayne's heart broke for Will and Seb: he, too, had experienced the utter devastation that followed losing a loved one. It had been over one hundred and fifty years, and he could still recall the pain as clearly now as he did then. The road to recovery was a long one, but Will and Seb would have support around them.

Dayne felt him coming before Seb galloped close by. Seb's magical aura glowed so brightly, it leeched into Dayne's heart, filling him with such life and joy that he felt like he was floating in the heavens. Seb wasn't aware of his magical abilities, of that Dayne was certain. He hadn't produced any magic, nor had he brought it up. Seb wouldn't be able to see or sense the aura, but Dayne could, and he wanted to explore it with him.

Dayne had felt immediately drawn to Seb the moment they met. His kind eyes and stunning smile began thawing the frost in Dayne's heart from the first hello. Dayne instantly fell back into his lively and charming self that had disappeared long ago. He knew Seb had lost someone whom he loved dearly, too: his friend Rupert. The loss was so recent that Dayne couldn't help but wonder, was Seb just looking for a distraction from the pain? Or did he feel something real too? He hoped Seb could feel something real, but after losing Rupert, his parents, and Aylise, Seb would need his own time to heal. Dayne would happily be that distraction for Seb, but that wouldn't be fair on either of them. Dayne would also happily be there to help mend his broken heart, even if he was just there as a friend, but when the time was right, he would happily help Seb explore his magic. Dayne smiled and quickened his horse towards the safety of Vandfall.

~ EPILOGUE ~

Every inch of earth was scorched. The ceilings of the underground chambers of the fortress had collapsed in, swallowing the earth into its dark depths. Fires continued to burn around the earth, and only a small section of the tower remained above the ground. Some of the stones still had a faint orange glow, although they were slowly fading back to black. Blackened and burnt bodies littered the earth, but piles of ash were all that remained of Haveena's royal guards. What had been an open green space had become a mass grave. Fires burned around the entrance to a hallway now exposed to the elements due to the sunken earth.

A lion emerged from the hallway. It paused at the entrance and sat there, surveying the area. It wasn't looking for prey, though there was enough around for a comfortable feast. No, it had travelled through the Amaranthine Forest because it had been drawn to the power that was pulsating from the fortress. It heard the call loud and clear and knew what it meant. Changes were nearing.

The lion's attention was drawn to the body of a dead woman lying in the middle of the pit. Deep down in the depths of the earth, flames licked around her body, and a large bloody wound marred her chest. The lion could smell the blood. Aylise's pale, lifeless body was lying on a glowing fragment of the fortress. The lion moved along the edge of the pit. Its eyes bore into Aylise as it leapt from glowing stone to glowing stone, navigating the winding path down to her body. Unlike the other skeletal bodies in the pit, she was whole: she had no visible burn marks, her flesh and meat seemingly untouched by the flames.

The power was strongest here: the lion could sense that. It leapt onto a stone close to Aylise's body and watched her from above. It never glanced away from her, until hot winds began to sweep through the pit. The winds were ferocious, like they were coming from the stones themselves. They swirled around the pit, like a vortex sucking the air towards the stone and the dead girl in the depths.

The stones began to glow brighter. It was too bright – almost blinding. It closed its eyes, shielding them from the light. Then just like that, the glowing stopped. The stones returned to their natural black state. The lion leapt back, startled by what it was seeing. Aylise was sitting up on the stone, the wound gone.

A ring of fire burned around her eyes.

ACKNOWLEDGEMENTS

This book has been a decade in the making. A journey that began with a single spark of an idea and grew into the story you now hold in your hands. The path to completing Rise of the Phoenix has been long, challenging, and deeply rewarding, and I could not have done it alone.

First and foremost, thank you to my husband, Damien: your unwavering belief in me and in Will's story has been a constant light. Through every late-night writing session, every moment of doubt, and every breakthrough, you have been my rock. You have stayed by my side every step of the way, championing me to share Will's story with the world. This book would not exist without your love and support.

To my editor, Dr Elise Ruthenbeck of RedStream Australia: you are an absolute powerhouse. Thank you for pouring your heart and soul into this book. Your wealth of knowledge, sharp editorial eye, and endless encouragement pushed me to strive for excellence. Thank you for challenging me, inspiring me, and helping shape this book into the best version of itself.

To Jaki Arthur, for that fateful night at the Clock Hotel in Surry Hills: from the moment you told me that this story needed to live on paper and shared with the world, it inspired all that came afterwards. Thank you, thank you, thank you.

To my incredible beta readers: your thoughtful feedback, keen observations, and enthusiasm for this story have been invaluable. You saw the potential in these pages and helped me refine them into something stronger. While I may know what's to come, and what motivates every character, you helped ensure readers could come along on that journey with us. I am forever grateful for your time, patience, and honesty.

To my friends and family who never stopped cheering me on: thank you for listening to me ramble about plot twists, for celebrating every milestone, and for reminding me why I started this journey in the first place. And to all my fellow marketers: your keen eyes, brainstorming sessions, creative minds and endless patience in reviewing cover mock-ups, fonts, colours and designs have been invaluable. Thank you for your help bringing the creative elements to life.

And finally to you, dear reader: without you, there would be no *Rise of the Phoenix*. Stories are meant to be shared, and it is an honour to share this one with you. Thank you for stepping into this world, for following these characters, and for making this journey alongside them. This is only the beginning, and I look forward to sharing these stories with you.

With gratitude,
Brendan

ABOUT THE AUTHOR

Brendan Arnold is a bestselling and award-winning queer author and **2025 Debut Author of the Year**. A lifelong lover of fantasy, he longed for more representation in the genre and set out to write stories that champion queer characters and strong, powerful women. Based in Australia, his debut novel won **2025 Young Adult Book of the Year**, **2025 Cover of the Year** and **Best New Adult Book of the Year**.

Brendan writes rich fantasy filled with emotional stakes, heartfelt angst, and villains you love to hate. He aims to craft stories that are easy to read yet layered with themes that resonate with both adults and younger readers.

From a young age, Brendan was known as the storyteller in his family, he spent countless hours creating new world and wondrous adventures to share with his family and friends.

His love of storytelling began at home. His grandfather taught him how to draw, sparking a lifelong passion for creating art. While his grandparents encouraged him to pursue every creative passion. Whether through writing, visual art, music, dance or performance, creating stories that entertain people has always been his passion.

When he isn't writing, you'll find him sketching new covers and character art on his iPad, buried in a good book, or deep in a story-driven video game.

To explore more of Brendan's work and the world of *Rise of the Phoenix*, follow him on social media and visit www.thebrendanarnold.com

https://www.instagram.com/brendanarnold/
https://www.tiktok.com/@thebrendanarnold
https://www.facebook.com/barnoldauthor

Brendan's
Bookshelf

Subscribe to Brendan's newsletter to
stay up to date with his latest projects,
follow along on his writing journey, and
get behind-the-scenes peeks at his
latest artworks and creative projects.

Brendan always has a book review or
two to share, a calendar of upcoming
appearances, and the occasional lame
joke or two.